About the author

After teaching history for more years than she will admit, G.C. Blair started writing books for children from years three to thirteen about Serious Subjects like Henry II, Elizabeth I and the United Nations. As much as she loved doing that, there weren't usually enough vampires, stunt princesses or pirates in them. Then whenever she sat down to write about Serious Subjects, Cid, Miss Fitz and Desmond de'Ath's pirate crew started butting in. By the time Vlad, PJ, Wilbur and the others had joined them, G.C. gave in and *The Miss Fitz Agency* was born.

GW00778154

THE MISS FITZ AGENCY

G.C. Blair

THE MISS FITZ AGENCY

Vanguard Press

VANGUARD PAPERBACK

A CIP catalogue record for this title is
available from the British Library.

ISBN 978 1 784658 26 7

*Vanguard Press is an imprint of
Pegasus Elliot MacKenzie Publishers Ltd.*
www.pegasuspublishers.com

First Published in 2021

**Vanguard Press
Sheraton House Castle Park
Cambridge England**

Printed & Bound in Great Britain

Dedication

For Zak, Jack and Georgie and in memory of their Grandad Paul.

Also, not forgetting Ultimate Uncle Alistair. 'Thank you' isn't enough.

Prologue
(Or Chapter Minus One)

Have you ever wondered where the story characters that nobody wants go? The ones that never get picked for books, plays or films? The Sleeping Beauties who snore? The ghosts that are afraid of people? The Rumpelstiltskins whose real names are Dominic or Nigel? Groups of eight or more dwarves? Fairy tale princesses who do their own stunts? Like Princess PJ, for example.

PJ lost her starring role in the film *Towering Hero*. It was another one of those totally predictable Rapunzel-type stories:

- Witch casts spell over princess.
- Witch locks princess in a very high tower.
- Princess waits for Prince Charming to come to the rescue.
- Prince Charming climbs up princess's hair (seriously?) and rescues her.
- They live happily ever after (except for the witch, but that bit is often left out).

Unfortunately, Prince Charming got himself tied up in tangles halfway up PJ's hair extensions, so she took a pair of scissors and them cut off. Charming plummeted to the ground. (I like the word 'plummeted'. It sounds like what it is: a sudden, heavy drop.) PJ, stunt princess, was sacked. Not that she minded – she hated the whole Prince Charming thing. Like she said, any self-respecting princess would simply make her bedsheet into a parachute and jump, not hang around waiting to be rescued.

So PJ, stunt princess, came to the only place for characters that don't fit in with what people expect: The Miss Fitz Character Agency. And it's my aunt, Fenula Fitz, who runs it. She takes characters that no one wants, that don't quite fit in, and helps them.

I help her during the school holidays, at weekends and in emergencies because I know something about not being wanted. I'm always the last one left when teams are picked for games at school or if we have to pair up in class. I try to look as if I don't care. (My top tip for this is to think about something like creating your ultimate sandwich or what it would sound like if a dinosaur burped.) Finally, there's only me left, so I'm not actually chosen at all.

Mum says it's because I've got what she calls 'the double whammy' of glasses *and* braces. I like my glasses, though, because I can menace people who are being annoying by pulling my specs down my nose and glaring over them. Actually, when I do this, all I see is a blur but no one knows that. I pretend that I don't care, but I never have my photo taken wearing my glasses and never, ever, smiling so my teeth show. To be honest, I try not to smile, especially in photos. Mum thinks I should grow my hair long and wear a pretty dress sometimes but I like my hair short and spiky and dresses are not practical. Plus, my legs are long and very spindly. My knees look like potatoes on sticks.

Being left until last used to bother me, until I worked out what was going on by making a flow diagram of my situation.

CID FITZ'S PROBLEM SOLVING FLOW CHART

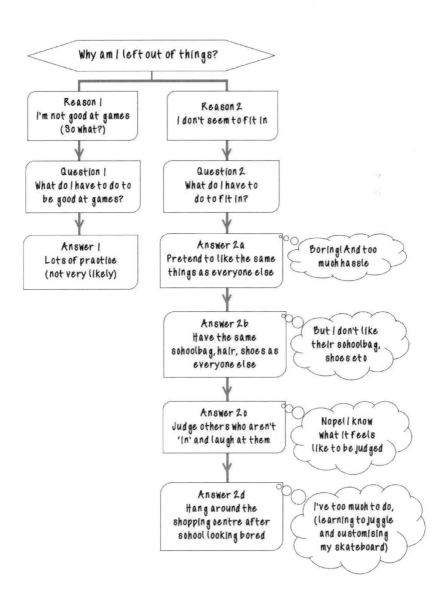

My older brother, Winston, told me it's things like this flow chart and building my stick insect farm that explain why I am left out so often. So I did what I always do when Winston gives me advice and ignored him.

Instead I looked at my chart and asked myself, 'Do I want to do any of these things, so I am included more?' And I said to myself, 'No, not really.'

Conclusion: fitting in *isn't* for me (although it's still embarrassing

being left until last). That's why I'm proud of my Aunt Fenula. You might have seen her adverts in magazines or as pop-ups on the internet?

I'm Cid Fitz. Actually, it's Clematis Iris Dahlia Fitz but I NEVER answer to that. Not even when I'm in trouble. Which brings me to Where It All Started: the first day of the last summer holidays.

Chapter One

The Miss Fitz Character Agency was in trouble. The sort of trouble that looks really bad until you take a closer look and realise that it's far worse than you first thought. I like working things out, so I was trying to help Aunt Fenula. From what she had told me I thought the agency was at 'Uh-oh.' 'Uh-oh' is Point 2 on my patented Ten Point Trouble Scale. It's very useful when working out how much bother you are in. Here it is:

1   Oops
2   Uh-oh
3   Things are Bad
4   Really Bad
5   It's going from Bad to Worse
6   It's Worse than that
7   I'm / We're up to my / our neck(s) in it
8   Disaster
9   Catastrophe
10 As serious as it gets

There's an optional eleventh point, too, in case you ever need it.

11 It's Nothing To Do With Me. I wasn't even there. Honest.

As I punched the numbers on my Digit Muncher X50 Super Calculator, waves of red figures were spewing from the printer and curling across the office.

'Cid? Cid?'

I could hear my aunt, but I couldn't see her. She was somewhere under the paper. I was too busy to look up. I was having one of Those Days. The sort where you wake up thinking it's Saturday but it's actually Thursday, and you have a big test and there's a really vomit-making smell in class, and it turns out to be you because you trod in something very brown and sticky on the way to school.

The more I worked, the worse things seemed. Far from being at 'Uh-Oh' on the Trouble Scale, I soon realised that things at the Miss Fitz Character Agency were actually Really Bad – a jump of 2 points and it wasn't even ten o'clock.

Finally, the sums were done and the printer stopped. Aunt Fenula popped up from the piles of paper.

'Are you sure this is right, Cid?' she asked. 'Have you added the fees from Vlad's role in *The Vampire Bites Back: Dracula's Revenge*?'

I checked my notes.

'No. We had to return them, remember? After we found out that it's not only mice and small spaces that scare Vlad. He faints at the sight of blood, too.'

'Even theatrical blood?'

'Yes.'

'Poor Vlad,' said Aunt Fenula. 'That must be very hard for a vampire, fear of blood.'

So I said, trying to be practical, 'He should have warned us.'

And she said, 'Well, actually, he did mention it. He told me it's why he had to leave his home in Transylvania. He said his family are *so* embarrassed by him and being expelled from the Vampire Academy was the last straw. Then his eyes started brimming with tears and…'

I love Aunt Fenula, but she's not got what my dad calls a Head for Business. It's one of his favourite topics of conversation. Although strictly speaking (ha ha) a conversation involves more than one person and Dad simply reels off what he calls advice in the form of Wise Old Sayings like: 'Fenula's heart rules her head. Always has, always will.'

Unfortunately, Aunt Fenula is also fond of Wise Old Sayings. When the two of them get together, it's a bit like they're playing top trumps.

Dad kicks it off. 'If you fail to prepare, Fenula, then you are preparing to fail.'

Aunt Fenula shoots back. 'I have the will, Nathaniel, and "Where there's a will there's a way," don't forget.'

Dad counters. '"The road to hell is paved with good intentions."'

Aunt Fenula blocks him. 'I have no intention of changing my intentions. "Do unto others as you would have others do unto you."'

Dad ups the stakes. 'But you must learn, Fenula, "Never a borrower nor a lender be". You'll end up in hot water and then where will you find yourself?'

(The answer, of course, is having a bath but it's easier not to say anything.)

Then Aunt Fenula hits Dad with her favourite: 'Don't worry about tomorrow, Nathaniel. It will take care of itself.'

At this stage, Mum usually gives me The Signal to remember something vital and rush upstairs. Then I ring her mobile. She says it's a call she has to take, answers, and then makes comments like, 'Oh no!' and 'Really?' and 'That's awful!'. Then she tells Dad and Aunt Fenula a combination of the following (delete as necessary):

'I would love to stay and listen but that was Mrs. Popplewell from the office / Great Uncle Franklyn at Sunny Ridge / Enderby's the dry cleaners on the phone.

There's been an emergency / a crisis / a trauma.

The tropical fish are eating each other / Ernie has pooped in his hat again / the duvets have exploded. Must dash.'

I'm not sure why the duvets would have exploded at the office because Mum works for an estate agent. Luckily, when they are in full flow, neither Dad nor Aunt Fenula are listening to anyone but themselves.

The thing is, Dad does have a point about Aunt Fenula's not having a business head. And it's a serious problem because if the Miss Fitz Character Agency goes out of business Aunt Fenula won't be able to help anyone. Princess PJ, Vlad and all the others will be out on the street, quite possibly along with her too. So part of my job is to help Aunt Fenula face the facts. Like the fact that signing Vladimir up to the Miss Fitz Character Agency was *not* a good idea.

'What jobs can a vampire who's afraid of blood, mice and confined spaces do?' I asked. 'No wonder none of the other agencies wanted him. We needed the fees from that film to keep the business going. We're almost bankrupt.'

'About that, Cid. There's something I've been meaning to tell you.'

I groaned. 'Not more bad news?'

But, suddenly, Aunt Fenula was gone.

Friday 23 July 10.02 a.m.
Trouble Scale 5

W h ᵃ m !

The agency door slammed open and shuddered against the wall. I felt a tickling prickle as something sprinkled onto my face. I looked up but didn't have much time to worry about the fact that the crack in the office ceiling had grown at least another five centimetres, as in walked a short gentleman wearing a black pin-striped suit, dark glasses and a white trilby hat with a black band around it. Looking back, this was when things hit Point Five: Going from Bad to Worse.

'Good morning, miss,' said the man, raising his hat. 'Forgive the manner of my entering but my partner, Marjorie, is stronger than she realises.'

The room darkened as Marjorie entered, which was quite something as it's dark enough already with its blackened oak wall beams. I had to crane my neck to look at the very glamorous, very large woman now filling most of the available space. I did a few quick calculations trying to work out how she was able to cram herself through the door, but I was too distracted by her clothing. Her pinafore was pinstriped and clashed with her polka dot silk blouse and a long, sequined scarf tied in a gigantic, sparkling bow. The flowery Dr Martens boots didn't quite go, but they certainly made an impression. No doubt about it, this was a Yuck Moment.

'We are looking for Miss Fenula Fitz,' said the man.

There was an Aunt Fenula-sized heap of paper in the middle of the printouts, but I decided to stall for time as I had never been in quite such a predicament before. ('Predicament' is a great word because it sounds sticky but serious, which is exactly how things felt).

'And you are…?' I asked.

'My card,' said the man.

'I'm Nudgebuster.'

'And I'm "& Co.",' said Marjorie. 'But you can call me "Big Ma".'

And she pulled her bright red, glossy lips into an alarming smile that almost reached her false eyelashes, but not quite. The abrupt air she had about her, coupled with a dress sense loud enough to drown the FA Cup Final, meant I couldn't *not* stare at her. As I did, I made another quick calculation, this time about the situation I was now in, and came up with an answer I didn't like. Aunt Fenula and I needed to have serious words. But that would have to wait.

'Can I help?

Mr. Nudgebuster was a curious man. ('Curious' is exactly the right word because it can mean nosy or strange and he was clearly both.) First, Mr. Nudgebuster peered around the office. Then he tapped one of the walls and stamped on the floor, causing more plaster dust to fall from the crack in the ceiling. He shook it from his sleeve before turning to me and saying,

'It's a delicate financial matter, I'm afraid. I really must insist on speaking with Miss Fitz.'

I needed to think what to say for the best, which is not easy when you're distracted by flowery boots. All I could manage was, 'Ah, I think she's, err, out. Yes. That's right. She's out. Can I – er – can I take a message?'

'I think someone's avoiding us. What do you think, Marjorie?'

'Let Miss Fitz know,' said Big Ma, reaching over the counter, taking me by the sweatshirt and dangling me in mid-air, 'that if she doesn't come up with the money—'

Suddenly there was a flurry of printouts as Aunt Fenula jumped up, leapt over the counter, grabbed Marjorie's arm by the bicep and cried: 'Let go of her, Big Ma, or…'

'Or what?'

I was quite impressed (and more than a little concerned) that both my aunt and I were now swaying from Marjorie's right arm.

Before Aunt Fenula could answer Big Ma, the door was flung open again. As the ceiling crack crept another centimetre, in strode one of the Miss Fitz Agency's signings, Dazzling Desmond Death, a pirate. You might think he sounds a bit scary, and you'd be right, but probably not in the way you are imagining. His captain's bicorn hat was so floppy that he kept it on his head with an elastic band; his long moustache was waxed, curled and had little bows at each end; and as for his ruffles – no self-respecting pirate has worn ruffles like that since … well, since forever. And (as he never stops telling people) it's pronounced Desmond de'Ath, not Death.

The tiny office was becoming crowded. There was some jostling and then Desmond made a declaration. Pirates like making declarations because it's more dramatic that way. 'Unhand her, madam!'

'To whom are you referring, my dear Captain?' asked Aunt Fenula.

Desmond looked puzzled.

'Isn't it obvious?'

'Not really,' said Aunt Fenula. She nodded at Big Ma. 'You see *she* has my niece, but *I* have her.'

'Are you sure?' replied Desmond. 'It looks like *she*,' he also nodded at Big Ma, 'has both you *and* Cid, Miss Fitz.'

'We could certainly use some help, Aunt Fenula.'

What happened next was all a bit of a whirl, but I'll try to describe it.

Desmond reached for his sword, tugging it hard and elbowing Mr. Nudgebuster into the counter.

'Ooof!' said Mr. Nudgebuster.

Desmond made another declaration. 'Unhand them, I said!'

This was a bit limp as declarations go, however, because Desmond was still tugging at his sword. It was stuck fast in its scabbard.

Big Ma dropped me, shook off Aunt Fenula and grabbed Desmond by the throat instead.

'That's better,' he choked, his toecaps scraping the floor as Big Ma lifted him up so she could eyeball him.

I wasn't convinced that things were better, but at least neither Aunt Fenula nor I were dangling any more.

'En garde!' spluttered Desmond, and then took everyone by surprise – himself included – as he finally pulled his sword from its scabbard with a …

W H O S H

Which was followed by a …

K - K - K - K R R R A A - Q

… as he hit the agency's front window. More expense!

'I think,' said Mr. Nudgebuster from somewhere under the counter, 'that we all need to calm down.'

He stood up, dusting off his suit, adjusting his hat and sunglasses and …

W H U M P !

… was promptly thrown back on the floor as the door was flung open for a third time. In barged Desmond's crew. They're not easy to describe. You've never seen such a muddle of shapes, sizes, hooks and false legs. There was a lot of shouting:

'Stop shoving, will you?'

'That was my toe.'

'Ouch! And that was my nose.'

'There was no need for that!'

'Who's pulling on my neckerchief? I can't breathe! Help!'

Someone needed to take charge. I climbed onto the counter.

'Everyone STOP!' I shouted.

The muddle froze. I looked at Desmond. Then I said what the school caretaker Mr. Spragg tells our teacher, Miss. MacLean, at about three thirty-one every afternoon: 'Captain, please tell your crew to exit in an orderly manner!'

Except Mr. Spragg doesn't call Miss MacLean 'Captain' and we're not her crew. But as he always sounds like he's in charge, it seemed like the right thing to say to Desmond. Unfortunately, all he could reply was,

'Kkh-kkkkhh.' His face had turned an interesting shade of red as it wobbled above Big Ma's fist.

Scared was now the main feeling pumping from my head down into my arms and legs. I channelled it into an angry roar. 'LET HIM GO!'

Chapter Two

Friday 23 July 10.37 a.m.

CＬ_UNＫ!

Desmond crumpled onto the floor, sword still in hand.

'All right, you chaps, you heard the young lady,' he said, eventually getting up after a great deal of coughing. 'Exit in an orderly manner. About turn!'

This was not as easy as it sounded.

'I can't move. I'm squished against the large lady.'

'Well I can't turn until you do.'

'But your hook's got caught in my button hole.'

'I can't see … I've gone blind! Help! Help!'

'Your patch has slipped over your good eye, idiot!'

It took a while, but finally only Aunt Fenula, Mr. Nudgebuster, Big Ma, Desmond and I were left in the front office. It was still a bit of a squeeze.

'If you wouldn't mind leaving, whoever you are,' said Mr. Nudgebuster to Desmond, 'we have business to discuss, Miss Fitz and I.'

'My card, sir. And I *do* mind!' declared Desmond.

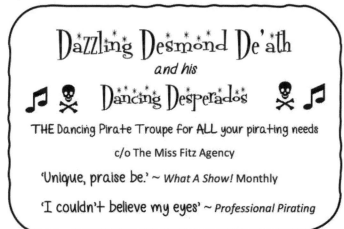

'You can't treat people like that,' he continued 'And neither,' he added, turning to Big Ma (who now had Aunt Fenula pinned against the wall), 'can you, madam.'

'Really?' sneered Mr. Nudgebuster, glancing at the pirate's card. 'Who's going to stop us? You? Do you think that because you're Captain Death you're going to scare us?'

He stood nose-to-nose with Desmond, who brandished his sword and made another declaration (although this one was less convincing).

'It's pronounced *de' Ath*. And I'm warning you, one step more and I'll use this!'

Mr. Nudgebuster took one more step, squashing Desmond against the wall alongside Aunt Fenula.

'I… I'm warning you, I will. I really, *really* will.' This was more of a gulp than a declaration.

'Not exactly sharp, is it?' chuckled Mr. Nudgebuster, grabbing the sword by the blade and throwing it over his shoulder.

'You can't be too careful.' said Desmond.

We all stared at him.

'Well, you can't. That's how accidents happen.'

I realised I would have to go through the Miss Fitz Agency's database later, to see which characters (if any) were actually able to do anything that might be expected of them. Survival can call for tough decisions. Aunt Fenula would have to face some facts like, for example, a pirate with a blunt sword wasn't going to cut it in the entertainment industry. (Ha ha).

By now the excitement had worn off and so had my patience. I decided to phone the police.

'One move out of you and the old lady gets it,' warned Big Ma.

'Old?' squeaked Aunt Fenula.

'There's no need to insult Miss Fitz. Apologise immediately!' Desmond was making declarations again.

'Who's going to make me? You?' And Big Ma laughed so hard that I was dazzled by the light bouncing off her fillings.

'No, but I will.'

Everyone turned again. This time PJ, stunt princess, stood in the doorway.

'That's a joke,' said Big Ma.

'I'm famous for not having a sense of humour,' replied PJ.

'It's true,' Desmond added. 'She never laughs. Not even when Clayton burps the national anthem.'

'Enough!' shouted Mr. Nudgebuster. 'This is between me, Marjorie and Miss Fitz. It's nothing to do with anyone else, so the rest of you – leave!''

I was not about to go anywhere.

'If it concerns my aunt, it concerns me. We're in this business together.'

Desmond went for menacing but didn't pull it off when he said, 'And I can't leave a damsel in distress. It's against my Code of Honour.'

PJ, however, not only sounded menacing but threatening: 'Looks like we're staying.' She drew her sword from its scabbard. 'I should warn you, I don't take kindly to people who mistreat old folk.'

'Old?' choked Aunt Fenula.

'Who are you to interfere in our business?' asked Big Ma.

'PJ, but you can call me "Your Royal Highness".'

Peta-Javana was actually Princess PJ's proper name. Peta means rock and Javana means graceful, but as Princess Peta-Javana is a bit of a mouthful, and Princess Graceful Rock is not much shorter, she is known as PJ. This is more practical. In a life and death situation, a name with a lot of syllables wastes time better spent escaping.

'It's time for you to leave, Princess Pudgy or whatever you call yourself,' chuckled Mr. Nudgebuster, grabbing PJ's sword.

Large drops of his blood dripped onto the floor.

'Ouch!' he yelped.

PJ thrust the tip of her sword under Mr. Nudgebuster's chin. She didn't take her eyes of him as she told Big Ma to... 'Let go of the old lady.'

'Old?' spluttered Aunt Fenula.

'Do it, Big Ma,' said Nudgebuster.

'For the record, everyone,' said Aunt Fenula moments later as she straightened her clothing, 'I am only 47!'

'And for the record,' snarled Mr. Nudgebuster, 'you owe us £20,000.'

'And for the record,' I replied, 'we don't have £20,000.'

'In which case, we…' Big Ma pointed at herself and Mr. Nudgebuster, '… will give you until the end of the month. That's one week and one day. Then we'll be back, and you…' Big Ma stabbed Aunt Fenula with her finger '…will be sorry. *Very* sorry. And that's also for the record!'

Nudgebuster & Co. slammed the door behind them. The window panes cracked more until they looked like a mosaic.

'Ha! Good riddance,' smiled Desmond. 'Can I be of any further service, Miss Fitz?'

'No, thank you, Desmond. You've done quite enough.'

'Think nothing of it, glad to be of service,' he said.

Then he went to remove his hat and bow low in a Very Grand Manner. Unfortunately, the elastic band holding it on pinged his hat back into his face right at the moment he tried to kiss Aunt Fenula's hand. PJ rolled her eyes and pulled him outside by his lapels.

'Poor Desmond,' said Aunt Fenula. 'He gets very nervous.'

'Especially around you,' I said.

'Me? I don't frighten anyone, as you have seen.'

'I don't think it's because he's scared of you.'

Aunt Fenula told me not to be so silly and to make a cup of tea.

As I sipped my tea, I went over everything that had happened during the kerfuffle. (I love 'kerfuffle'. It sounds very muddly and we were definitely in a muddle.) As I made some new calculations what Big Ma had said finally sank in. I suddenly realised we were at number six on the Ten Point Trouble Scale – it was Worse Than That – and I blurted out,

'We owe them £20,000!' Which I followed with, 'When were you were going to tell me that, Aunt Fenula?'

Aunt Fenula winced. 'I really did mean to, Cid. The bank wouldn't lend us any more money, so I asked Mr. Nudgebuster instead. I thought we'd be able to pay back at least enough to keep him happy with Vlad's fees but…'

'… but Vlad's afraid of blood. And mice. And confined spaces.'

'Yes. Then Big Ma said I was lying when I told them I didn't have any money. I came back one day to find the office and my home had been turned over. They even threatened Vlad and some of the others. Then Mr.

Nudgebuster agreed I could have one month to find the money as long as I agreed to give the Agency buildings to Nudgebuster & Co. if I couldn't get what we owed. But now, suddenly, they're only giving me a week.'

'Let me get this straight,' I said, hoping that if I repeated what I thought I'd heard, Aunt Fenula would tell me I'd got it all wrong. 'You've borrowed £20,000 and the terms are pay it back in a month or Nudgebuster & Co. get *all* the agency buildings? They're worth ten times that!'

Unfortunately, Aunt Fenula didn't tell me I'd got it all wrong. She shook her head and sighed. She looked like she'd already given in.

'I was desperate, Cid. If I didn't have the money by the end of the day, we wouldn't be opening the next morning or ever again. And at least with Nudgebuster's deal I wouldn't have to pay any interest, just what I borrowed. It seemed like a good deal. I was sure Vlad would earn enough in fees to more than cover what I borrowed.'

Apparently, when someone lends you money you pay back more than you've borrowed and that's because interest is added on. It's a bit like being paid money for having money. For Nudgebuster & Co. the deal with Aunt Fenula was very interesting indeed. As for Aunt Fenula…

'Dad's right,' I said. 'You don't have a Head for Business!

'What am I going to do?' Aunt Fenula sighed. 'Do you think you'll be able to come up with one of your plans? You're good at those.'

Friday 23 July – Lunchtime
Trouble Scale 6

I felt angry. The sort of angry when you feel like you're swelling up into a big red ball of yell that you're too furious to get out. I needed to shout but I couldn't work out at whom: Nudgebuster & Co. for threatening my favourite aunt; my favourite aunt for getting herself into such a mess; or me, because I couldn't see how I *wasn't* going to disappoint her. So I counted to ten and then breathed out slowly, until I had deflated into what felt like a saggy balloon.

The only thing that might help was for me to try to be practical. I started scrolling through the Miss Fitz Character database, hoping a solution would jump out. It didn't.

'It's hopeless,' I said after ten minutes. '*They're* hopeless. We need some normal characters for hire.'

'What's so great about "normal"?' asked Aunt Fenula.

Like I said, I know what it's like to be left out and not picked for teams or birthday parties, but we could only help the Miss Fitz characters if we stayed in business.

'OK,' I replied, '"normal" isn't the word, but we need some characters on our books who do what people expect them to do, who are like people want them to be.'

Even I winced at what I was saying. That sounded worse. After all, I'm not the sort of daughter my mum was expecting and certainly not the kind of sister Winston wanted and I'm very happy about both of those facts. I tried again. 'How about "traditional"?' I said. 'Let's say we need some "traditional" characters.'

'But if we didn't take in the likes of PJ, Vlad, Desmond and the rest, what would become of them?'

I sighed. 'If we don't have £20,000 by this time next week, we'll find out. So will they.'

There were some big decisions to be made. Head versus heart decisions. We'd have to drop some of the acts from the agency's database. I knew Aunt Fenula would hate it, because I did, but I was there to help her 'face facts' as Dad had told me. So I suggested getting rid of Dazzling Desmond and his Dancing Desperados.

'There's a lot of them,' I pointed out. 'We could make a big saving. Maybe even enough to keep all the others on until we find them work.'

'Cid, we can't. Not after they helped us, surely?'

Aunt Fenula's eyes looked wobbly with tears. I felt awful but there was no other choice. If the agency shut down, PJ might survive in the Real World, but the others wouldn't.

Aunt Fenula can't help herself; if there's a good cause to champion she's the one championing it. This is one of the things I love about her. But it was also why the Miss Fitz Agency was in so much trouble. The visit from Mr. Nudgebuster and Big Ma had showed how serious things really were. In fact, on the ten-point Trouble Scale, I reckoned we were currently hurtling towards point seven.

'Pleeease.' Aunt Fenula wasn't going to give up.

I screwed all the courage I could find into a tight little ball. 'I don't know what else we can do, Aunt Fenula. We need £20,000. If we can show we are trying to cut costs, maybe the bank will lend it to us. Otherwise we'll have no chance of getting Mr. Nudgebuster's money by next week and we'll lose the agency.'

Chapter Three

Friday 23 July 8.00 p.m.
Trouble Scale 6+

By eight o'clock that evening, Aunt Fenula and I were exhausted. We had been working out ways to save money. The biggest and easiest was still to get rid of Desmond and his crew.

Aunt Fenula yawned. 'Time to go home,' she said. 'Pizza, ice cream and TV are what's required now.'

She locked up the front office and we went out of the back door.

Home for Aunt Fenula is what she calls a flat. Really it's a portacabin on top of another portacabin across an old cobbled courtyard behind the main office. I think there must have been a coaching inn or something here at one time. There's not much left of it now except the courtyard and two of the buildings that once surrounded it. In one of the old buildings is the Miss Fitz Agency offices and the costume hire shop next door. They make up one side.

The other old building is an 'Antique Furniture Emporium'. It should really be called the Broken Furniture Warehouse, but then nobody would ever go there. Anyway, it makes up the second side of the courtyard.

As we walked towards Aunt Fenula's flat, I saw a couple of dark figures peering over from the multi-storey car-park that is behind the portacabins and makes the third side of the courtyard. I couldn't be sure, but the bigger, lumpier of the two looked like a Big Ma shaped heap. The short, squat, pepper pot shape next to it could certainly have been Mr. Nudgebuster.

'Who's that up there?' I said to Aunt Fenula, who was walking towards the once grand wrought iron gates that were the fourth side of the courtyard.

As she turned to look, however, the figures ducked down and all that was left was a bit of a mound where the larger one had stood.

'I could have sworn I locked these gates,' she said, as she held up the padlock and chain we used to secure them.

I shrugged.

'And has someone moved the bins around?'

I looked into the far corner next to the portacabins, by the Antique Furniture Emporium. Not being the sort of person who pays much attention to bins, I couldn't be sure, so I shrugged again.

Aunt Fenula began fumbling around in her large handbag but I was too tired to wait, so I pulled my keys from my jeans' pocket and went to lock the gates for her.

We hurried over to the portacabins. There's something about the courtyard when it's dark that I don't like. It's the old outside toilet by our office back door. To be fair, I'm not that keen on it when it's daylight, but that's because of the giant spiders that live there. I often think a tarantula would be an effective guard dog, but I'd be too scared to own one. Anyway, it's rumoured that the toilet is haunted by a brown, misty spirit that floats up from beyond the U bend if anyone pulls the flush. It is not the idea of a ghost that bothers me so much as what a brown mist in an old toilet might be made from. Frankly the spiders are enough to keep me away.

The portacabin underneath Aunt Fenula's had a sign on the door in fluorescent paint that read FFAFA. Underneath was written in red marker pen: 'The Fenula Fitz Academy of the Fictional Arts. Rehearsal Studio.' There was a light on inside.

As we walked up the outside steps to Aunt Fenula's flat, we could feel the FFAFA studio shaking. Something was definitely up.

'I think,' said Aunt Fenula, 'that we ought to make sure everyone's all right.'

There was a great deal gossiping and fidgeting and pacing going on, but not much else. None of the agency's characters had had anything to rehearse in a long time. We stood to the side of the studio's open window, so that we could watch and listen without being seen.

'What was it all about today, Desmond?' Arthur, the Nearly Invisible Man, was asking the question but for obvious reasons it wasn't easy to tell.

'I couldn't possibly say,' replied Desmond. 'Pirates' Code and all that.'

Arthur didn't give up. 'Who was the large lady? I'm sure the studio walls shook when she walked into the main office. She put me off my practice and I reckon I almost had it then, too. Another two seconds and – woof – I'd have vanished.'

'I wish you'd stop practising in here, Arthur,' moaned Vlad. 'It's disgusting.'

Arthur's straining to become invisible usually resulted in a lot of grunting and some strange smells that couldn't be ignored.

'It was Nudgebuster & Co. Miss Fitz owes them money,' said Princess PJ.

'That was against the Pirate Code,' said Desmond.

'But I'm not a pirate,' said PJ. 'And the others have got a right to know. Plus, we all know that Shuggy can't keep a secret.'

'It's true,' said a short pirate with impressive dreadlocks and large hoop earring hanging from his left ear lobe. 'Secrets seem to take on a life of their own in my mouth.'

'We'll all be out on the street next week,' wailed Vlad. 'No one wants a vampire who's afraid of tight spaces.'

'And mice,' added Arthur.

'And faints at the sight of blood,' PJ continued.

'Who needths a big, bad wolf wiv no teef?' said Wilbur. He's a wolf, but a thin, scraggy one. 'Eshpeshly one who can't shee wivout his glasshes.' Unfortunately, Wilbur was also quite vain and didn't like wearing them.

'Gums can be quite scary, Wilbur,' replied Spud. He's another one of Desmond's pirates. 'My great grandmother had no teeth and when she kissed me it was like she was sucking a boiled sweet.' And he shuddered.

PJ looked at him. 'Yes, but it doesn't take much to scare you, Spud. No offence, but you and Dazzling Desmond Death's other Dancing Desperados aren't much like *proper* pirates, are you?'

Desmond's parrot, Prendergast, looked offended and squawked loudly. Desmond stood as tall as he could to look PJ in the eye.

'It's pronounced *de' Ath*, as you well know.'

In that moment he did seem to be a 'proper pirate.' Then, just as quickly, the magic broke and he was Desmond again.

'And I think you'll find that dancing pirates will be the Next Big Thing. All we need is to be discovered...'

'All any of us needs is to be discovered, Desmond,' grumbled Princess PJ. 'But who's going to give a stunt princess like me a job? I can climb, walk the tight-rope, hang-glide, ski-jump, sword fight,' and she sliced the air with her sword. 'Plus I have a knock-out punch. Instead I have to put up with vain, boastful Prince Charmings, Aladdins and knights in shining armour saving the day while I have to do all the squealing and mushy stuff. YUCK!' And she kicked a chair across the room.

'Ouch!'

'Sorry, Arthur, didn't see you there.'

'What will become ov uss?' Wilbur cried. 'I'll never sssurvive in da wild.'

'What about your false teeth?' Shuggy suggested.

'Vey don't eksssactly fit well.'

That was true. One time when Wilbur had the hiccups, he swallowed the bottom denture. PJ had to do the Heimlich manoeuvre on him, which not only saved his life, but cured the hiccups too.

'Should we tell them what we've decided?' Aunt Fenula whispered.

I chickened out and shook my head.

Aunt Fenula closed the door gently.

'You're right. Let's not upset them any more today,' she said.

Saturday 24 July 10.00 a.m.
Trouble Scale 6-

The next morning, things seemed a teensy bit better than they had done the night before (teensy is a bit of a silly word, but it feels very small). We had drawn up a Five Point Plan to take to the bank. If they liked it, they might lend us some money.

The Miss Fitz Character Agency Five Point Business Plan.

By Cid Fitz, with 'help' from Aunt Fenula

1. Check down the back of the sofa, under the filing cabinet, in the bottom of Aunt Fenula's handbag and under her bed for any money we might have missed.

2. Increase the fee for characters joining the Miss Fitz Agency to £100.

3. Go through ALL the 'Help Wanted' ads for characters, on showbizizuz.com *and in* That's Showbiz! *weekly. Apply for EVERYTHING!!*

4. Cut costs e.g. Desmond's Dancing Desperados.

(I couldn't bring myself to write down what number 4 really meant in any detail.)

5. Take this plan to Mrs. Flush at the bank to see if they'll lend us any money.

Aunt Fenula and I were at the bank and in Mrs. Flush's office by 10 a.m. She was studying the plan carefully.

'They wouldn't lend me money before,' whispered Aunt Fenula in a low voice. 'That's why I ended up with Nudgebuster & Co.'

I nudged her with my elbow, hoping she'd understand and keep quiet. It worked.

Finally, Mrs. Flush asked, 'Did you find any money down the back of the sofa, under the filing cabinet or anywhere else totally inappropriate?'

While Aunt Fenula was counting out the £11.35 we had collected onto her desk, Mrs. Flush stared at us over her glasses. I wondered if she could actually see us or if she was doing my trick. I thought about turning my eyelids inside out to see her reaction. I have never met anyone who likes the eyelid thing. If she didn't flinch, I would know she was pretending and it was all for effect. I didn't do it, of course, but it was very tempting.

As Mrs. Flush discussed the rest of the plan, I noticed that her nostrils flared whenever her voice became louder. She said she approved of point two. She said she couldn't believe that we didn't do point three 'as a matter of course, Miss Fitz' (her nostrils flared widely) and she wanted more details on point 4.

'Who is Desmond, what are his Desperados desperate about and why are they dancing?'

Aunt Fenula left me to explain, as she was very teary.

When I had finished Mrs. Flush exclaimed, 'Really? How extraordinary!' and her nostrils reached maximum flare.

'Do I have to tell Desmond and his crew they've got to go?' Aunt Fenula asked.

'If you wish the bank to lend you the money, then yes,' Flush answered.

'Why you unfeel…'

I pushed Aunt Fenula through Mrs. Flush's office door before she could say anything more as I knew whatever it was she was going to say, or worse, do, would get us thrown out of the bank. On the way back to the Miss Fitz Agency offices, she was very glum. She said very little other than repeating, 'But do we *really* have to tell Desmond and his crew they've got to go?'

And I would say, 'Yes. It's tough but it's show business.'

Finally, because I didn't like seeing her so upset, I added, 'But maybe there'll be a miracle, like in the films.'

You've probably already guessed that some sort of a "miracle" was going to turn up. And it did. Except "miracle" is too strong a word in this case. In fact, "good luck" might be pushing it. But it was definitely luck. Of a sort.

Chapter Four

Saturday 24 July 12.38 p.m.

I was sitting in the back office of the Miss Fitz Agency at about lunchtime, working through yet more sums, when the main office door opened (quietly this time). I peeped though a crack in the back office door as a round, fidgety man with brown hair and a ginger beard entered. Next to him was a boy with a floppy blond fringe.

'Are you sure this is a good idea, Rory?' the man said. 'Look.' And he pointed at the cracked front window held together by duct tape. 'That's not the sign of a successful business.'

So far, not so good, and that wasn't only because I knew Rory from school. 'Knew' is a bit strong. Rory Birkwhistle is always picked first for team sports and games, when he isn't doing the picking, that is. He was captain of the boys' football and basketball teams, in the gymnastics squad and could make Holly Prickles (yes, really – there ought to be a law or some kind of names test parents have to pass) go red and giggly.

Holly is editor-in-chief of our Leavers' Year Book, which means Rory would probably be on the front cover and most of the inside pages, while I will be lucky to get a mention on the 'Students Who Wore Uniform On Non-Uniform Day' page. Really that should be my own special page as: 1. it was only me and Edwin Dorstrapp who turned up in school uniform and he ran home again; 2. I did it again the following year. I blamed Winston for 'accidentally' deleting all the school emails. Mum would not listen when I told her that 'accidentally' deleting did not delete them from the 'Bin' folder too, which is what Winston had done. She said if I didn't know what was going on in my own school it was all my fault anyway. One more example of her siding with Winston.

'I'm positive, Dad,' said Rory. 'Anyway, what else can we do? We're running out of options *and* time.'

That sounded more promising. For us, anyway. I decided to stay in the back office in case seeing me might put Rory (and therefore his dad) off using the agency. Assuming he recognised me of course, which he probably wouldn't, but I dare not take the risk. I crouched down and continued watching through the crack in the door.

Mr. Birkwhistle rang the bell on the counter. They jumped as Aunt Fenula popped up from behind like a burnt bun from a toaster. She had been grubbing around in the dirt looking for more lost change, so it wasn't the most professional introduction. For starters, her hair resembled unravelled wool.

'Greetings,' she said. 'I'm Miss Fitz.' And she beamed her best smile. Luckily it didn't put Mr. Birkwhistle off. 'Who can I do for you?'

Aunt Fenula loves to ask this question because she thinks it's funny. It isn't. It's auntie humour. Mr. Birkwhistle was baffled.

'Who can you... what... huh?'

As we later discovered, Mr. Birkwhistle was easily baffled. He said it was because he was a creative genius, too busy thinking Great Thoughts. Lucky for him that Rory turned out to be a surprisingly practical sort. I listened closely.

'We are looking for pirates, aren't we, Dad?' said Rory.

'You've come to the right place then, Mr...?'

'Birkwhistle. Byron Birkwhistle. And this is Rory. Here's my card.'

Birkwhistle Universal Media Productions

Excelling in entertaining

'When only an all-round artistic genius will do.'

www.byronbumptv.com

HOLLYWOOD < > MUMBAI < > PARIS < > BOGNOR

Aunt Fenula squealed with excitement. 'THE Byron Birkwhistle? Of BUM Productions?'

'I prefer BUMP. And yes.' Mr. Birkwhistle wiped the sweat from under his glasses before adding, 'So, do you have any pirates?'

'For *Pirate Premiership Knockout* I assume? Look no further!' Aunt Fenula replied. It seemed that our miracle had arrived, and not before time. *Pirate Premiership Knockout* was the unexpected television hit of the summer.

'The thing is,' said Rory, 'they have to be able to beat Putrid Pete Pukebreath.'

'If not the deal's off,' added Mr. Birkwhistle. 'There's potentially millions of pounds at stake. Are you *sure* your pirates are up for the challenge? You've seen him on TV?'

I held my breath, waiting for Aunt Fenula to reply. If she told the truth, we were in danger of plungin straight to number 7, or more, in the Trouble Scale.

Aunt Fenula smiled again – I really must tell her not to, especially not if she's going to show ALL her teeth. Mr. Birkwhistle began pacing.

'He's got to be stopped! The public love to hate him, and that's fantastic for our viewing figures, but now we need him to lose. That same public will want him to get his comeuppance in the grand finale. And we want everyone talking about it. We want them downloading, uploading and re-loading it. We want it viral. But if Captain Pukebreath wins, everyone is disappointed and, more importantly, Graffham H. Scrope IV won't buy *Pirate Premiership Knock-Out* for American television.'

I was a bit puzzled by this. Of course I wanted a large slice of triple layered luck with jam and cream filling landing on our plate, but this wasn't right. The competition was supposed to be decided by the runner-up in the *Pirate Premiership Knockout* league table playing the top crew. Surely BUMP only needed to make sure the runner-up won?

Luckily Aunt Fenula asked the question. I stayed hidden.

'The runners-up are refusing to take on Pukebreath in the finale,' Rory explained. 'And they aren't the only ones. None of the other crews is willing to go against him either and it's becoming impossible to find any new ones to take him on.

'So,' said Mr. Birkwhistle, 'if you can't help us…'

Aunt Fenula nodded thoughtfully. 'Do you mind if I consult with my assistant for a moment?'

Then next thing I remember is falling into the main office as Aunt Fenula pulled open the door. I wanted the floorboards to splinter wide and swallow me whole. Instead they held firm, so rather than scramble to my feet in a fluster, I lay back and propped my head up on my hand and smiled up at everyone. Looking back, I can't believe it seemed like a smooth move at the time.

'You've caught me taking a break,' I said.

Rory and his father stared at me then looked at each other, while Aunt Fenula's unravelled hair seemed to be frizzing as she glared at me.

'If you wouldn't mind stirring yourself, Clematis,' she snapped.

By now, I wasn't feeling quite so smooth. I hoped that hearing me called 'Clematis' instead of Cid would confuse Rory into thinking I was someone else (although the thought of two people looking like me made me feel sorry for whoever the other one might be).

'Aren't you the girl…?' Rory began.

Thankfully Aunt Fenula bundled me into the back office before he could finish his question.

'I take it you were listening?'

I nodded.

'Well?' she whispered excitedly, 'This could be that miracle you were talking about. They are desperately in need of pirates for the finale of *Premiership Pirate Knockout*.'

'You have met Desmond?' I said.

Of course she had. What I meant was that he wasn't suitable. Not at all. Not in any way.

'But Mr. Birkwhistle, *Premiership Pirate Knockout* – it has to be that miracle you mentioned, Cid!' Aunt Fenula wasn't going to give up easily.

So I said, 'You know there's no dance round on *Premiership Pirate Knockout*?'

Of course she knew. What I meant was that Desmond's crew's pirate skills were certainly not the best (and in fact were probably the worst) ever seen. *Premiership Pirate Knockout* was all about proper pirating and swashbuckling, whatever a "swash" is.

'Desmond's talents are more in the song and dance area,' I whispered. 'And his crew don't really have any talents of any sort.' Harsh but true. My worry was that Aunt Fenula was getting us into a situation that might make me do something I had never done before and never wanted to: jump to point 11 on the Trouble Scale.

'But if Mr. Birkwhistle can't find any other crew willing to take them on the whole thing will be scrapped and that won't help anybody. It has to be worth a try.'

I scribbled down a quick flow chart of our options.

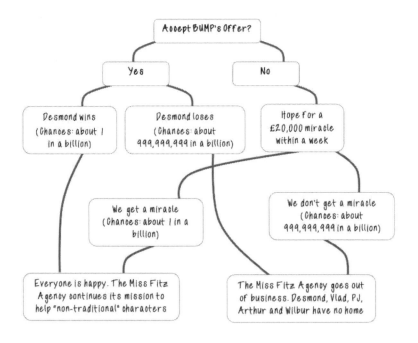

CID FITZ's PROBLEM SOLVING FLOW CHART
Problem No. 43 Do we accept BUMP's offer?

Mr. Birkwhistle poked his head into the back office. 'Well? Is the Miss Fitz Agency up to it? If not, say so as I've no more time to waste.'

As I heard what Aunt Fenula said next the cold, lumpy custard of dread plopped into my stomach.

'Indeed we are, Mr. Birkwhistle. Let me assure you that we have a crew on our books that is unlike anything you or Mr. Pukebreath will have come across before. Ever. I can safely say they'll take him by surprise.'

That was true, at least.

'Wonderful,' Byron Birkwhistle replied. 'Without a replacement crew before Monday, we'd have to cancel the finale and Pukebreath would get the prize without even a fight. And then it's all over.'

'We need to discuss terms,' said Aunt Fenula. 'Fees and such like. I know it shouldn't really matter when it comes to art, but business is business.'

'What fees did you have in mind?'

Aunt Fenula is a good actor. She used to be one when she was not much older than I am. When she replied, '£20,000,' my glasses nearly slipped off my nose. I thought she'd ask for about £5,000, but £20,000 – that was way more than usual. Mr. Birkwhistle's eyeballs seemed to be inflating, which told me he thought the same.

'That's more than we err… usually… are you sure?' he stuttered, lifting his glasses and wiping away some beads of sweat.

'We here at the Miss Fitz Agency pride ourselves on finding unique characters with unexpected qualities,' said Aunt Fenula.

Translation: 'We here at the Miss Fitz Agency take on characters no one else wants because they are too different. In fact, they are not what you'd expect by any stretch of your imagination.'

Usually, when directors and producers discover our characters' unexpected qualities (like vampires fainting at the sight of blood) they are sacked. Very rarely, however, someone comes along who is so desperate they are willing to try anything. Aunt Fenula can sense this – it's a bit like a superpower. I could tell she sensed desperation in Byron Birkwhistle.

Mr. Birkwhistle took out his mobile. He tapped and swiped the screen for a couple of moments. Aunt Fenula winked at me.

'£20,000 is not acceptable, Miss Fitz. I'm afraid we'll have to go elsewhere.' He walked back into the main office. 'Come along, Rory.'

As he turned to leave, Rory grabbed his sleeve. 'But, Dad!'

Aunt Fenula winked at me again before going to hold the door open for Mr. Birkwhistle.

'Goodbye. We are sorry to see you go, Mr. Birkwhistle.' Then she paused, seeming to work something out in her head before adding, 'But if you sign up with us today on our Gold Service Scheme, I can give you our special promotional offer of a 50% deduction for new customers.'

Aunt Fenula is good at thinking on her feet. For starters we don't have any schemes, let alone a Gold Service. And we certainly don't have promotional offers because we can't afford them.

'£10,000?' said Mr. Birkwhistle. 'Payment would not be until the completion of the finale.'

'And an extra £10,000 if they win?'

'An extra…I'm not sure if… but that's still £20,000 in total.' The beads of sweat were appearing under his glasses again.

Rory gave his dad a little shove and a serious Look before saying, 'Of course, Miss Fitz, it'll be worth every penny if—when–they win. Won't it, Dad?'

Mr. Birkwhistle was too busy wiping under the rims of his glasses again to answer.

Aunt Fenula smiled. 'That seems most acceptable, Mr. Birkwhistle. Let's sort out the paperwork.'

Sunday 25 July 9.30 a.m.
Trouble Scale either 1+ (Aunt Fenula) or 7 (Me)

Aunt Fenula left the agency early the next morning to finalise the deal with BUMP and find out what was to happen on Monday morning, when the filming of the grand finale began.

'You can tell Desmond the good news while I'm gone, Cid,' she had said as she shut her coat in the office door. 'He'll be delighted,' she had added when she opened it again to free herself. That was when I noticed she was wearing one green and one yellow shoe, but it was easier not to say anything. So I didn't.

I made a large bowl of Nutty-Oaty-Choco-Crunch and thought about Saturday afternoon. It had all happened so fast, I had felt dazed. Now it hit me, what we had done. We'd made a deal to supply pirates to win the grand finale episode of *Premiership Pirate Knockout*. I felt too nervous to have more than two bowls of cereal. Dazzling Desmond de'Ath and his Dancing Desperados? Against Putrid Pete Pukebreath? It wouldn't end well. Desmond might be very sweet, but that was a problem. Pirates aren't meant to be sweet.

'Don't see problems, Cid, see opportunities.'

Why one of Dad's Wise Old Sayings popped into my head at that moment, I don't know, but I decided to do something I'd never done before: listen to it.

So I asked myself, could we find a way to make Desmond and his Dancing Desperados being sweet on *Premiership Pirate Knockout* work? After all, they were irresistible in an unexpected, confusing sort of way. Once the audience saw them, they might love them even if they didn't win. And if the audience loved them, Graffham H. Scrope IV would surely buy the TV series for America and we'd be saved. *Premiership Pirate Knockout* could be our miracle. Sorted. I had a third bowl of cereal.

I felt quite bouncy as I walked over to the FFAFA portacabin. Desmond was there, taking his crew through their paces.

'First position... good. Second position... and arms... Third position...'

In case you are wondering, arms means arms as in arms and legs, not as in weapons. And the positions are ballet positions. Ballet is well known for being extremely tough and, to be fair, Desmond is quite good at it. There were two big problems, however.

First, there is no demand for dancing pirates.

Second, even if there were, Desmond's crew were not cut out for ballet. Carlos could be quite skilful (when his peg leg was under control) but Clayton had the grace of a sack of coconuts. Spud was fairly nimble (when he didn't get his hook caught) but Shuggy was clumsy. Finally, Gruff was as strong as a box (but also looked like one), and Barry was too thin and wispy (although he described himself as 'willowy', which is also how Mum usually describes me to her friends.)

Once his crew had done all five basic ballet positions, Desmond moved them onto jumps. This was not successful. To start with they looked like a net full of frantic fish freshly landed on a trawler. It finished with a pile up after Gruff landed on Shuggy's foot. Shuggy went to kick him but missed and took out Carlos's peg leg making him grab hold of Barry who knocked over Spud who got his hook caught in Clayton's belt and pulled his trousers down to his knees as they fell. Wilbur, Princess PJ and some of the others started giggling.

By the time Desmond had sorted them out, one half of the crew wasn't talking to the other half.

'I, for one, cannot endure under such circumstances!' sniffed Carlos. 'I feel most discombobulated.'

Typical Carlos! I wasn't sure what dis-com-bob-thingied meant either, but Barry made it clearer.

'I too am unable to continue,' he said. 'I feel quite distressed.'

'Me three. I've had enough,' finished Clayton, as he pulled up his trousers. 'I feel like a right 'nana.' Then he added, 'And they're my lucky pair, too,' as he pointed at his kitten underpants.

I told Desmond I needed a word with him. I explained that Aunt Fenula was talking to a new client who was looking for pirates to take on Putrid Pete Pukebreath in the grand finale. He beamed.

'I knew that dear lady recognised talent when she saw it.'

PJ almost exploded. 'Are you seriously suggesting you go up against Putrid Pete Pukebreath? Your crew? As in that lot over there?'

She jerked her thumb in the direction of the other pirates. An argument over who had caused the pile up during ballet practice had turned into a fight. Sort of. It was mainly a lot of shoving, poking and running away shouting, 'Can't get me.'

I began having second thoughts. I decided that Desmond's crew wouldn't survive more than a couple of rounds of the *Pirate Premiership Knockout* grand finale.

Then a little voice in my head said, 'Don't see problems, see opportunities. Be positive, Cid.' So I had third thoughts. What were a few minor injuries if it meant that the Miss Fitz Agency was saved, along with Vlad, Wilbur, Princess PJ, Arthur and the others? We'd have to make it work.

I told them the news.

'Aunt Fenula is over at BUMP productions, signing a contract for you. 'It's kind of a pirate reality television thingy...'

And that was as far as I got.

'This is our big break into show business,' Desmond cried, pirouetting around the room. 'I always knew "The Biz" was my true calling. We're going to be stars, my hearties!'

There was much cheering and whooping among the crew. They were so excited that I got caught up in The Moment and decided against going in to details. There was plenty of time for them to find out what they were doing. And who they were competing with.

Sunday 25 July 2.15 p.m.
Trouble Scale 7+ (I was right.)

The Moment lasted until Aunt Fenula returned from the BUMP studios with the filming schedule. She handed copies around before reading it out.

PREMIERSHIP PIRATE KNOCKOUT

Putrid Pete Pukebreath And His Pustules (Team Screaming Skull) v.
Dastardly Desmond Death And His Desperadoes (Team Seahorse).

Desmond put up his hand. 'Shouldn't that be "Dazzling Desmond De'Ath and his Dancing Desperadoes?"' he asked.

I frowned at Aunt Fenula but she said it was simply a typo and continued going through the schedule.

Episode Six Filming Schedule

Monday: Day 0

Meet the teams. Film 'getting to know you' pieces and footage of teams relaxing and training to be used in introductions and fill-ins for the programme.

Raft race – fun contest to build up the rivalry. Film more fill-in shots.

Tuesday: Day 1

Pirate Skills Competition.

Each team can earn 5 points for winning and up to 5 additional points for style. Day 1 maximum total possible = 40 points.

1. Rope swinging
2. Climbing the rigging
3. Hoisting the main sail
4. Cannon firing

<u>Wednesday: Day 2</u>

Treasure Island competition. Each team can win up to 10 points for pirate skills used in finding the treasure. Day 2 maximum total possible = 10 points.

<u>Thursday & Friday: Rest Days</u>

<u>Saturday: Grand Finale</u>

Battle between Team *Screaming Skull* and Team *Seahorse*.

Winner gets 50 points and the *Premiership Pirate Knockout* Trophy and a golden treasure chest full of £10, £20 and £50 notes.

No points for second place, style or skills. Grand Finale maximum total = 50 points.

Shuggy gulped. 'But that says we're up against... Putrid Pete Pukebreath!'

Then panic broke out.

'We'll be puréed,' said Carlos. 'Like tomatoes.'

'We'll be scrambled,' added Barry. 'Like eggs.'

'We'll be mushed,' finished Clayton. 'Like that!' And he smashed his right fist into his left hand. 'Ow!' Then he added, 'And that *really* hurts.'

I looked frantically at Aunt Fenula, who gave a gritted teeth grimace that made the tendons in her neck stand out like handles. PJ jumped in to save us.

'The important thing is to know your enemy,' she said.

'But we do,' warbled Spud. 'And that's the problem. Everyone knows Putrid Pete Pukebreath. We're doomed!'

'Nonsense,' said Desmond. 'A positive attitude is all that's required.'

PJ raised her voice to be heard over the panicky pirates. 'All you need are a couple of good strategies and some practice. It's the little things that count. Make sure your gun deck is well organised and the areas around the cannons are tidy.'

'We can do that,' Desmond beamed.

PJ carried on. 'Blast the opposition quickly, before they get time to realise what's hit 'em. Then blast them again. When you attack with your swords, make sure your lunges have strong follow through – be able to stretch that little bit further when they step back.'

'Ah,' said Desmond. 'Those things there…'

'The strategies?'

'Yes. They're not really our thing.'

'So what is?'

'Well, as pirates we like to rely on good map reading, fair shares in the treasure and efficient sail management. Look at the schedule. Victory on days one and two is well within our grasp.'

'What about battles and fights?'

'We avoid those. Too dangerous. Someone always gets hurt.'

'I've got a battle strategy,' said Gruff. 'I shout "look behind you" and when they do, I run.'

'Except last time you tried that, you tripped over your sword and fell flat on your face,' said Barry. He turned to PJ. 'It's true. I took three splinters from his nose.'

The 'good news' bouncy feeling from earlier had melted into squishy niggles wriggling through my insides. This was not going to end well. I did a few new calculations. Dazzling Desmond taking part in the finale of *Premiership Pirate Knockout* could send the Miss Fitz Agency to at least number 8 on the on the Star Trouble Scale. Possibly 9. In fact, I had the feeling things might even be heading for 10.

Chapter Five

Monday 26 July 8.00 a.m.
Trouble Scale: 8 (0 according to Aunt Fenula!)

The following morning, everyone was to arrive at the docks to begin filming *Pirate Premiership Knock-Out*. Aunt Fenula had given me the job of making sure Desmond and his crew made it to the set. She was on her way to Nudgebuster & Co. to tell them the good news about the £10,000 fee and the bonus for winning. I gave her a repayment plan that I had worked out for the other £10,000 in case (when!) Desmond didn't win. Aunt Fenula was feeling a lot more enthusiastic about it than I was. She seemed convinced that our worries were over.

'Once I tell them they can have £10,000 by the end of the week, I'm sure they'll agree with this plan of yours about the rest.'

'And if Desmond and his crew don't make it to the end? Or if they lose? You weren't there for the strategy discussion yesterday.'

'You worry too much, Cid.'

Aunt Fenula was probably right about that. On the other hand, if she had worried a bit more maybe we wouldn't be hovering quite so high on the Ten Point Trouble Scale.

I set off for the dockyard where the filming was to take place.

As I walked through the gates, I could see cars, caravans, trucks and trailers parked well back from the dock. Usually there were cargoes for ships piled on the quayside but today, people were unloading equipment and even some scenery from the trucks. Others were popping in and out of caravans and a tall woman with short, curly hair, was shouting instructions about the placing of lights, boom microphones and rails for cameras to roll along. Later, I would find out that she was Delia Drummond, and was in charge of filming.

When I arrived, Desmond and his crew were already aboard their ship, *Seahorse*. As I rounded the building where the Maritime Museum was, I could see only two ships anchored alongside the quay and as soon as I saw them I knew that Desmond's just had to be the one with the sagging rigging, flabby sails and wonky crow's nest. It was topped off with a tatty skull and crossbones. The skull was smiling, but not in a sinister, timber-shivering way. It looked … happy.

On the other hand, the crew looked nervous, and they weren't the only ones.

'Don't worry, Cid,' Desmond had said at breakfast. 'We've a few jitters, but that's healthy before a big performance. I gave them my second best pep talk. I'm saving the best for the big battle finale. Still, they're well pepped and ready to go.'

A long limousine with dark tinted windows drew up on the quayside. Out stepped a large, round man with enormous, very dark sunglasses. He was wearing a bright blue suit and blowing bubble gum bubbles. Mr. Birkwhistle scrambled out of the car after him.

'What do we have here, Birkwhistle?' asked the man, watching Desmond lead his crew down the gangplank. I was counting them to make sure they were all present and correct.

'That's Team *Seahorse*, the crew that is going to win *Pirate Premiership Knock-Out*, Mr. Scrope.'

Of course I had heard of Graffham H. Scrope IV – who hadn't – but to see him in the flesh was … interesting. His sunglasses were so dark that anyone daring to look him in the eye would see two distorted reflections of themselves. And his suit was so bright and so blue that you could see it for a long time after you shut your eyes. It made you want to look anywhere but right at him. That gave Mr. Scrope another advantage (as if he needed one). The person talking to him was never able to look him in the eye yet they felt his sharp, cold stare drilling into them like… well, like a drill. The bubble gum was a bit much, though. There are some things older people simply shouldn't do and blowing bubble gum bubbles is one of them. Another is skateboarding, especially wearing slippers and goggles. (Aunt Fenula.)

Splat! A large bubble burst and Mr. Scrope's tongue stuck out to scoop it back in before it stuck to his chin. He looked like a blue bullfrog catching a fly. I shuddered.

'They'd better, Birkwhistle,' Scrope drawled, poking a stubby finger at him. 'The public has loved hating Pukebreath and his *Screaming Skull* team. But now he must get his comeuppance. The baddies have to be beaten. That's what our audience expects. If not, I'm pulling out of the deal.'

'Dastardly Dezzy Death and his crew are fearless, Mr. Scrope,' replied Mr. Birkwhistle. 'Aren't they, Cid?'

I felt 'clueless' might be more truthful, but I had all my fingers crossed and said, 'Yes, Mr. Birkwhistle.'

Mum says there are two reasons to cross your fingers: for luck, or when fibbing. (Fibbing sounds less serious than lying, and I think it was OK anyway because my fingers were crossed for both reasons.)

Mr. Scrope and Mr. Birkwhistle went over to the pirates, where Rory was waiting with the clapperboard. I slunk along behind them wishing I could turn invisible or at least a bit hazy, like Arthur.

'All set, Rory?'

I wondered how long Mr. Birkwhistle would sound that confident.

'Yes, Dad. I think everyone's ready.'

The pirates nodded enthusiastically.

'So, kid, what's on today's schedule?' Mr. Scrope asked.

I had been so mesmerised by Mr. Scrope's bubble gum, that I hadn't seen Rory standing there. He checked his clipboard. 'It's all the filming of "getting to know you" segments and footage to use as fillers when we put the final programme together – training shots, that sort of thing. We've a fun raft race to help break the ice this afternoon and a "Meet 'n' Mingle" buffet this evening. First, however, the new crew has to introduce themselves, sir.'

'About that,' said Desmond looming into the conversation from behind Rory. 'We have been working on a little something.' And he nodded at Barry, who was holding an accordion. 'Take it away, lads!' And as he began playing, the pirates started to sing.

'I'm Shuggy.' (Shuggy stepped forward and shook his dreadlocks.)

'I'm Clayton.' (Clayton waved.)

'I'm Gruff.' (Gruff looked at the camera and winked.)

'As pirates we can be quite tough.

We like finding treasure

For us it's a pleasure,

We love all that sparkly stuff.'

The song continued as the others introduced themselves.

'I'm Barry.'

'I'm Carlos.'

'I'm Spud.'

And the treasure we dig from the mud

We then share with the poor,

So we always need more,

Being pirates is deep in our blood.'

Then Desmond stepped in front of them, and sang:

'I'm captain of this fine, strong crew,

As we sail the wide ocean blue.

We love a good quest,

Always give of our best

And we're very polite as we do.'

'We could,' said Desmond, as the tune came to an end, 'add a bit of a jig if you like. Nothing too fancy.'

He stood on tiptoe and stretched his arms above his head. 'Spin, turn, kick, pirouette. And repeat,' he muttered to himself as he did his little dance. 'What do you think?'

I winced. Rory gasped. Mr. Birkwhistle gulped. Delia, who was in charge of filming, clamped her lips tight to stifle a giggle. Everyone turned to look at Graffham H. Scrope and held their breaths. He chewed his bubble gum for a few moments until…

'I like it! It's new, different, modern – pirates who give to the poor. It'll get the public right behind you.'

The Dancing Desperados high fived each other. At least they looked less nervous.

'Yes – I can see it now,' Scrope continued, spreading his hands wide in a giant arc. 'Goodies versus baddies. Heroes versus villains. Plucky underdogs against the vicious bullies. Pukebreath gets his comeuppance.' And he slapped Mr. Birkwhistle on the back. 'It's going to be quite the fight, yes siree. A real battle royal. Let's grab a coffee.'

Monday 26 July 10.15 a.m.

As Mr. Birkwhistle and Graffham H. Scrope IV drove off again in the stretch limousine, leaving me nowhere to hide, Rory looked up from his clipboard and stared at me.

'It's… Clematis, isn't it? You look exactly like this girl at my…'

But before he could finish, I heard myself blurt out, 'Hiya, Rory.'

Then my arm decided to do its own thing too and I watched helplessly as I gave him an open-palm, circular wave. I cringed. Who waves like that? And who says 'hiya'? Even now the whole thing is playing back in my head, on a loop, in slow motion.

'It *is* you. The one in Miss MacLean's class who came to non-uniform day in her school uniform.' And he grinned.

Why are popular kids popular when they're so … like Rory was being? It all seems to be about image with them. Unfortunately, I don't have much of one. Well, I do, but not the right kind of image, as the 'hiya' and the palm wave had proved.

Rory chuckled. 'And you did it twice. Even Dorky Dorstrapp remembered last year.'

'That was not my fault. My brother deleted the school emails.'

'Who needs an email to remember it's non-uniform day?'

Okay, now he was starting to sound like my mother and that was really annoying. I glared at him as I waited for my brain to come up with something better to say than, 'Me, obviously.' It was still working on it when Spud, Carlos, Shuggy, Gruff, Barry and Clayton shuffled over to speak to Rory.

'Errr… about the battle,' said Spud. 'The Captain says it's all special effects, body doubles and make-up. That's right, isn't it?'

'Of course not,' said Rory. 'Where did you get that idea? It's *reality* television. It's true that there is some make-up involved…'

'Oh good,' Carlos whispered very loudly to anyone who was listening. 'I always worry that my lips are too thin and my eyelashes don't stand out enough.'

'… but you won't need body doubles,' Rory continued. 'There's nothing you're going to be doing that you expert pirates can't cope with. A bit of rope swinging, sail rigging, plank walking – that sort of thing.

Pirates who've earned the name "Dastardly Dezzy Death and his Crew" have nothing to fear. This finale is going to be the biggest TV ratings hit of the year.'

'Expert pirates?' asked Shuggy.

'I think you've got it wrong,' said Gruff. 'We're not Dastardly Dezzy Death and his crew.'

'But that's what Miss Fitz told us.' Rory searched the emails on his tablet. 'Yes – here it is.'

To: Byron.Birkwhistle@byronBUMPtv.com

From: fennyfitzcharacters@themissfitzagency.com

Subject: Pirate Premiership

Dear Mr. Birkwhistle,

Good news. Our pirates are very eager to do your show.

Dastardly Desmond "Dezzy" Death and his crew can start tomorrow as agreed. I'm sending Cid with them to help settle them in. I'll send you our bill as soon as I have typed it up.

'Dastardly?' said Carlos. 'She meant "Dazzling", surely?'

'Dezzy?' said Barry. 'He only ever answers to "Desmond".'

'Death?' said Clayton. 'It's "de'Ath" – definitely *NOT* "Death".'

Rory glared at me. 'Your aunt has sent us the wrong crew. I should have known there'd be a screw-up if you're involved.'

And he pulled out his phone to call his dad. Moments later, the stretch limousine was back. Mr. Birkwhistle got out and began waving his arms, splashing coffee everywhere, demanding explanations and threatening to ruin us.

Chapter Six

"You'd better explain yourself, young lady,' Rory's dad hissed, trying not to alert Graffham H. Scrope to the fact that something was wrong. I was too discombobu-thing-ied to complain about being called young lady. I could feel us shooting up the Trouble Scale so I had to think fast.

'Of course she hasn't, Mr. Birkwhistle. The "Dazzling Desmond de'Ath" thing is all part of the act… their act that is.'

I was quite pleased with my own ingenuity ('ingenuity' is a complicated, intelligent kind of word, so I think it's better to use than creativity in this case). Then I lowered my voice as if letting him in on a great secret.

'They pretend to be hopeless. It makes Putrid Pete think they're a walkover. It's very clever really. It gives them an important strategic advantage if their opponents think that they're incompetent wusses.'

There was a dazzling flash of blue as Mr. Scrope stepped out of the limo, followed by silence as everyone watched him take a lump of soft, squidgy bubble gum from his mouth and hand it to Mr. Birkwhistle. Another Yuck Moment. I think he was looking at me when he said, 'Brilliant idea, young lady. You clearly know about ratings. The *Premiership Pirate Knockout* finale will be an even bigger wow with the audience. And that means shed loads of dollars.'

Mr. Birkwhistle, still holding the used lump of bubble gum, began agreeing with Mr. Scrope. What a crawler. Except 'crawler' is too lame for him. He was being a sycophant. It's a strange word but totally the right one as it means mega-crawler. And Mr. Birkwhistle was making me feel sick with an amount of crawling the size of an elephant. So he was clearly being a sick-o-phant. Except the dictionary spells it 'sycophant'.

I have to be honest, I smirked. A lot. Rory wasn't smiling though.

'All I can say,' said Rory, 'is that it must take a great deal of acting skill for your pirates to appear *that* incompetent.'

He looked me straight in the eye. I held his gaze. There was too much at stake to worry about what might happen at school.

'It does.' I said. 'They do incompetent very well.'

And, to be fair, that is the truth. They're brilliant at it. Which is why I was able look Rory in the eye. But there was another reason, too. I was starting to feel quite protective of Desmond and his Dancing Desperados, and it was more than simply feeling sorry for them.

At the same time, I was very worried about what would happen to them, and all the others, if they didn't win the contest. I couldn't bear the thought of Nudgebuster & Co. throwing everyone onto the streets and squandering what was left after Aunt Fenula had worked so hard to help out of work entertainers and characters that no one wanted.

'Sometimes,' Aunt Fenula had said to me that morning, 'when you meet someone who is not quite what you expected, it helps to find out a little more about them. And as Desmond is not quite what anyone expects in a pirate captain, I'm going to tell you a little bit about him.'

This is Desmond's story as told to me by Aunt Fenula.

'To say Desmond was a bit of a disappointment to his parents is like saying the Arctic is a bit chilly, or the poisonous man-eating razer-back Omni monster is a bit dangerous. You see, there was "Something" about Desmond from the day he was born. The sort of Something that everyone knows but never mentions. Except possibly his Great Aunt Marylin. But then it was often whispered that Desmond was "Just like *her*".

Desmond was born a pirate. That wasn't the Something. Desmond's family were all pirates. Even their cat, Nine Tails, was a pirate.

Desmond's dad (Drastic Diego) and little sister (Lawless Lindy) were really good pirates. His mother (Pitiless Pearl) and big brother (Marvin the Marauder) were bad pirates. Really, really bad. Stinky, cursing, battle-scarred, harder-than-nails type of bad. They all pronounced their surname "Death" and everyone thought that it was very fitting. Except for Desmond. He always preferred "de'Ath". He was never going to be a traditional pirate, as his report from *The Isambard Pugnacious Academy for Pirates And Desperadoes* showed:'

THE ISAMBARD PUGNACIOUS ACADEMY
FOR PIRATES AND DESPERADOS

Graded "Truly Terrible" by OfSCAM

'The worst establishment we have ever inspected. Its corrupt leadership, vicious staff and imaginative punishments produce vomitingly vile villains.' -OfSCAM*

* Office for Standards in Crimes And Misdemeanours

Report for: **Desmond Death (de'Ath???)**

Form Tutor Comments:

Desmond is a sensitive sort of a pirate. He is exceptionally light on his feet and can carry a tune well. However, he is always picked last for team games and competitions due to his total lack of ability in every other area of pirating.

Progress in Pirating Skills

Climbing the rigging	*Desmond is more of a dangler than a climber.*
Swashbuckling	*'After you, I insist' is NOT how pirates start fights*
Cannon Firing	*Desmond must stop screwing his eyes shut and sticking his fingers in his ears. Especially while aiming and firing the cannon.*
Sword skills	*Carving vegetables into birds and animals is no substitute for slashing and thrusting skills.*
Sea Shanties	*Singing – excellent; composing – Desmond's lyrics lack menace.*
Dancing a jig	*Excellent. Desmond's swift and nifty footwork made him top of the class.*

There was a PS on the other side that read, The Isambard Pugnacious Academy feels that Desmond has needs we cannot meet. Here's the number for the Bedazzled School of Stagecraft: *0478884111. Ask for Cynth. Please ring6 them ASAP. Please, please, PLEASE!!!!*

'Desmond was actually rather proud when he got this report. He hoped that everyone would finally listen to him when he said he wanted to be a dancer rather than a pirate. And *that* was the Something that everyone knew about but no one mentioned.

'When Desmond's mother read his report, however, she did something she had never done before. She wept.

'No! No, no, no, no, no! It's not going to happen. No child of mine is going into show business! Never, never, NEVER!'

'With the final "never!" Pearl grabbed grandpa's wooden leg, much to his surprise, and flung it through the kitchen window and into the street beyond the garden, narrowly missing Nine Tails, but hitting a passer-by. The passer-by's shout of 'Ouch! What the...?' was followed by a whoooosh, thud and 'Miaow, miaOW, YOW!' as grandpa's leg flew back in through the kitchen window and straight into the swing bin, taking Nine Tails with it.

'Desmond's parents refused to give in. They started looking for a new pirate school for him. Every one they rang, however, seemed to be suddenly full. Apart from one: the Mungo Mump Academy for the Pirating Arts. According to its blurb it had "A New Approach for Modern Pirating." Drastic Diego knew about Mungo Mump. He was an old friend of his mum's.

'"Mum said he was very loyal, that she'd trust him with her last doubloon ..." (if you think about it, this isn't really that good a thing to say about a pirate – they are supposed to be mean and greedy, after all) "... I've heard of Mungo's new approach to pirating. It might be just the thing for Desmond."

'Pitiless Pearl looked at the brochure. She didn't like it, but the only other choice was sending Desmond to stage school and there was no way she was going to allow that!'

The Mungo Mump Academy for the Pirating Arts

A New Approach for Modern Pirating

Class included at no extra cost:

pirate fashions | sail origami
shanties & jigs | aromatherapy

'It truly stands out from other pirate schools' –
What Pirate? Schools Guide

The **only** pirate school to be graded
'Defies Description' on the last OfSCAM school inspection

'When Desmond said he was excited about learning origami, Pitiless Pearl did something else she had never done before. She blushed. Not even when she and Diego had been courting had she blushed. But then, she had never been so embarrassed before.

'I think,' Aunt Fenula said at this point, 'that the Mungo Mump Academy made a great impact on our Desmond.' She explained why. 'If Desmond wasn't a typical pirate pupil, Mungo wasn't a typical pirate teacher.

'"I don't hold with the old ways," he used to say. "Times are changing and so must we. I believe in Motivational Pirating. I like my crew to share their ideas, their feelings."

'"He needs a firm hand, captain," said Desmond's mother as she shoved him forward. "Don't spare the cat."

'Pirate legend has it that Mungo actually dared to give Pitiless Pearl a long, hard stare before saying, "Cat? Are you perhaps referring, madam, to the cat o'nine tails? Rewards, dear lady, are better than punishments!"'

(The way Aunt Fenula told it, Mungo Mump sounded just like Desmond.)

'Desmond's dad cut in quickly, before Pitiless Pearl exploded at Mungo.

'"Treasure is the reward, eh captain? And rum, of course."

'"I prefer to use star charts and awards. Perhaps you'll be Pirate of the Week, Desmond? You could win a luxury spa break."

'"Now, Desmond," Drastic Diego said quickly, before his wife could say anything, "drink your rum and remember – the maggots in the ship's biscuits are a valuable source of protein, so don't spit them out."

'"Rum?" cried Mungo. "Maggots? Avocados are a much healthier source of protein, and of essential oils too. In any case, our ship's biscuits are always freshly baked – I hope you like double chocolate chip cookies, Desmond."

'Those who were present said that Pitiless Pearl began hissing like a pressure cooker. "And what's wrong with maggots? They never did me any harm."

'Drastic Diego gave Desmond some good luck gifts. "Here's some extra strong gunpowder I made for you. And a whetstone for sharpening your sword."

"'I'll take those," said Mungo. "We don't practise with *real* gunpowder. I have my own concoction that gives off puffs of fluorescent coloured smoke instead. And as for swords – haven't you heard of health and safety? Those things are sharp! We don't want any nicks or cuts."

'It is said that although Pitiless Pearl opened and closed her mouth, no sound came out.

'Before they left, Drastic Diego gave Desmond some advice.

"'Don't make the same mistakes you did at Isambard Pugnacious. Never, ever cry even when you get splinters or rope burn."

"'That won't be a problem,' said Mungo. 'All our trainees wear fleece lined gloves and have a weekly allowance of hand cream. Now, Desmond, do you have any questions?"

"'Will there be music and dancing lessons?"

"'Of course. We at the Academy for the Pirating Arts are renowned for our all-singing and dancing extravaganzas when our pirates graduate."

"'Stop! I can't take any more! Diego, are you sure there's nowhere else for our boy to go?"

"'What about the Bedazzled School of Stage Craft?" Desmond suggested.

"'No!" both his parents shouted.

"'But I want to be a dancer."

'Desmond had actually said it out loud. The thing everyone knew about but never mentioned. There was a thud as Pitiless Pearl passed out in shock.'

By the time Aunt Fenula had finished I understood Desmond a bit better, especially why he had such a different approach to pirating compared with, say, Putrid Pete Pukebreath. Putrid Pete was not a pirate who liked shanties and jigs. Or good manners. He was more likely to trip you up and run off with your dinner money. Which is exactly what he did to Desmond immediately they were introduced later that morning.

'You need to be careful there, Cap'n,' said Pete as he offered a hand to help Desmond up, only to let go and watch him fall back to the ground.

'And you, sir,' replied Desmond as he got to his feet and brushed down his jacket, 'need to learn some manners!'

'I am *so* sorry. So very sorry.' In fact, Pete didn't sound sorry at all.

'Aren't I sorry, Scurvy Sam?' And Pete grinned at his first mate, who had crept up behind Desmond.

'Aye, Cap'n you are,' replied Scurvy Sam, grinning broadly. One of her teeth was gold and it glinted in the sunshine. 'I don't think you realised quite how special Dastardly Dezzy Death is.' And she flicked imaginary dust from Desmond's shoulders.

'It's Desmond de'Ath,' corrected Desmond. 'And you need a manicure, Ms. Scurvy.'

'I've heard,' continued Sam, 'that Cap'n. Death's crew have an exciting new pirate sea shanty.'

Sam said 'exciting new sea shanty' in a tone of voice I call fake enthusiasm. I hear it quite a bit, especially if Holly Prickles and her best friend Summer Relish are around. Frankly, with a name that sounds like it belongs in a cheese sandwich, I don't think Summer ought to be patronising anybody but as she wears all the best brand names and has a pony called Pippin everyone rates her as not only the coolest kid in our class, but possibly the whole school. So when Summer says something like, 'Great T-shirt, Cid,' in a too positive voice, I know she doesn't mean it. I'm trying to build up a 'Response to Summer Relish' weapon bank of zingy come-backs, but as yet I haven't got any.

'It's pronounced de'Ath,' said Desmond. 'And yes, we do.'

'Go on then,' Putrid Pete said. 'Let's see it. One pirate can learn a lot about another from his sea shanty, and I'd like to get to know you better.' And he winked at Scurvy Sam.

So Desmond summoned over his crew and they performed the sea shanty again. And Desmond finished with his little jig again. Pukebreath's pirates fell about laughing. Desmond's crew was indignant.

'What scurrilous rapscallions!' declared Carlos.

'What insolent riff-raff!' added Barry.

'What cheeky monkeys!' finished Clayton. 'But don't tell them I said so.'

At this point I closed my eyes. I couldn't bear to watch any more. This *Premiership Pirate Knockout* thing was going to be a disaster.

Chapter Seven

Monday 26 July, Lunchtime
Trouble Scale 9-

I phoned Aunt Fenula to find out how she had got on with Nudgebuster & Co. After the morning I had had I needed some good news.

'It didn't quite go the way I had hoped,' said Aunt Fenula.

Aunt Fenula uses the word 'quite' when what she really means is 'really'. As in 'It really didn't go the way I had hoped.'

'They don't even want to wait until the end of the week. They say they've heard things about Desmond and he is a complete no-hoper.'

If they knew, how long before Mr. Birkwhistle or Rory found out? Aunt Fenula went on,

'I tried to persuade Mr. Nudgebuster – Big Ma was having none of it. I said we had a plan that was bound to make Mr. Birkwhistle and Mr. Scrope see Desmond's potential for other TV work.'

'What is our plan?' I asked, surprised that we had one.

'That by the time they find out that Desmond and his crew are not quite what they wanted, they'll like them so much they'll want to use them again.

'I've thought about it a lot, Cid. It really could work! In fact, I told Nudgebuster & Co. that Desmond and his crew could end up more famous than Putrid Pete.'

I was more focused on the fact that Desmond and his crew were not "quite" what Mr. Birkwhistle wanted. What would happen if he decided to get rid of them before he'd had a chance to get to like them? After all, the Grand Finale was only five days away and Putrid Pete had to lose. It's hard to like someone or something that's doing the opposite of what you want them to do. It's why I'm picked last for teams in PE.

'Did you get anywhere at all with Nudgebuster & Co?' I asked.

'Not really. They said if they think they're not going to get the money back, they'll be round to the agency to start measuring up for new carpets and curtains before the weekend.'

I couldn't think of anything positive to say.

'Can't you tell them how unfair the deal they made you sign is?' I asked.

'But they didn't "make" me sign it. I was so sure we'd be able to pay it back from Vlad's fees that I agreed. It looked like a big piece of luck to me.'

'It was,' I agreed. 'Bad luck.'

There was a pause then Aunt Fenula put on her Happy Voice.

'In other news, I've got someone for you to meet. He's going to be a great addition to the agency. I think you'll like him.'

I hoped I hadn't heard her correctly. 'Say that again.'

'I said, I think you'll like him.'

'No. The bit before.'

'He's going to be a great addition to the agency.'

'Yes. That bit.' I swallowed my shout and tried hard to keep my voice down. 'We're in debt, likely to be out on the streets by the end of the week and you've signed on someone new? Who is "He" exactly?'

'His name's Dusty and he's a professional skeleton. He's a bit down on his luck at…'

Skipping over the fact that I was not certain what a 'professional skeleton' was, I groaned.

'Aunt Fenula, what have you done?'

'He's very good, Cid. Really gets into a role, especially when his allergies are under control. Oh, and he's a bit ticklish.'

So we now had a ticklish, allergic, professional skeleton on the books. I tried to explain to her how serious the situation with Desmond was. I couldn't seem to make her see that Dusty was a step too far.

'This time it's NOT going to be all right, Aunt Fenula! Desmond's crew are not right for this job and Mr. Birkwhistle nearly found out this morning. I was able to come up with something for the moment, but I don't know if it'll be enough. It depends how long your plan of him growing to like them takes to work. If it works, that is. Rory Birkwhistle is already suspicious.'

I explained what had happened to Aunt Fenula, who was trying very hard to believe that there wasn't really a problem.

'Brilliant! Don't worry, Cid. It sounds like you said exactly the right thing. That's why I need your help. You're always full of good ideas. I'm sure it'll work. And by the time they find out they won't care because they'll know how sweet Desmond and his crew are.'

'It'll take more than that if they're going to give Putrid Pete a real fight,' I said. 'As for "sweet" pirates...' I was lost for words. Aunt Fenula is one of the few people who can do that to me.

'Come on, Cid. We can do this!'

I sighed.

'There's what Rory calls a "fun" raft race to their ships this afternoon,' I said. 'It's filmed to use in trailers for the show.'

'Is there anything you could do to help Desmond and his crew out? Make them feel good about themselves and they might surprise you.'

That was not what I wanted to hear. I had had enough surprises already. Then Aunt Fenula changed tactics. 'And think about all the others here at the agency, dear,' she said. 'They're counting on us – on you – to help them. If we can pull this off, the agency is saved. And it could mean a lot more work for everyone else.'

Talk about playing dirty! She knew there was no way I would want to let down Arthur, Vlad, Wilbur and the others.

Suddenly I heard myself saying, 'I'll see what I can do. Mr. Scrope likes them at the moment, so if we can do enough to keep him happy...'

'That's my Cid! I'll see you down at the quayside this afternoon to see how things are going for myself.'

Monday 26 July 1.45 p.m.

By the time Aunt Fenula arrived after lunch, I was already sitting with Rory in a speed boat out in the bay, a raft anchored on either side of us, waiting for the race to begin. I watched as two launches made their way towards us, each with one of the crews on board. Rory looked over at me.

'So, Cid, if I understand your plan, Desmond's crew will lose this race to fool Putrid Pete into thinking they're no threat?'

'Well done! You're keeping up so far.' I had snapped at him but it was nerves more than anger.

'Keeping up?' replied Rory. 'I know exactly what's going on. In fact, I'm at least one step ahead of you.'

'Good,' I said. 'Then you won't have any more questions, will you?'

My stomach felt like a barrel of overactive electric eels. I read somewhere they can give each other electric shocks and I could definitely feel sharp sparks as well a horrible swirly feeling. I wanted to tell Rory to shut up and mind his own business but, unfortunately, this was his business.

I turned away from him and tried thinking Positive Thoughts. Then I tried visualisation. Princess PJ says it's something sports stars do. She uses it before a dangerous stunt. Basically, you imagine in detail how you want things to go, so I imagined Desmond and his crew coming a close second to Putrid Pete. They needed to be good enough to stop Rory being suspicious. Then I watched them trying to get out of their launch and onto Team *Seahorse*'s raft and imagined even harder.

'Help! I'm slipping off!' cried Spud.

'That's because you're all at one end of the raft,' I shouted at them. 'Spread out!'

Rory sniggered. 'They so convincing, they don't even look like they're acting,' he said.

Then Shuggy started grumbling, 'I don't see why we have to do this.'

'Because you do,' I said in my best Miss MacLean voice. 'So get on with it.'

Desmond was still on the launch searching through a canvas bag, as Putrid Pete Pukebreath jumped onto the other raft to give Team *Screaming Skull* a pep talk. Actually, it was a pep shout. And it wasn't pep so much as threats.

While Putrid Pete's crew sat to attention, Team *Seahorse* was a knot of jostling, jiggling and fidgeting pirates. No one wanted to paddle. I tried to give them a bit of a pep talk myself.

'Come on, Team *Seahorse*, you've got this. You can do it if you all pull together.'

'I'll get rough hands!' sniffed Carlos. 'I'll need hand cream.'

'I'll get backache,' moaned Barry. 'I'll need ointment.'

'I'll get sweaty and smelly,' finished Clayton. 'I'll need a bath.' Then he sniffed his armpits. 'Too late!' he added, and pulled a face.

Desmond finally jumped onto the raft and took charge. 'Come along now, chaps. It's not too far to the *Seahorse*.'

He was wearing luminous orange armbands that had been inflated to an alarming size.

'We don't want to let Cid and Miss Fitz down, do we?'

'On your marks,' called Rory through a megaphone, 'get set … Go!'

Putrid Pete's rowers quickly set a steady rhythm towards their ship, *Screaming Skull*. Scurvy Sam shouted warnings of very nasty punishments.

Over on Desmond's raft, Barry stabbed at the water sulkily with his oar. Carlos was very precise – and deliberately slow. Clayton did at least try. The raft bobbed and wobbled in no particular direction, not helped by the others shuffling, nudging and elbowing each other trying to get comfortable until I couldn't stand it any longer.

'Stop!' I shouted. 'You're just going round in circles, and small ones at that!'

It was time for me to take charge. Even if Mr. Scrope and Mr. Birkwhistle were satisfied with what I had told them about the strategy of being deliberately useless, I could tell Rory wasn't. And if Desmond and his crew were to eventually win as Mr. Scrope wanted, they needed to sharpen their skills and their confidence. Jumping in the water I swam to Team *Seahorse*'s raft. It didn't take more than thirty seconds before I was hauling myself aboard.

'Right, on the count of three… one… two… three and paddle! In… Out… In… Out…'

'That's the way, chaps!' beamed Desmond. 'And the rest of you sit still, or there's no cocoa tonight.'

Even with an extra body on board, we started making progress. Although we gained slightly on Putrid Pete's crew, however, it was nowhere near enough. By the time we reached the *Seahorse* Barry, Carlos and Clayton were exhausted. The only sound I could hear above their huffing, puffing and wheezing was Putrid Pete's crew laughing at them.

We didn't have long enough to get annoyed, let alone recover, before the cameras started rolling again.

'We want a few shots of the pirates training,' Rory explained. 'We give them a coach then film the team being put through their paces. It's part of the programme's opening five minutes, another way for viewers to get to know Team *Seahorse*.'

A coach? That would be the quickest way for everyone to find out how hopeless Desmond and Team *Seahorse* were. I gave Aunt Fenula a Look and we stepped into a huddle. (I know two people don't make much of a huddle, but it sounds very secretive and we certainly had a big secret to keep.)

'What are we going to do?' I hissed.

'Could you coach...?' Aunt Fenula started to ask a question to which there was only one answer as far as I was concerned.

'No,' I said, before she could finish. 'I don't know the first thing about it.'

'It's all about being positive.'

We jumped as Rory came up behind us and asked if we would like to meet Team *Seahorse*'s coach.

Without even a glance in my direction Aunt Fenula said, 'About that. My niece, Cid, will be the crew coach. She's been working with them at the agency, helping them with their "hopeless pirate" act. We don't want someone else interfering, messing it up.' Rory opened his mouth but got no further before Aunt Fenula carried on. 'You see, what we thought is that if they pretended to be not very good, it'll do two things. First, the audience will feel sorry for them. That means they'll really get behind them. Second, Putrid Pete will be lulled into a false sense of security.'

Byron Birkwhistle appeared from nowhere. 'I love that plan,' he said.

'But Dad...' Rory began, but Mr. Birkwhistle carried on.

'More importantly, Mr. Scrope loves it, and he's the one with the big money. When Desmond shows his true colours in the finale and Putrid Pete gets his comeuppance, the show will become the stuff of legend. And that's important because Mr. Scrope will only buy *Premiership Pirate Knockout* if Desmond beats Putrid Pete. The baddies winning is a definite no-no with him.'

After seeing Desmond in the raft race, I knew we were setting ourselves up for a big fall. All I could do was glare at Aunt Fenula and then head up the *Seahorse*'s gangplank and on to the poop deck, where

Desmond was trying to assemble the crew. Shuggy had tangled his dreadlocks in some rigging and Gruff had Carlos in a headlock while they argued about when to load a canon with gunpowder.

'Come on, chaps,' Desmond was saying. 'Time for some training. Let's sharpen those reflexes and hone our skills!'

As I looked at the shambles of a crew in front of me, I knew that the only thing I could do was to try to make this crazy scheme work. 'Pull yourself together, Clematis Iris Daisy,' I said to myself – as you can tell, things were bad. In fact, it felt like we might hit point 9 on the Ten Point Trouble Scale.

Delia, BUMP's chief camera operator, headed a small group up of behind-the-scenes people up the gangplank.

'Mr. Birkwhistle has sent me over to film a few scenes of Dezzy's crew getting ready for the competition,' she said. 'He says there's a plan to make Pukebreath think they're rubbish?'

What could I do but smile? 'It's a sure-fire success,' I lied.

It didn't take long for the recording equipment to be set up. Certainly not as long as it took me to line up Team *Seahorse*.

'Okay, crew,' I said, trying to sound positive, 'I'm going to start with some basic drills. Let's try standing to attention. On my command… A-ten-hut!'

The crew didn't move.

'Ten-hut!' I shouted.

'Ask nicely,' sniffed Gruff.

'Quite right,' smiled Desmond. 'Good manners, Cid, are what modern day pirating is all about.'

I said 'Please!' through gritted teeth.

The crew straightened up, although it didn't look much like standing to attention to me. Anyway, I began the inspection. I stopped at Carlos.

'Take off that ridiculous eye patch,' I said. 'You don't need it.'

'It's menacing,' said Carlos.

'It's threatening,' continued Barry.

'It's posing,' muttered Clayton.

Carlos glared at him but before he could add anything further Clayton pulled the patch away from Carlos' eye and then let go …

S_NA_P!

Carlos howled in pain.

A breakdown in discipline already. What would Miss MacLean do? I couldn't keep Clayton in at break time because there wasn't one. Write a letter to his mum? A bit of an overreaction. Then I thought, 'What would a Mrs. Foster-Grimes, my PE teacher, do?'

'You'll run ten circuits of the deck for that when we're finished, Clayton!' I said.

Carlos laughed. 'Serves him right.'

'And you'll do five, Carlos, for not obeying orders when you're given them.'

Before either could complain, I asserted my authority before I lost it again.

'By the left, quick march!'

Gruff and Spud turned smartly and stood nose to nose.

'She said left!' hissed Spud.

'This is left!' said Gruff.

'Not her left!'

'Then whose left did she mean?' Gruff looked confused.

'*Left* left. Like me!' Spud shouted.

'Why should I go to your left? You're not the boss of me!'

Meanwhile the others wandered off in an array of different directions.

'Wow,' said Delia. 'They've got this incompetence thing off to a fine art.'

If only she knew.

I sorted out the muddle and made Spud and Gruff shake hands.

It was time for star jumps. The crew groaned. I don't blame them – I hate star jumps too, but they had been so annoying that, if I am completely honest, a little part of me enjoyed making them do some. There was no left or right or backwards or forwards involved, so what was there to go wrong?

Plenty.

Every time Shuggy, (who was quite short,) brought his hands up he hit Barry, (who was rather tall,) in the mouth. Every time Barry brought his hands down he slapped Shuggy on the head. Then one shoved the other and the other shoved back. Within seconds their arms were flailing as they tried to slap each other. The whole line ending up in a tangled heap.

Once I had sorted the muddle out and made Barry and Shuggy shake hands, Desmond suggested I tried them with lunges.

'On my command… Right leg – lunge! And back. Left leg – lunge! And back. Right leg – lunge! Well done, Gruff – good work! Call that a lunge, Carlos?'

Gruff sniggered.

'Show him how it's done, Gruff,' I ordered.

Gruff pulled himself back to the starting position and then, with a flourish, sprung forward with his left leg.

'There! See how it's done, Carlos?' I asked. 'And back, Gruff.'

Gruff didn't move.

'Relax, Gruff,' I said.

'I can't!' he said, his eyes watering. 'I think I over-lunged.'

'Let me help,' said Carlos, pushing down on the top of his head.

Gruff screamed as his legs slid into the splits. The others winced. I went to help him.

'I can feel a draft,' said Gruff once he was upright again.

'I'm not surprised in those old undies,' chuckled Carlos.

Gruff's trousers had ripped wide open. He jumped on Carlos, who fell backwards into the hold. Gruff dived in on top of him and, with a cry of 'Bundle!' the others piled in too.

Once I had sorted the muddle out (again) and made the pirates shake hands (again), Desmond decided they should take a break.

'They need some shaping up,' he said, 'but they've got spirit!'

'And not much else,' I thought, but I didn't say anything.

While the recording equipment was being packed up, Delia walked over to me. She was wiping her eyes and breathless with laughter.

'Team *Seahorse* is brilliant!' she said. 'Where did you find them? Their comic timing is pure genius. They deserve their own show.'

Perhaps Aunt Fenula was right. Perhaps Desmond and his crew would win over Byron Birkwhistle if not Mr. Scrope. Even if BUMP offered them some TV work in this country we'd have enough to pay back Nudgebuster & Co. Then we could start paying off the agency's other debts, too. I decided to be positive for once.

I should have listened to that little voice inside my head that tried to remind not to get too carried away because whenever I do, I'm soon brought back down to earth with a splat. In fact, a series of splats.

Chapter Eight

Monday evening's "Meet 'n' Mingle" buffet was the next thing that, to use Aunt Fenula's words, 'didn't quite go' as we might have hoped.

Mr. Birkwhistle sidled up, Rory tagging along behind him. Aunt Fenula had been cornered by Desmond and I was trying to rescue her.

'I've seen what Delia shot of Desmond's team this afternoon,' Mr Birkwhistle said. 'They are beyond incompetent. Their bungling has me fooled completely, and I've seen quite a few pirate crews over these last weeks. But perhaps they could do a proper drill? Show us their real skills, to give us an idea of how they will beat Pukebreath in the end. Mr. Scrope is feeling a little anxious.'

There it was – Splat! I was brought back down to Earth.

'What do you mean? That was some of their best...' began Desmond.

Another Splat was on the way so I took evasive action. If saying 'evasive action' makes it sound like I have a plan for these situations, I do.

The Cid Fitz Strategies for Escaping Awkward People

Option 1. Tell them someone wants them. Boring but good to use on parents, teachers etc.

Option 2. Eat pickled onion flavoured crisps and belch loudly.

Option 3. Sniff your armpits and pull a face.

Option 4. FO1. (Farting Option 1). This is the best option, but you need to drop one that is SBD (Silent But Deadly). Then you sniff the air, look at the other person with disgust and move away from them. That way they think that you think it's them.

Option 5. FO2. Be loud and proud. Only use this if you absolutely have to because everyone will know it's you and is likely to avoid you too.

Winston tells me to use the Ultimate Deterrent. This is the pick your nose option. The consequences are far too serious though, no matter how you get rid of whatever you find up there. However, 1. I have enough problems with other people as it is and 2. I'm not stupid enough to listen to Winston, let alone trust his 'advice.'

As it was a "meet 'n' mingle" buffet, I went with option 1.

'I think Shuggy needs you, Desmond,' I said. 'He's trying to explain how ballet-robics works to Scurvy Sam and it's not going well.'

I had avoided a Giant Splat, but the danger wasn't over yet. As Desmond hurried off, Aunt Fenula barely had time to catch her breath before Mr. Birkwhistle was asking about 'proper drill' again.

'What you have seen so far,' she said, 'is some of their best acting. It takes a *lot* of practice to be that inept and, as you have seen, they are really "in the zone". If we ask them to go back to being ruthless, cutthroat pirates they might drop out of character completely.'

Aunt Fenula has a talent for making things up as she goes along and getting people to believe her. Luckily, she didn't decide to become a nefarious con artist. Although it means despicable, 'nefarious' sounds a much sneakier word to me, and I was realising that Aunt Fenula has a very sneaky streak.

Mr. Birkwhistle nodded the kind of nod that people who want you to think they're very clever give when they don't understand what's going on.

'Wonderful! Marvellous! Well, keep up the good work.' And then he rushed off to a meeting calling out, 'Mr. Scrope will be pleased,' as he went.

Rory frowned at Aunt Fenula.

'It is certainly true that Pukebreath thinks they are a complete joke,' he said. 'And that will give Dezzy's crew an advantage. But I can't help wondering about what Carlos, Barry and Clayton said yesterday.'

Rory was not letting go of his suspicions. Cue Aunt Fenula to the rescue.

'They are under strict orders not to come out of character. If they blow their cover, they lose their advantage,' she replied quickly. 'It's called "method acting". They play the role of incompetent pirates 24 / 7 so their performance is really convincing.'

Rory gave the kind of nod that people give when they are weighing you up. He said, 'They've certainly convinced me. Anyone watching them would think they're hopeless.'

Aunt Fenula was on a roll now, and playing her part well too. 'It's better if no one else knows they are really "Dastardly Dezzy Death's Despicable Crew" in case Putrid Pete finds out.'

Finally, Rory said, 'Wow. You really know your stuff. Dad can relax. America here we come!'

There was something about the way he said it that worried me. I couldn't decide if he believed us or not. He sounded a bit too positive, like he was being patronising.

We queued up at the buffet table. Desmond was balancing cubes of cheese and pineapple on cocktail sticks on top of a heap of spicy chicken wings when Scurvy Sam, Putrid Pete's first mate, wandered over. She smiled at Desmond, which was odd.

'What a beautifully curled moustache,' she said.

Her voice was too positive. In fact, she sounded like Summer Relish herself. Poor Desmond fell for it.

'Do you think so, Miss Scurvy?' he asked, smiling.

'Oh yes, it makes you look gorgeous.'

'I use tiny curling tongs, especially for moustaches, and then wax it with coconut oil.'

'You ought to just strap the coconut over your face,' replied Scurvy Sam. 'Faster and much better looking.'

Before I could go to Desmond's rescue, Clayton beat me to it.

'I can recommend coconut,' he said. 'It's good for the complexion. Try this.' And he thrust a coconut cream pie in Scurvy Sam's face.

Aunt Fenula sidled up to me and whispered, 'Well it's going better than I thought it would.' Then she ducked as a mini quiche flew past. The buffet had lasted a whole twenty-two minutes before the food fight broke out.'

Monday 26 July Midnight

Even though the food fight had worn me out, I did not get a good night's sleep. Partly because I could still smell cheese and pineapple, and partly because I was worrying about Dusty, the agency's latest signing. He had got on very well with everyone and Aunt Fenula was very excited about him.

'We could advertise him and Vlad together as a Halloween special offer. Two for the price of one.'

At first I thought this was a great idea. Then I read his file. Dusty was allergic to dust. Before you say, 'But that's not a big deal,' think about the kinds of places skeletons turn up in films and stories: vaults, crypts, attics and graveyards. Oh, and cupboards, apparently. Dusty's last role had been playing a skeleton in a closet. An old, dirty closet. Not only did he sneeze but the door opened, he fell out and landed in a heap. Bones everywhere. That's the thing about skeletons. They only stay together through willpower and once that's gone they collapse.

If that had been the end of it he might have kept his job, but Dusty has another problem. It turns out he's not very good at putting himself together again. He got his skull on the wrong way round and smacked into the back of the closet when he was supposed to spring out and surprise the hero. Safe to say it was Dusty who was surprised, first by the closet and then by the sack.

My head said, 'I can't see how Dusty will help the Miss Fitz Agency at all.'

My heart said, 'Poor thing. Not only was he unwanted, but he was literally considered rubbish and dumped in a box by some bins.'

I knew my heart would win. It did. But was that a good thing?

Chapter Nine

Tuesday 27 July 8.00 a.m.
Trouble Scale still stuck at 8-9

Early next morning, the BUMP film crew was setting up the equipment ready for a busy day of filming. The *Screaming Skull* and *Seahorse*, had been anchored in Bilgewater Bay. Anchored nearby, was a massive yacht, complete with a speedboat and a helipad on which was a small helicopter. By the time we reached the quayside, worries were already racing round my stomach like socks in a tumble dryer. This was not as bad as electric eels in a barrel, but it was early yet.

Mr. Birkwhistle had called a meeting on the quayside, to make sure that Aunt Fenula and I understood what was going to happen. First, he gave Rory his instructions.

'This is a big responsibility, Rory. You're in charge of starting and finishing every race. I'll be here until Mr. Scrope arrives. We're going to watch from his yacht.'

I felt a bit irritated that Rory was being left in charge. I was also worried that he still didn't buy the whole "method acting" story. He looked and sounded very efficient and took us through the rundown of events.

'We're starting with the rope swinging competition. Then climbing the rigging, sail hoisting and cannon firing.'

Delia came running over to Mr. Birkwhistle. 'Putrid Pete has scared off his team's coach. Again. He says if we try to give him any more coaches, he'll make them walk the plank.'

'That's the ninth coach this series,' said Mr. Birkwhistle. 'You sort it out, Rory. I can't be doing with pirate tantrums this early in the morning.'

Delia left, but came running back over two minutes later.

'Prendergast is in sulking because he wants to wear stage make-up and Fang is flapping around making fun of him and getting in everyone's way.'

Mr. Birkwhistle looked confused. 'Prendergast? Fang?'

'The parrots,' explained Rory. 'Prendergast belongs to Dastardly Dezzy and Fang to Putrid Pete. He's a vicious bird, that Fang.'

'Parrots? Make-up? You sort it out, Rory. You're good at that sort of thing,' said Mr. Birkwhistle. 'I can't be doing with parrot tantrums this early in the morning.'

It wasn't long before Delia came running over a third time. This time it was the judges. 'Gloria Golightly is upset because her breakfast bacon butty has been served on a blue plate when she asked for white. And Nifty Nikolai Gnashjaws says his boiled egg is the wrong way up. He insists it's pointy end down.'

'Pointy end? Do eggs have a pointy end?' said Mr. Birkwhistle. 'You sort it out, Rory. I can't be doing with celebrity tantrums this early in the morning.'

Tuesday 27 July 10.00 a.m.

By the time things were ready for the first contest I was very nervous. I had to admit that Prendergast was now very happy but I'm not sure the shock of seeing a parrot wearing false eyelashes will ever wear off.

'Right,' shouted Rory through a megaphone. 'The first contest is swinging from a rope. Each of the pirates must swing from the stern to the main mast, holding a knife in their teeth. First crew to finish wins five points. There are also up to five points that the judges can award for style and effort.'

'We've got some hope then,' I said to no one in particular.

Desmond smiled. 'Hope? Of course there's hope. I can safely say my crew oozes style, Cid. Remember their sea shanty.'

'It would be hard to forget it,' I said.

'Exactly!'

As the crews and coaches set out for their ships, the judges climbed onto a special platform on the quayside. They had high powered binoculars and live feeds streaming from cameras placed around each ship. Rory and Aunt Fenula sat alongside them.

The expert judge was Nifty Nikolai Gnashjaws, a retired pirate who owned the Shivering Timbers Pirate Academy. I hadn't heard of Gloria Golightly, but apparently she was the second runner up in last year's "Come Glide With Me".'

Aunt Fenula and I had looked blank when Rory told us.

'You know, the over 70s ski dancing show,' he said, rolling his eyes. 'Didn't you watch it? It's another one of Dad's productions.'

I can't believe anyone would have watched over 70s ski-dancing, but then I again I'm always left out of games and groups at school, so what do I know?

A cannon fired. The competition had begun.

Shuggy went first for Team *Seahorse*. As he stood on the poop deck, knife between his teeth and grabbing the rope confidently, he looked the part. That was as far as it lasted. He grinned at the others as he swung through the air and the knife fell. Clayton howled as it plunged into his boot, pinning him to the deck.

'Ooops!' said Shuggy, as he headed to the bow, missing the main mast altogether.

'Sorry…' as he swung back towards the stern.

I shouted, 'Let go now!' as he passed over the middle of the main deck again.

'What did you say?' he called.

'I said "let go!"'

'What?' he shouted as he swung back.

'Let go!'

'What did she say?' he called out as he once more headed towards the bow.

'Let go! NOW!' the crew yelled.

Shuggy was last seen flying out beyond the ship's bow.

S ^{P} $_L$ A ^{S} H !

'Man overboard,' said Spud, and started giggling.

I got the lifebuoy and threw it at Shuggy. And I do mean I threw it *at* him, not to him.

Gruff went next. He ran with the rope and came lunging towards the others with quite some force – so much, in fact, that he overshot the landing spot and collided with a barrel of greasy, smelly slops, sending its contents all over the deck. Barry and Spud rushed to help him up, but slipped and slid all over the place, falling flat on their faces.

I started panicking. How could they be this bad? They weren't going to get any points, not even for style. I couldn't see Rory's face, but I wondered what he was thinking. I was sure he hadn't believed Aunt Fenula's method acting explanation for Desmond's crew's performance and the rope swinging round wouldn't have convinced him. It's not that method acting isn't an Actual Thing – it is – but Team *Seahorse* wasn't acting.

Amidst all the kerfuffle, there was a shrill, rolling blow on a whistle. The first round was over. Putrid Pete's crew had already completed the task.

The judges conferred, but I don't know why. The result was never in doubt.

'Putrid Pete's team won,' shouted Nifty Nikolai, ignoring his microphone. 'So they get the five points. They also get five points for style. That was some proper pirate rope swinging.'

'And for Team *Seahorse*,' said Gloria Golightly, 'Two points for effort. One point for the swinging...'

'And that's too generous,' interrupted Nikolai.

'... giving a total of three points.'

The judging was interrupted by wailing coming from *Seahorse*. It was Clayton, still attached to the deck by Shuggy's knife.

'Oi! What about me?'

Luckily, Shuggy's knife had only pierced the toecap of Clayton's boot, not his actual foot. It didn't stop Clayton milking it, though. There was a lot of limping and moaning.

After a short break, the crews of each ship were lined up on their main decks.

I looked at Desmond's crew and tried to do the Positive Thinking thing but I don't think it worked very well.

'Back to basics,' I said. 'Climbing the rigging. You can ALL do this, surely? It's a pirating essential.'

The captains read out the instructions to their crews.

'Each pirate must climb the rigging and hang a different coloured banner from the crow's nest. Then the pirate must climb back down and "tag" the next in line. The first team to get all its banners up there wins. The scoring is the same as before.'

The starting cannon fired. The race was on.

Carlos and Clayton went first for the *Seahorse*. They were slower than the *Screaming Skull*, but they did it. Shuggy made it halfway up but then got a nosebleed and had to come back down. Barry was better at putting his feet through the holes than on the rope rungs.

'What *is* the matter with him?' I asked.

'He's afraid of heights,' said Spud. 'He's doing it with his eyes shut.'

Then it was Spud's turn. As he was within an arm's length of the top a seagull carrying a fish flew by his ear. Spud let go of the rigging and waved his arms at the bird, trying to get rid of it. It shrieked and dropped the fish down Spud's back. He began crying.

'Get it out! Get it out! Get it away from me!'

'He's got fish-phobia,' said Carlos, wisely. 'It's irrational.'

'He has a fear of fish,' explained Barry. 'It's silly.'

'He freaks out at chips too,' finished Clayton. 'Weird.' Then he added, 'Now dumplings, they *are* scary.'

Meanwhile, Gruff scuttled up the rigging. He climbed over Spud (who was now dangling upside down hanging on by his knees) but before he could tie his banner to the crow's nest the whistle blew. Another victory for the *Screaming Skull*.

'Putrid Pete's team won,' shouted Nifty Nikolai. 'They get the five points plus five more for style. Very nifty footwork, get it?' And he roared with laughter at his 'joke.'

'Team *Seahorse* gets three points. All for effort,' said Gloria Golightly. 'There was no style.'

By now I needed a big, triple fudge muffin with chocolate swirls. As I ran down the gangplank, I saw Rory.

'This is all going to plan, right?' he asked, narrowing his eyes and peering at me like I was an unidentified sample of something unpleasant.

'Of course!' I crossed my fingers, hoping he wouldn't notice. 'This will have the viewers feeling sorry for them.' At least that's true, I thought.

Tuesday 27 July 11.45 a.m.

A little while later as I was walking back from the catering caravan I saw Rory standing behind the portacabin where the make-up was done. He was having a serious discussion on his phone. I crept along the side and listened.

'They say it's all going to plan but I'm not... Yes, I know there's still tomorrow's contest and then the battle finale, but... Yes, Dad. I do understand how...'

From what I could hear I reckoned Mr. Birkwhistle was still happy with Desmond. So far, so good. As I listened further, I could tell by Rory's voice that he was beginning to give up.

'I know Miss Fitz says Dastardly Dezzy's crew is "method acting" ... Yes, I know what it means... Yes, I do! ... It means they stay in character as useless pirates to fool... Yes, they are very good at it... No, you'd never guess they weren't hopeless...'

I tiptoed away, over to the dockside where the ships were moored. Putrid Pete was shouting at Desmond about the next contest which was hoisting the mainsail.

'I assume your crew knows what that is?'

'Would you like a head start?' asked Scurvy Sam.

'There's no call for that, Samantha,' said Desmond. 'We have won awards for our sail management.'

'"Sail management"?' repeated Scurvy Sam. 'Oooh, get you!'

My job of preparing Desmond's crew for winning the grand finale was becoming harder. While the crew of the *Screaming Skull* was laughing and jeering, Team *Seahorse* were looking glummer and glummer. Time to cheer them up.

'You've got this next one,' I said. 'It's hoisting and bringing in the sails. Remember what the captain said – you've won awards for sail work. Come on, Team *Seahorse*.'

Nothing.

'Gruff, I want you up top to wave the skull and cross bones when the mainsail's done. After that, you all bring the sails down and stow them neatly. Job's a good 'un!'

A few nods.

'But you have to be quick. And I mean *quick*! No hanging around because Clayton has snagged a nail or something.'

Some sniggering and more nodding. Progress at last.

The teams got off to a good start. Shuggy had toilet paper stuffed up each nostril and Barry even kept his eyes open, although he wouldn't look down and clung to the rope so hard he got rope burn. Gruff was shouting instructions and encouragement. This contest was actually going their way. Until…

There was an argument at the top of the mainsail and Carlos was left clinging to the yardarm, kicking his legs and shouting threats at Barry and Clayton. The others stopped to watch and let go of the sail, sending it crumpling and tumbling onto the deck below. Then – white out.

The whistle blew on yet another defeat for the *Seahorse*. The next thing I knew was Desmond shouting instructions. There was a flash of sunlight followed by a blurry crowd of red faces looming over me. I groped for my glasses.

'How many fingers am I holding up?' Spud asked me.

'None!'

'She's fine,' Spud said to Aunt Fenula, still waving his hook in front of my face.

'Are you all right, Cid dear?' she said.

'Yes – unless you can die of embarrassment.' Which at that moment felt like an Actual Thing.

Tuesday 27 July 12.33 p.m.

A minute or two later (still dazed) I was watching the live feed of the judging with Aunt Fenula and Rory. It was taking longer than was needed to come to the obvious conclusion that Team *Screaming Skull* had won, but then I have never seen a reality show or contest where the judges didn't stretch out their part of the show. The pauses before the results are announced are long enough to make a mug of tea and the cup-cakes to go with it. Rory was looking fed up, but I guessed that was more to do with the conversation he'd had with his dad. I reckoned this was a good sign because it must mean that Mr. Birkwhistle still believed the whole "method acting" thing.

'Putrid Pete's team won,' said Nifty Nikolai, finally stating the obvious. 'They get the five points plus five more for style. Their sail unfurled as smoothly as cream pouring from a jug.'

Whereas ours had plummeted into a heap of exactly my height.

'Team *Seahorse* gets…' Gloria Golightly began when a face loomed up to the screen and there was a tapping sound. It was Desmond, peering down the camera, all teeth and nostrils.

'Is this thing on, Delia?' he asked. She nodded.

'Wait please, Ms. Golightly,' he said. 'Look here.'

The image on the screen swerved as he tugged Delia's arm. Rory spoke to Delia through the microphone attached to his headpiece. He didn't sound best pleased.

'What does he want? Move the camera, Delia.'

Delia panned round only to focus on Desmond beaming next to a giant origami butterfly, made from the *Seahorse*'s mainsail. It was actually pretty good.

'Five points for style to Team *Seahorse*,' announced Gloria Golightly.

Desmond's team cheered and I gave a sigh of relief. Progress at last.

'It looks quite exquisite,' said Carlos, edging his way in front of the camera.

'It looks quite beautiful,' added Barry, pushing in front of Carlos.

'It looks quite crumpled,' finished Clayton, shoving Barry out of the way. 'What's it supposed to be?'

Rory stared at me, opened his mouth, closed it again, opened it and then seemed to seize up, like his battery had gone flat. I was glad. If he had questions about what was going on, I certainly didn't have the answers.

Chapter Ten

The last test of the day was cannon firing.

'They can't be pirates and not know how to fire a cannon,' said Aunt Fenula, trying to lift my spirits.

'Even you've been amazed at what they **don't** know,' I said. 'And the only person I know who knows anything about firing a cannon is Princess PJ.'

'Excellent idea!' And before I knew it, Aunt Fenula had disappeared.

After lunch Desmond and I lined up the crew of the *Seahorse* below decks in pairs. Suddenly there was a call of 'Look out below!' as PJ grabbed the handrails of the ladder down to the gun deck and slid down, her feet in the air.

PJ went off to inspect the cannons while I explained the next round to Desmond's crew. Basically each pair had to load and fire their cannon one after the other to hit a bright yellow buoy bobbing about in the sea. Simple. I hoped.

Princess PJ finished inspecting the cannons, wiped her hands on her jeans and gave Team *Seahorse* a few top tips.

'Remember, make sure you've your equipment close to hand – powder, wadding, rammer, you know the sort of thing.'

'What about cannon balls?' asked Spud.

PJ rolled her eyes. 'Obviously!' she huffed before continuing. 'Don't forget, do NOT stand behind the cannon when firing. The recoil is fierce. We don't want to be mopping squished pirate off the gun deck. And swab out the cannon with a damp swabber. I don't want to see any flaming torches pulled out from the barrels because you forgot to wet it.'

'What about the cannons?' I asked.

Having seen the state of repair of the rest of the ship, I was worried about the cannons working at all.

'We have a strict cleaning rota; don't we team?' said Desmond.

'Aye cap'n!' came the reply, followed by a loud 'Huzzah!'

At least they sounded confident

Tuesday 27 July 02.00 p.m.

The siren sounded. I wouldn't say that Team *Seahorse* were expert, but they all seemed to know what they were doing and how to do it, which was much better than they had done so far. Gunpowder bags, then cannon balls were rammed in before the fuses were lit. The cannons were fired quickly, one after the other. There were no arguments, nose bleeds, ripped trousers or showing off.

BOOM – BOOM – BOOM

There was choking, blinding smoke and a moment's silence, followed by:

Thud – Thud – Thud

Heavy iron balls dropped from the cannons and rolled slowly to the side of the deck. As the air cleared, and the rotten egg smell of gunpowder with it, there stood Team *Seahorse* like a rack of barbecued sausages: hot, smoky and singed round the edges.

'Whose turn was it to see the cannons were cleaned?' asked Desmond.

One by one, each pirate turned and pointed to the one next to him, except for Barry, who was at the end of the line. Before he could think up an excuse the siren sounded again.

Putrid Pete's team had won (of course) and scored another ten points (of course) – five for winning and five for hitting the target with all three cannon balls. Team *Seahorse* scored zero, zip, zilch and however else you want to say nought.

Tuesday 27 July 2.09 p.m.

I sat on the quay staring into space. There was no way I could see of Desmond and his crew beating Putrid Pete in the grand finale. My first day in charge had been a total disaster. I had been positive, I had been shouty, I had been encouraging. I had even been 'peppy' at times. I didn't know what else to do. How would we get through tomorrow? A full score of forty for Team *Screaming Skull* compared with …

'At least they got eleven points,' said Aunt Fenula, smiling. She had reappeared from wherever she had gone in time to hear the results announced.

'That's a start,' added PJ.

'But you've seen what they're like,' I said. 'And Rory is very suspicious. We're lucky that so far his dad hasn't listened to him.'

'But Delia likes them,' replied Aunt Fenula. 'As long as they get some kind of work with BUMP we'll be okay. If she can help us persuade Mr. Birkwhistle…'

'But Rory doesn't see things Delia's way, and his dad will listen more to him than her. Plus, he already thinks I'm nothing more than a joke.'

Aunt Fenula shook her head. 'I think our plan will work.'

At that moment, Rory came rushing over to gather everyone together to listen to Mr. Scrope. He was making an announcement at exactly 2.30 p.m. A Very Important Announcement.

Tuesday 27 July 2.30 p.m.

We gathered around the judges' podium on the quayside. Mr. Scrope was there, Mr. Birkwhistle by his side, grinning broadly and blowing impressive gum bubbles.

'I have decided to make tomorrow's treasure hunt skills round a little more interesting,' he said. I could see a lump of pink gum sticking to his teeth and falling as he spoke. I wondered if he did that on purpose, to hypnotise people into doing what he wanted.

'There is real treasure in the chests,' he continued, 'and you can keep it, if you can find it before sunset.'

'Yes!' shouted Team *Screaming Skull*.

'Huzzah!' shouted Team *Seahorse*. Somehow they were not at all phased by the cannon firing defeat and seemed more determined than ever. I felt a tiny tickle of pride. It takes a lot to keep going when the odds are against you. Although I'm not sure Desmond and his crew realised just how against them the odds were.

Once the cheering had died down, Mr. Scrope carried on.

'There is £10,000 in gold coins in each chest. All you have to decide is how to spend it.'

Delia camera panned round to the cheering pirates and Rory stepped in with a microphone.

'Captain Putrid,' he asked, 'what do you say to that announcement.'

'£10,000? That's nothing to successful pirates like us. We might have a party. We might even invite Dancing Desmond and his crew, so we can cheer them up after they fail to find their treasure chest.'

Desmond's dander was up. That's an Aunt Fenula phrase. I am not sure what a dander is, but it sounds a very Desmond-y way of getting angry. 'Ha!' he barked, suddenly.

Delia swung the camera round to him.

'What do you say to that, Captain Death?' asked Rory.

Desmond's dander went full on. 'It's pronounced de'Ath, young man,' he said in that way some teachers and parents have (you know the one, when they make 'young man' or 'young woman' sound like a put-down). 'And what I say is this. Captain Putrid will be laughing on the other side of his whiskers. My team will be £10,000 richer by the end of the day.'

'And what will you do with the money? Our viewers would love to know.'

'Usually we give half to charity and then share out the rest between us.'

'Usually? You sound like you have other plans this time.'

Desmond turned to his crew. 'What do you say we give *all* the money to charity?'

'But Captain, if I have to look at Spud's belly drooping over his trousers for one more day, I'll throw up,' said Gruff. 'He needs a new pair.'

'*I* need a new pair?' asked Spud, spinning round to glare at Gruff. 'At least I didn't split mine.'

The pirates sniggered.

'Seriously, team. I think we ought to give our treasure to the Miss Fitz Character Agency.'

'That's not a charity,' said Barry.

'No,' Putrid Pete interrupted, 'but it might just as well be. They take on all the rejects and no hopers, like you lot.'

'Yeah, Dizzy Dezzy and the Dunderheads,' shouted Scurvy Sam.

It was my dander's turn to be up, and I yelled, 'Come here and say that!'

Scurvy Sam sauntered over and repeated, right in my ear (which was a real Yuck Moment): 'Dizzy Dezzy and the Dunderheads.'

Aunt Fenula and Desmond each took one of my arms before I could land a punch and my legs didn't reach far enough to kick Scurvy Sam as she strolled back, grinning at me over her shoulder. Seeing her smug face was another Yuck Moment.

Graffham H. Scrope IV was excited. 'Don't hold back! This is going to make *great* viewing. Audiences love a grudge match.'

Desmond saw things differently and I worried he might be giving the game away. After all, serious pirates don't come out with things like, 'This is all most unseemly!'

'We'll see who's laughing when we win tomorrow's contest,' said Gruff.

Shuggy nodded. 'We'll show 'em what's what, Captain!'

'Yeah. I feel like we can really do this,' said Spud. 'For Cid and Miss Fitz and all the others.'

I could tell from his face that Mr. Scrope was loving every minute of what he was seeing. And that meant Mr. Birkwhistle was too. Maybe the Miss Fitz Agency was on its way down the Ten Point Trouble Scale at last. With the £10,000 fee and Desmond giving us £10,000 we could pay Nudgebuster & Co. back and keep the agency open even if he lost the grand finale.

'Things could be going our way at last,' I said to Aunt Fenula. 'Desmond says his crew is good at map reading and they find lots of treasure. And they don't have to beat Putrid Pete. They simply have to find and dig up their treasure by sundown.'

Tuesday 27 July 2.56 p.m.

We had a full ten minutes of peace before the next kerfuffle broke out.

Before I explain, I want to make my position very clear: if you wear legwarmers outside a dance studio, you're asking for trouble. Mum told me they were very fashionable when she was growing up but not to ask anyone about it (like Aunt Fenula) because people who wore them (like Aunt Fenula) don't talk about it. It's some kind of honour code, I think.

Anyway, Desmond had decided to take his crew through some warm down exercises after the day's work. Not being someone who does a lot of sporty-type stuff, I didn't know warming down was an Actual Thing, but Desmond insisted.

'It helps the body recover after strenuous activity, Cid.'

Before I had time to even wonder if I should say something about Team *Seahorse* not seeming to have done much exercise, strenuous or otherwise, the cheering started. Except it was more jeery than cheery.

'It's Dazzling Desmond de'Ath and his Dancing Desperados,' shouted Putrid Pete at his crew.

'They look desperate all right,' laughed one.

'They're not Desperadoes so much as Dodos,' cried another.

'It's Dazzling Desmond de'Ath and his Desperate Dodos!' yelled Scurvy Sam, before snorting with laughter.

Putrid Pete could barely manage to shout 'What *are* they wearing?' for laughing.

'Oi!' Gruff shouted at Putrid Pete. 'I knitted these legwarmers myself for the entire crew.'

And he had. Even Carlos was busy snapping an elastic band around the luminous green and blue striped legwarmer on his peg leg.

'Ignore them,' Desmond said. 'People always mock what they don't understand.'

That's the kind of thing Mum or Aunt Fenula tell me if I've had one of Those Days at school and, to be fair, I think it's very true. But it's NOT the kind of thing you say to someone like Summer Relish or anyone who thinks it's okay to laugh at someone else's misfortune. And the legwarmers Team *Seahorse* were wearing looked very misfortunate.

Things went downhill from there. Putrid Pete and Team *Screaming Skull* made fun of Desmond's crew, mimicking their stretches and lunges, jumps and leaps until Desmond snapped. Actually snapped. Everyone was stunned into silence, even Putrid Pete, as Desmond stomped – STOMPED – up to him.

'You think you can do a better job, do you, Pukebreath? I doubt it, judging by your mimicking.'

Desmond's voice was seething. Seething is definitely the word. It's furious but also sounds long and a bit dangerous. Like when teachers are so angry they go dangerously quiet before really, really shouting. Desmond was seething for sure when he challenged Putrid Pete to a competition.

'Well? Are you up to the challenge, sir?' The way Desmond said 'sir' wasn't like you would say it to a teacher (unless you *wanted* a phone call home). He made it sound like an insult.

Now Team *Seahorse* was jeering and cheering. Putrid Pete had little choice but to accept.

'Fine! I'll take your challenge. But I want an impartial judge.'

Rory, who had come over to see what the fuss was about, went to ask Gloria Golightly. She agreed, but it turned out that the winner was never in doubt.

The first round was twirling on the spot on one leg. Actually, the technical term is 'spotting' but it's basically twirling, although it's not as easy as it looks. To 'spot' properly, your head goes round at a different speed to your body. Don't ask how it's done, it looks impossible to me. It was certainly impossible for Putrid Pete, who couldn't even spin around on both legs without stumbling. Desmond was A-MAZ-ING. He went faster and faster and Team *Seahorse* cheered louder and louder until Gloria Golightly called 'Enough' and said he was making her dizzy.

'Dizzy Dezzy,' said Putrid Pete and laughed, although it was a limp laugh. No substance.

Entrechats came next. That's the 'jumping-on-the-spot-while-crossing-and-uncrossing-your-legs' thing. I can see why they need a shorter name for it but 'entrechat'? Anyway, the more times you cross and uncross your legs before landing, the better.

Desmond went first. He jumped and managed five times. I tried too, but only managed twice.

Then Putrid Pete jumped. He managed to cross his legs but he couldn't uncross them and fell in a heap.

'That's not proper jumping,' he complained. 'It might impress in ballet school, but it's not pirating. Crossing your legs and jumping is what you do when you need the loo.'

Team *Screaming Skull* chuckled, but Desmond won the round. He won the next two as well: who can jump the highest from standing still and who can leap the furthest. By this time Team *Seahorse* was cheering and they lifted their captain onto their shoulders.

'I've not got time for this nonsense,' Putrid Pete shouted. 'We'll see who wins tomorrow, when it's real pirating and it really counts.' Now it was his turn to stomp, except he stomped off in a huff, his crew mumbling and grumbling behind him.

Rory came over to me. I wasn't in the mood to argue and I felt my eyes roll.

'What do you want?'

'Nothing really, it's just that display Desmond put on.'

I was tired so I let my mouth do its own thing.

'Stop right there!' it shouted. 'I know what it's like to be made fun of because I do things a bit differently…'

'A bit different? Desmond's completely unexpected. I think Putrid Pete…'

'But that's just it, you don't think, do you? You're too busy being captain of this, that and the other to bother about…'

'I'm trying to tell you…'

'I am NOT going to tell Desmond to apologise. You don't know what it's like…'

If we'd listened to each other our conversation might have been a lot shorter. As it was my brain was coming up with a lot of stuff it needed to say and Rory kept talking over me and I kept cutting him short and so it went on until:

'Enough already, I give in!' Rory held up his hands like he was surrendering. It took a while for my brain to register this but a few seconds later my mouth trailed off, mid rant.

'All I wanted to say is that Desmond was amazing back there. Putrid Pete didn't like it one bit.'

'He's not apologising,' I said, determined to leave Rory in no doubt.

'Who wants him to apologise?'

'You do.'

'I never said that.'

'You did! You said…' and then I stopped. Rory was right. He hadn't. By now I was sure I looked like Holly Prickles does around Rory, but for a completely different reasons. Typical! The one time I actually say what I feel and I get it wrong. I embarrass even myself sometimes.

'Oops.'

It was all I could think of to say. I wasn't prepared to give Rory a 'sorry' after he had been a patronising grump most of the last two days.

'Those ballet moves are tough. They take a lot of strength and practice. I was never able to cross my legs more than four times when I did an entrechat.'

Typical Rory, he could do four and I could only manage two. Then it hit me.

'You do ballet?'

Rory looked a bit embarrassed. I'd never seen him like that before. It made him seem quite friendly.

'Not exactly,' he said. 'But my mum was a dancer and she tries to teach me the basics. She says it will help with my sport, make me stronger and more flexible.'

'Does it?'

Rory nodded. 'It's improved my game. I'm even being scouted by some big teams. Mum took me to the ballet once too. I actually enjoyed it, though I never let on. She can't really teach me very much ballet anymore, not since she's been ill. That's why I'm here helping Dad out. She needs to rest sometimes. Plus, it's not easy moving around old pirate ships in a wheelchair.'

'Oh,' I said. 'Sorry.' I wasn't sorry about what happened up until now, but I was sorry about his mum's illness. It sounded serious. I wondered what was wrong with her but I figured if he wanted me to know, he'd tell me. Things like that can be harder if people make a fuss, no matter how nice they try to be. Anyway, whatever it was that had annoyed me earlier, seemed really silly now.

'Doesn't matter. But don't say anything to the others, will you? About the ballet and stuff.'

'Others?'

'At school. Summer, Holly and the rest of them.'

'Oh, yeah, right. Summer and Holly. They're always wanting to hang round with me. It's annoying really.'

Rory looked at me for a moment, then laughed. But it was a good kind of a laugh. It was an 'I understand' kind of a laugh that told me perhaps he wasn't as much like Summer and Holly as I had thought. On the other hand, he didn't want anyone to know he wasn't 'one of them' so perhaps he was, if you see what I mean. Either way, I wondered for the first time if there were more to Rory than I realised.

'I shan't,' I said. 'And you're not to tell them about the agency either, especially not my mad aunt.'

Although I had a horrible feeling it would be all over social media when the grand finale of *Premiership Pirate Knockout* was shown, whatever the outcome.

Chapter Eleven

Tuesday 27 July 6.30 p.m.

Desmond and his crew were in a good mood back at the agency that evening. They were the only ones, except for Aunt Fenula, who was trying to be Very Positive, which was annoying PJ.

'I can't see how they're going to get very far with ten points.' she said. 'Not if today's performance is anything to go by.'

'If Desmond completes the filming, we get £10,000,' said Aunt Fenula. 'If he finds the treasure, we get another £10,000. Our problems will be over.'

PJ sighed. 'But this is Desmond you're talking about.'

'But even if we get £20,000, all that does is pay off the money we owe Nudgebuster & Co.,' I said, feeling bad about being so glum. 'We need more than that to stay in business. We need the bonus, otherwise the Miss Fitz Agency will probably still have to shut down.'

'How many times do I have to say it?' replied Aunt Fenula. 'We don't necessarily need them to win. Mr. Scrope likes them – all we need is for him to like them enough to buy *Premiership Pirate Knockout*. Or he might hire them for some other show. Desmond and his crew are different and that's a big selling point.'

I wasn't convinced. I mean, I know that being the same as everyone else is boring and I love what Aunt Fenula is trying to do. I understand the cards and posters in school about being an individual or not following the crowd. I'm not happy being a sheep, but other people don't always make it easy, do they? They might say 'be yourself' but my question is, how far do they *really* mean it? Suppose Desmond was too different for Mr. Scrope? He knew exactly what he wanted – plucky underdog defeats dastardly pirate – and only one thing was for sure: Desmond was far too un-pirate-like to beat Putrid Pete.

Then Aunt Fenula let out a wobbly, gurgling sound. She had gone pale and was looking at her phone. I peered over her shoulder and read out the text message she had got from Nudgebuster & Co.

'We hear today was a DISASTER! Don't know what nonsense you told Birkwhistle about Dizzy Dezzy, but you WILL be found out and we will get what we want.'

'How do they know about what happened today?' asked PJ. 'I thought the filming and results were supposed to be secret.'

'They are,' I said. 'Someone's been blabbing.'

'What's worrying me,' said Aunt Fenula, 'is that they say they're going to get what they want rather than what they are owed.' I was too worried to ask what the difference might be.

'Desmond better win then,' PJ said, but she didn't sound encouraging.

There was work to be done, however, so we didn't waste any more time on the threatening text. Aunt Fenula, PJ, the pirates and I began looking at some of the day's footage on my laptop in the FFAFA Studio. PJ had asked Delia to send it over to help Team *Seahorse* to 'sharpen up their tactics'. Carlos, Barry and Clayton, however, were already off task.

'I come across as rather magnificent,' said Carlos. 'This footage embodies my quintessence as a performer.'

I'm not sure what a quint-thingummy is either, but that's Carlos for you.

'I come across as quite striking,' added Barry. 'This footage defines the heart of my performance,' added Barry.

'I come across as a right chubster,' finished Clayton, sucking in his cheeks. 'This footage gets across how big my bum really looked. But when I asked, you all said it was fine.' And he turned his back in a huff.

When Gruff, Spud and Shuggy began arguing about how much time they each had on camera, I had had enough. Vlad, Wilbur, Arthur and the others weren't around. They had gone out for an evening stroll, which seemed like a good idea, so off I went to the chip shop.

Tuesday 27 July 7.56 p.m.
Trouble Scale heading for 10!

In fact, it was a bad idea. I came back to find the FFAFA studio door hanging off its hinges, with a big hole punched through it. From inside I heard a voice shouting:

'One more squeak from you, Pudgy, and Fancy here gets nutted.' It was Big Ma's voice. I translated what she had said into: 'Keep quiet, Princess PJ, or Carlos will be head-butted.'

I dropped my chips and crouched under the open window. Then I stretched up until I could see Big Ma with Carlos in a headlock under one of her substantial arms. Her other hand had PJ by her hair.

I looked around at the chaos. Nudgebuster had brought what he called "a little bit of muscle" round with him and Big Ma. A little bit? They weren't the sort that people say 'He's only a lad' about. They were the other sort. If their fists had been brains they'd have all been geniuses, especially Madeleine, although Rocky and Herbert weren't far behind.

My heart was pounding so hard in my head that my throat throbbed with each beat, the sound blocking my ears. I needed to get closer, to work out who was where and what was going on. I crawled along to the next window and kicked something that rattled and wobbled as it spun on the cobbles. I held my breath, not daring to breathe.

'Psst.'

I jumped, which isn't easy when you're squatting under a window. I peered into the room, but I couldn't see anyone who was able to 'psst', let alone who knew I was there.

'Psst.'

I looked down. There was Dusty – well, Dusty's skull. I picked him up.

'What happened?'

'They "dropped in on the off chance" was what they said. Called it a "social visit".'

Clearly it was anything but social. Dusty carried on.

'Then they said they knew today had been a disaster. Then they started ransacking the place. They said it was as good as their property and there was nothing we could do. They were right about the last part. I've never seen such big biceps.'

'Why is your head out here, Dusty?' I asked. 'Where's the rest of you?'

'I had found a comfortable drawer to sleep in in the old dresser at the far end of the studio – I don't need much space – and, to be honest, I decided to stay in there. Then everything started to rattle and sway as the largest scary one…'

'Big Ma?'

'Yes… well, she came over to the dresser and started pulling the drawers right out, tipping them upside down, checking their backs. She tipped me on the floor and grabbed a heap of old paper that I was using for bedding. I told her to stop and one of their goons drop-kicked me through the window. So here I am. Well, my head. The rest of me is around somewhere. What's going on?'

'Aunt Fenula borrowed £20,000 from them. If we can't pay by the end of the week, they get everything including the agency buildings.'

'There are more valuable things in there than my bedding. Why did they want that so badly?'

I shrugged. 'Who knows? People like Big Ma don't seem to worry about having reasons for what they do.'

Dusty was quiet for a moment then said, 'What happens to the agency if Miss Fitz can't pay? Where do we go?'

'If the agency is shut down, you all have to go elsewhere.' I looked at Dusty. 'Whatever happens, I promise not make it easy for Nudgebuster.'

'Count me in, Cid. Did your aunt tell you that she found me in a damp, cardboard box by some bins outside the back of the film studios? I wasn't able to pull myself together until she came along and helped.'

Dusty's story decided it for me. There was ABSOLUTELY NO WAY I would let Aunt Fenula down. I peeped through the window and held Dusty up so he could see too. The rest of him was scattered far and wide. If he tried to pull himself together, well, bones moving across the floor would be a bit of a giveaway.

'Roll me over towards the gate, Cid. That way I can at least warn the others when they get back.'

I did as he asked and then turned back to what was happening in the FFAFA studio. Nudgebuster had Desmond by the arm, an arm that was being forced so far up his back Desmond was standing on tiptoe.

'Where is it?' Nudgebuster asked.

'I keep telling you, I don't know what you are on about.'

Aunt Fenula's voice was muffled. She was squished into a corner behind Big Ma, who was holding PJ by the hair in one hand and Carlos in the other.

Nudgebuster forced Desmond's arm further up his back. Desmond breathed heavily through gritted teeth. From the wince he gave I guessed he was trying not to cry out in pain.

'WHERE IS IT?' Nudgebuster shouted.

Aunt Fenula's voice was strained. She sounded angry, weary and scared.

'How many more times? I don't know what you are on about!'

PJ simply sounded angry. 'If Miss Fitz says she doesn't know then she doesn't know! Don't assume everyone else is a cheat and a liar just because you are.'

Big Ma wound her hand into PJ's hair, so she had to twist and bend to stay upright.

'And you are also a bully, sir!' added Desmond. 'A bully and a yellow cowardy-custard!'

Saying things like that only make situations like this worse. But Desmond was Desmond, and this was his style. Nudgebuster twisted his arm further.

Anyway, by now I couldn't tell if I was furious or terrified. Herbert and Rocky were sitting astride an upturned sofa. What looked like Gruff and Shuggy were peering from under the wooden arm rests and another was waving a hand through another gap – until Herbert stomped on it. From the squeal I could tell it was Spud.

As for Madeleine, she had at least two people shut in a cupboard, judging by all the banging and thudding. I couldn't see any sign of Barry or Clayton, so it had to be them.

'Where's that niece of yours?' asked Big Ma, so suddenly that I gasped. I immediately clamped by hand over my mouth. Why do people do that? I mean, it's too late by then.

'I don't know. Out somewhere.'

'Do you want me to send some of The Lads round to her parents' house?' Herbert asked Mr. Nudgebuster.

'They're on holiday,' Aunt Fenula mumbled.

'I'm not sure I believe you,' Nudgebuster said.

'It's true,' shouted PJ. 'Now, let us go.'

I stretched my neck for a better view but I must have made a noise or something because Big Ma swung round, twisting PJ's hair and taking Carlos's head with her.

I ducked down, but couldn't be certain that she hadn't seen me.

PJ was saying things that I can't repeat, but safe to say she was swearing revenge. Carlos was making a strange gargling sound.

'Shut up, Fancy,' said Big Ma, tightening her grip. 'You too, Pudgy.'

Then there was a lot of banging as the cupboard started rocking. I couldn't hear what Clayton and Barry were saying but I could guess. There was a crash as Madeleine shoved the cupboard forward and pushed it over.

Silence. But not only from Clayton and Barry. I held my breath and listened. Nothing. What was happening? I needed to crawl to the door for a better look. Crouching had made my feet go numb and now I had pins and needles, but I edged along slowly.

The silence was making me uneasy. Uneasy enough to take a risk. I peered round the door, then further, a little more … I nudged the door very slightly. But that was all it took for its last hinge to give way. By the time I knew what was happening it was too late. Nudgebuster dropped Desmond and lunged, grabbing at me. I managed to pull free before he got a grip. I dodged around the remains of the furniture – overturned table and chairs, smashed coffee mugs, broken photo frames – with Nudgebuster matching my every move as we circled around the upturned furniture.

Desmond meant well. He always means well. Unfortunately, when he stuck out his foot it was me he tripped, not Nudgebuster. I fell, sprawled across the floor.

'Good evening, Clematis,' he sneered. 'So glad you could drop by after all.'

'How long were you out there?' asked Big Ma.

'Long enough to know you think we have something valuable here. No wonder you're so eager to get your hands on the agency.'

I tried to sound twice my height and a good deal heavier but I don't think it worked.

'It's what your aunt agreed,' said Nudgebuster. 'And judging by today's performance from Desperate Dezzy and his Dingly Drongoes, the Miss Fitz Agency is not going to be able to pay back what it owes.'

I have no idea what a 'dingly drongo' is but that was the last thing on my mind.

'How do you know what happened today? Who told you?'

'Never you mind. You just concentrate on what's happening to your friends here. Might help to focus your mind.'

'Just look at them,' laughed Big Ma. 'Oh, silly me. I forgot. You can't see most of them because they're grovelling under the sofa or shut up in a cupboard.

Nudgebuster pushed Desmond's arm even further up his back. Sweat trickled into Desmond's eyes, but he wouldn't cry out. 'If you want to help your friend here,' said Nudgebuster as he glared at me, 'you'll tell me where it is.'

'I don't know what you're on about,' I said. 'But if it's all going as badly as you think, you can come and look after the filming is over.'

Then I had a thought. It calmed me down enough to sound like I had regained my control even though I hadn't, not by a long way.

'But it's not going as badly as you thought, is it? Otherwise why all the rush?'

It's funny how fast your brain can work when it's running on adrenaline, but I suddenly realised that Desmond's courage showed he had sticking power. I felt sure he'd see the filming through, come what may. That would give us £10,000 to start paying off Nudgebuster & Co. And Desmond was confident in his crew's map reading and treasure finding skills. In fact, with £10,000 from the treasure hunt we didn't need Desmond to win. We could pay off Nudgebuster & Co. in full and the agency would be safe. Then I thought of something else.

'Do you think if we had something valuable we'd have got into debt with someone like you?'

Nudgebuster smiled. 'Good point. Maybe you really *don't* know what I'm on about. But it's not going to stop us.'

'I'm calling the police,' I blurted.

'Go ahead.'

Nudgebuster's response immediately made me suspicious.

, 'I shall, I mean it.'

'I'm not stopping you.'

As I began tapping my phone Big Ma turned to Nudgebuster, 'How do you think Mr. Scrope will react, Kenneth, when he finds out the police have been involved with one of *Premiership Pirate Knockout*'s contestants?'

'I shouldn't think he'd like it, Marjorie. Scandal is not good for family television shows.'

I paused.

'But,' I said, 'it's not us that's breaking the law. It's you that's done this… this… damage to property.'

'And to arms,' said Desmond.

'And to throats,' choked Carlos, still in a headlock.

'And to hands,' cried Spud.

There was thudding from the cupboard.

'It's nothing more than high spirits,' said Mr. Nudgebuster. 'Madeleine, Rocky and Herbert do get a bit over excited.'

I started tapping in the phone number again.

'How do you think it will look, Marjorie, when the Miss Fitz Agency is splashed all over the media for being bankrupt?'

I stopped tapping.

'Not good, Kenneth. I can't see Mr. Scrope wanting it playing any part whatsoever in the grand finale of *Premiership Pirate Knockout*. It would ruin the brand image.'

'He wouldn't want to be associated with such a business, would he? And that would be a shame, as it's the only way the Miss Fitz Agency has got a hope of surviving.'

'But it's not fair!' shouted Shuggy from under the upturned sofa. 'You can't come in here and do this. All my drawers emptied, my old mum's wedding dress ruined.'

'Who cares?'

Suddenly, there was a roar and a blur of grey as Wilbur leapt from the shadows through the door and clamped his jaws around Nudgebuster's arm. Nudgebuster yelled and shouted frantically for us to call him off. Big Ma rushed to help him and then laughed.

'What are you afraid of, you big wuss? Being gummed to death?'

As she grabbed Wilbur by the tail to pull him off, Vlad came swooping in through a window, purple-lined cape flying out behind him and fangs gleaming. Big Ma screamed, immediately dropped Wilbur, who fell flat on his face, which started a nosebleed, which made Vlad squeal and faint, collapsing into a heap under his cloak.

Nudgebuster started laughing. 'Character Agency? It's a freak show!'

But his laughter turned into coughing and spluttering.

'What is that disgusting smell?' he choked.

Then Big Ma was retching and gagging. We are used to Arthur's dematerialisation problems, but even by his standards it was disgusting. Still, it did the trick. The Lads rushed outside, gasping at fresh air.

Big Ma had let go of PJ and Carlos to pinch her nose and hold onto her stomach. 'Which one of you is responsible for this foul, eggy sandwich, sewer stench?'

'I'm… warning… you,' belched Nudgebuster, looking around.

He couldn't see who was to blame and he couldn't wait any longer to find out. Nudgebuster & Co. couldn't leave the portacabin fast enough. They fought each other to get through the doorway first then fled, shouting something about drains and getting the council on to us.

'I did it!' shouted Arthur. 'I really did. I went invisible!'

But there was no one left to listen. We were all outside, gasping for fresh air.

Tuesday 27 July 11.20 p.m.
Trouble Scale back down to 7+ (Things looked better for Wednesday)

It took a couple of hours simply to make sure everyone was all right and set the furniture upright again. We checked that everyone had a bed to sleep in (including a basket for Wilbur and a drawer for Dusty). Then Aunt Fenula made cocoa. It was only as I turned out the light that I realised two things:

Firstly, whatever Nudgebuster & Co. thought they'd find on our property must be worth much more than the £20,000 we owed them.

Secondly, now we knew about it they couldn't risk us finding it before they did.

When I combined these two points with the knowledge that they had someone on the 'inside' of *Premiership Pirate Knockout* and the experience we had had that evening, a third thing was clear: the agency was in even greater danger now.

Chapter Twelve

Wednesday 28 July 9.30 a.m.

By the time Aunt Fenula and I had arrived on set the next day, Rory had already gathered the pirates and the cameras were rolling. I hadn't told her of the conclusions I had come to the night before. She would have gone into melt down and that would not be good for anyone, especially me.

Rory waved us over when he saw us and actually smiled at me. I was not sure whether to trust this change in him or not. I guess the big test will be if he does it when we're back at school or if I'll go back to being 'The One In Miss MacLean's Class Who Wore School Uniform On Non-Uniform Day. Twice.'

Standing next to Rory, also smiling, was his dad, who greeted us with, 'So how's the plan going?'

Aunt Fenula came out with one of those phrases adults use that can mean anything you want it to.

'It's going as expected.'

'You should've seen Desmond challenge Captain Pukebreath yesterday, Dad,' said Rory. 'He was a-maz-ing. Putrid Pete was no match for him. I think the plan will work really well.'

I guess being good at everything himself, Rory didn't realise some of us only have one or two things we're good at, if we're lucky. He seemed to think that if Desmond was an expert dancer, he must be an expert pirate.

As Rory and his dad went to check the filming schedules, Aunt Fenula gave me a thumbs up and a big grin. I gave her a half smile. It was all I could manage.

'What's the matter now? Rory is coming round to Desmond. With him and Delia on our side we stand a better chance of BUMP signing them up even if they don't win *Premiership Pirate Knockout*.'

'"If they don't win"? When! And Rory has only changed his mind because he seems to think if Desmond is good at dancing he must also be good at pirating. What happens when he finds out that's not true?'

'But it won't matter. Either way the agency will be saved and we can send Nudgebuster & Co. on their way.'

It mattered to me, though. There was one person Aunt Fenula had forgotten about and that was Graffham H. Scrope IV. He would NOT take kindly to being fooled. Yes, Mr. Scrope was willing to pay a lot of money to buy *Premiership Pirate Knockout* for his American viewers – but only as long as he got the ending he wanted. What would he do when it didn't happen? And then what would he do when found out the truth about Desmond?

I get that business can be ruthless (What is "ruth"? Clearly if you don't have it you're not very nice.) I get that you have to be hard-headed. And of course I knew what it would mean for PJ, Arthur, Vlad and the others if we didn't make some money or get a contract ASAP. But something was nibbling me. It wasn't niggling, it was definitely nibbling, like a tiny worm munching my stomach lining, and I knew that feeling well. Something, somewhere, wasn't right with any of this. There was no time to work out what at that moment however.

Delia panned the camera round Team *Seahorse*, filming the first shots of the day. As soon as he saw her, Carlos adopted what he considered was a heroic pose.

'He can't help himself,' Aunt Fenula whispered to me.

'My quest is not for gold, but for glory,' said Carlos.

'I seek not jewels, but honour,' added Barry.

'I'm after as much loot as I can get my hands on,' finished Clayton. 'And I've got big hands.'

'That's the spirit,' Desmond was saying. 'We've got this, Team *Seahorse*. Digging for treasure is something we definitely are good at.'

Aunt Fenula looked at me. 'You see, Cid? Look how positive they are today after that little contest yesterday afternoon. Everything is still to play for. After all, it's "not over 'til the fat lady sings".' Which is a weird thing to say, but that's Aunt Fenula for you.

'If there's a fat lady singing, she's bound to be on Desmond's crew,' whispered PJ.

I laughed and that made me feel much better. At least the treasure island contest was not a race. Each team was to be judged on teamwork and, of course, finding their treasure. Once Team *Seahorse* had dug up the £10,000 we could pay off Nudgebuster & Co. half of what we owed. By the end of the week threats like 'we'll tell everyone you're bankrupt' and 'what would Mr. Scrope think if the police were involved?' would no longer work. I began dreaming what we could do if Desmond's crew actually won. We'd have money in the bank! I already had plans for it. Firstly, teaching the Miss Fitz characters some useful skills. And buying in some quality filming equipment. That would need a better computer. And there was a special effect and make-up course I wanted to go on. And... so much more. Even if Desmond didn't win, we only needed to hold on for four more days.

Wednesday 28 July 10.00 a.m.

Mr. Birkwhistle handed a large parchment scroll to each captain.

'Team *Screaming Skull*, your treasure is buried in the eastern side of the island and Team *Seahorse*, yours is in the west. There are picks and shovels already there, but each captain may pick three extra items from the Quartermaster's Stores to take as well.'

While Desmond joined Putrid Pete in the stores, I gave a pep talk to the *Seahorse* crew.

'You need to do this,' I said. 'Today's points are vital if you are to stand a chance in the grand finale. And don't forget, five of the points are for teamwork, so no quarrelling.'

'Quarrel? asked Carlos.

'Us?' continued Barry.

'You've seen how well we all get on...' Clayton began. Then he paused. 'Fair comment,' he added.

Putrid Pete was first out of the Quartermaster's Stores. He had chosen a barrel of rum for his first thing (no surprise), a barrel of rum as his second thing (again, no surprise) and you can probably guess what his third item was.

'How's this, me hearties?' he shouted to his cheering crew. 'Plenty of rum for all!'

Then Desmond appeared dragging an enormous picnic hamper with an accordion balanced on top of it and a beach umbrella. I groaned. Couldn't Desmond do something pirate-y for once?

Rory and his father were more than happy, however. Mr. Scrope had turned up in time to see both Putrid Pete and Desmond leaving the Quartermaster's Stores. He was pleased with Desmond's choices as they would go down well with family audiences, but did not approve of Putrid Pete's barrels of rum.

'Still,' said Mr. Scrope, 'it means audiences will love it even more when Desmond gives Putrid his comeuppance in the grand finale.'

As Mr. Scrope spoke, he worked a large lump of bubble gum around his mouth. I couldn't not stare. It was like watching the one red thing in a white wash going round a washing machine.

'If Mr. Scrope is happy, Dad is happy,' Rory whispered to me.

'It's all going according to plan, Mr. Scrope,' Byron Birkwhistle said. 'Isn't it, Miss Fitz?'

'Yes, it's all going according to plan,' repeated Aunt Fenula.'

Scrope chewed his gum furiously for a moment then stopped suddenly.

'About that plan, Birkwhistle,' he said. 'It's time to move things up a gear, make it more of a contest, build up the tension for the grand finale.'

'A quite brilliant idea, Mr. Scrope. Tell us your vision.'

Aunt Fenula rolled her eyes; I snorted as I tried to swallow a laugh and Rory blushed. His dad was being a total sick-o-phant.

'It's time for Team *Seahorse* to show us what they can really do. Give Putrid a bit of a wake-up call, make him realise this contest isn't all going his way. I want shots of his reactions when Desmond's crew scores full marks and narrows the gap between them. He might be shocked or angry or scared. Whichever it is that's when we roll the credits before the grand finale episode. Everyone will be talking about it; we'll have record breaking viewing figures.'

The cold, lumpy custard of dread plopped into my stomach again. Worse still, Rory was smiling at me.

'This is going to be great,' he whispered while Mr. Birkwhistle talked strategy with Mr. Scrope. 'I wasn't convinced by your plan before. To be honest I thought it was some kind of scheme to get money out of

Dad. But after seeing Desmond in action last night, I'm convinced. He'll run rings around Putrid Pete.'

I nodded. What else could I do?

I was still in shock from that when another, bigger, nastier surprise was delivered. Mr. Scrope had finished explaining 'how it's gonna be, Birkwhistle' and was about to get into his stretch limo when he turned around and called out across the quayside, 'Don't forget, Birkwhistle: no win, no deal; do deal, no fee!'

And he blew and popped an extra large bubble of gum.

I felt sick. Clearly there was also a lot riding on this for BUMP too, and therefore for Mr. Birkwhistle, Rory and his mum. I gave Aunt Fenula one of my speciality side-long glares. They're not easy as you feel like your eyeball might slide out of your ear, but the situation was serious enough to do one.

We were surely about to hit point 9 on the Trouble Scale.

Chapter Thirteen

Wednesday 28 July 10.17 a.m.

As soon as I could, I pulled Aunt Fenula behind the portaloos near the catering caravan.

'What are we going to do?' I whisper-shouted, or shout-whispered or whichever way round it is.

'There's not much we can do.'

'Mr. Birkwhistle isn't going to find Desmond very funny when he loses his fee from Mr. Scrope,' I hissed, 'no matter how much they make Delia laugh.'

'It's a shame, but at least we'll get enough to pay Nudgebuster & Co. and save the agency. PJ, Wilbur, Arthur, Dusty and everyone will still have somewhere to belong.'

Then another thought struck me.

'And I doubt Rory will be laughing either. At least before all this he didn't know who I was, but now he does and he'll hate me.' I groaned. School was going to be a nightmare. And my nightmares are scary.

'I'm sorry, Cid but saving the agency is our top priority right now.'

Before I could point out that at least it was all right for Aunt Fenula as she didn't have to worry about Summer Relish or Holly Prickles there was an uproar from across the quayside.

'Ooh look, at his parasol.' Scurvy Sam was pointing at Desmond. 'Are you wearing your swimming cozzies or are you changing under your towels?'

Team *Screaming Skull* fell about laughing.

'Disregard them,' said Carlos, sticking his nose in the air.

'Ignore them,' added Barry, turning his back on Putrid Pete's crew.

'La-la-la,' sang Clayton, and stuck his fingers in his ears.

Wednesday 28 July 11.20 a.m.

I climbed into the boat taking both teams of pirates and two camera operators to the island. I was there as Team *Seahorse*'s coach. Team *Screaming Skull* had, of course, made it very clear what they thought of coaches by getting rid of all theirs.

Once we were under way, Rory filled in more details about the contest.

'We will take you to your starting points and leave you with your camera operator and coach – if you have one – before returning to the mainland,' he said. 'Your coach is there to observe, keep up morale and get in touch with the mainland if there are any issues.'

'Desmond's Dipsticks haven't got a clue how to get into trouble,' growled Putrid Pete. 'Real trouble, that is. *Pirating* trouble.'

'Modern pirating is not about causing havoc,' replied Desmond. 'It's about skill, tactics.'

'And you haven't got any of them, either!' shouted Scurvy Sam.

Putrid Pete's crew started howling with laughter again and it all kicked off. Fang squawked right in Prendergast's face. Prendergast flapped and hopped off Desmond's shoulder to begin pecking Putrid Pete's kneecaps.

'Oi, Desmond, call off your mangy bird,' shouted Pete, kicking at Prendergast, missing and stumbling into Desmond, who dropped his map as he grabbed onto me to steady himself. Before we knew what was happening, Fang had snatched the map and flown off with it to the launch's stern. He appeared to be studying it. I know parrots are meant to be clever, but even my dad can't read a map. At least I think that's why he never uses one, even when Sat. Nav. takes us down a track so narrow that the car ends up wedged between hedgerows.

Suddenly, Fang squawked and scratched at the map with his claws.

I felt a rush of anger, like a lava fountain had suddenly been turned on in the pit of my stomach. Have you ever felt that? I swear I grew taller as it surged up inside. I stood on tip-toe and poked Putrid Pete's shoulder. Then I did that teacher low-voice trick, the one where you know they really, really mean it.

'If that parrot does *anything* more to that map,' I hissed, 'I'll make sure you forfeit the race and Desmond gets your points as well as his own.'

Putrid Pete glared at me, but I was ready for that and stood my ground. 'Really? They won't listen to a silly little girl like you.'

The phrase 'silly little' winds me up more than almost any insult you can think of. So much so that I didn't know what I was going to say until the words were out of my mouth.

'Yes, really. Shall we put that to the test? I think you'll find Mr. Scrope would like Desmond's team to win. It seems his audience wants to see flea-bitten, rancid pirates like you, lose. And Mr. Birkwhistle needs to please Mr. Scrope.'

Putrid Pete continued glaring at me for a few seconds but then yelled at his parrot.

'Fang! Get back 'ere, you naughty bird. And give the nice gentleman his map back.'

Fang did as he was told.

I felt like I had won a glorious victory.

Meanwhile, Prendergast was perched on the bow, his back turned to us. He was refusing to budge. Desmond asked Putrid Pete to apologise to Prendergast for kicking him. Putrid Pete refused. I can't repeat what Putrid actually said because it was what Mum calls 'colourful language'. Let's say his words weren't pastel shades like Powder-Puff Pink or Baby Blue and leave it at that.

So, what should have been a test of individual pirating skills and teamwork had already become a bad-tempered grudge-match. Luckily the two teams would be several miles apart otherwise the whole thing could have become a bloodbath. Okay, so that's a bit of an exaggeration, but it wouldn't have been pleasant. Not that Putrid Pete and his crew could ever be called pleasant.

'We'll be watching the film feeds with the judges back on the mainland,' Rory said as we approached the east side of the island. 'You'll find out your scores when you get back.'

As Putrid Pete followed his crew off the boat he stopped by me and whispered, 'Nudgebuster and Big Ma are "associates" of mine. They told me all about you, your aunt and that no-hopers' agency of hers. Don't think I don't know what's going on. I'd think twice before you're rude to me again.' And he jumped onto the shore.

Have you ever had that hot-cold-prickly feeling of 'what have I done?'. It raced down my arms and legs before filling my stomach like a bucket of cold sick. It wasn't only that Putrid Pete was in cahoots with Nudgebuster & Co. that bothered me. 'In cahoots' sounds much more exciting than 'in league with' (which sounds like football) or conspiring, (which is too much like perspiring, which Mum says is what ladies do instead of sweating). Although I was feeling more than a bit hot and sweaty by now because I wasn't sure what to make of Putrid Pete saying he knows "what's going on" either.

I didn't have long to think about all this, though as a few minutes later, the boat dropped off Team Seahorse on the west side of the island. Delia began filming immediately and Desmond became very captainly. He gathered his crew and stood on the enormous hamper to address them. Address is a bit of a pompous way to say 'speak' when someone is standing on a picnic hamper, but Desmond in captain mode *is* a bit pompous (in the nicest possible way, of course).

'I think we all know how serious this is. It's about much more than treasure. It's about our honour and indeed, the honour of the Miss Fitz Agency and all our friends there. And they are counting on us. They need us to win more points today. So, it's not simply that we *want* it more than Team *Screaming Skull*, but we need it more than they do. Isn't that right, Cid?'

I nodded and went a bit captainly myself.

'We have to face facts. Things are tough. If you can put on a good show today and again tomorrow, even if you don't win the grand finale we think we can persuade Mr. Birkwhistle to give you some more work of a different kind. And that means we'll all have a future. The £10,000 treasure from today will really help with that too.'

Desmond dabbed his eyes with a handkerchief. 'Bravo, Cid. I couldn't have put it better myself. Let's do it, team!'

'Triumph is within our grasp!' exclaimed Carlos, clapping his hands.

'Victory awaits!' cried Barry, punching the air.

'Oosh!' shouted Clayton, raising his arms and jumping forwards so his belly bounced into Spud, which pushed him into Desmond who fell off the hamper.

Desmond sat up and spat out rather a lot of sand. Carlos gasped in horror.

'A portent!' And he clasped his hands together while glancing at the camera.

Barry grabbed Carlos while looking directly at the camera and loudly whispered. 'An omen?' And then brought his hands to his face.

Clayton shoved Carlos and Barry as he wailed, 'No, no – it's a sign!' And he loomed at the camera lens, getting closer and closer until all that could be seen were his quivering nose hairs. 'We're doooooomed!'

I glared at the three of them. 'Pull yourselves together, stop over-acting and MOVE IT!'

Wednesday 28 July 1.15 pm

It took Team *Seahorse* quite a while to study the map and agree on a route. For starters, there was a rhyme to work out, as if there wasn't enough pressure already:

Through undergrowth you have to hack
The path you want, no turning back
Until you reach the place you need;
So think on this and please take heed.
Where white meets blue in shades of grey,
And darkness rules both night and day,
Deep inside you'll find the chest,
It's yours if you can pass this test;
Unlock it quick before sun down
If not, your smile becomes a frown.

'So we set off into the jungle,' said Gruff. 'C'mon, let's go.' And off he ran leaving the others standing in a group around Desmond, who was holding the map.

Desmond called him back.

'Which direction were you going to go in, Gruff?'

'To the place where blue and white meet and it's grey and dark.'

'Which is where on the map exactly?' Desmond asked.

Gruff shrugged, loped back to the group and kicked sand over Barry's shoe. Barry then barged into Gruff, who barged back and sent Barry flying.

'Teamwork!' I shouted, and I made Barry and Gruff shake hands before the kerfuffle could turn into anything more. The last thing we needed was to have points docked for silly squabbles.

'What's white?' asked Shuggy.

'Snow,' said Gruff.

'Ice cream,' said Clayton.

'Sugar,' said Barry. Then he kicked off his shoe. 'This sand gets everywhere. It's already in nooks and crannies I didn't know I had.'

'Sand!' shouted Spud. 'This sand is white.'

'And the sky is blue!' cried Clayton. 'And clouds are grey.'

'But there are no clouds,' said Desmond. 'It's hardly ever cloudy here. And even if it were, which clouds? They move as the wind blows.'

'Ooh, ooh, ooh!' cried Gruff, jumping up and down, his hand in the air. 'I know! The sea! The sea is blue. And it can be grey, too.'

'Not here,' said Desmond, sitting on a rock as he studied the map further.

'That rock is grey,' pointed out Carlos.

It didn't take long to decide that we were looking for a white, sandy beach with grey rock caves. In a cave, as Desmond pointed out, 'darkness rules both night and day'.

Finally, after a lot of discussion during which the map was looked at from every possible angle, Desmond took charge.

'It's this way, crew!' he shouted, pointing into the undergrowth. 'Come on!' And he strode off.

There was a lot of pushing and shoving as the others rushed to be the pirate immediately behind him. Actually, that's not strictly true. They were trying to be the pirate immediately behind and to the side of him. Why? Delia was concentrating on filming Desmond leading the way through the undergrowth and the others wanted their share of the limelight. No sooner had one of Team *Seahorse* jostled into place then he was nudged aside or pulled back or mysteriously fell as another pushed into his place. Prendergast meanwhile was sitting on Desmond's shoulders, claws dug in, determined not to budge and squawking regularly.

Finally, there was such a surge of pirates behind him, that Desmond was pushed into Delia who was backed into tree.

'CUT!' she yelled.

The pirates froze.

'And get off me!' Delia shoved back and the pirates behind Desmond fell like skittles.

As the filming had stopped I used my low teacher voice to remind Team *Seahorse* of what was at stake, that there were points for teamwork and we needed every point we could get.

I was already worrying because their behaviour hadn't been great. Delia (who was connected to the mainland via a little headset) told me it was no better on the east side of the island. In fact, it sounded worse. She said that, after a lot of shouting, Scurvy Sam and Fang had gone off on their own.

Meanwhile, Team *Seahorse* began to work well together.

Wednesday 28 July 2.39 p.m.

At last, Desmond led us to a clearing where he pulled out his compass. Delia panned in for a close up. Desmond turned around a few times, then studied the map and peered into the undergrowth. He did this for every point on the compass, until Delia and I were dizzy. Next he rested his chin on his fist and pulled his brows down, before saying 'aha' and sticking a finger in the air. If there were an overacting Oscar, Desmond would have won it.

Finally, Desmond came to a decision.

'This way!' he cried, and marched off.

No one followed. Even Prendergast had flown off his shoulder. Desmond, still overacting furiously, swung around and twiddled his moustache.

'What's this, me hearties? Mutiny?'

'No,' said Shuggy. 'but that's the way we came. Look – you can see where Clayton fell on that big flowery bush, the one that's squashed flat.'

'Fell? I was pushed!'

Desmond bit his lip, then coughed. 'Well done, Shuggy. I was wondering who would be first to notice.' Then he turned to talk to the camera directly. 'Little tests like this are an important part of keeping my crew at the peak of their performance.'

Not only was that quick thinking, but he kept a straight face.

'This way!' Desmond walked off in the opposite direction, his crew behind him and Prendergast flying overhead. Delia didn't move, however.

'What's wrong?' I asked.

'Just wait,' she said.

The chatter and noise of Team *Seahorse* grew quieter until there was silence. It was as if Delia and I were the only two people for miles around.

Before long there was rustling and then a low hum. It grew louder until, moments later, out walked Desmond into the clearing, the others right behind him.

'Another test, Desmond?' asked Delia.

'Captains need to know that their crews will follow them wherever they go,' he said, before putting his nose in the air and giving his best haughty look.

I went over to Desmond. I turned my back to the camera and whispered, 'I thought you said you were good at map reading and treasure hunting?'

'We are,' he hissed. 'But look at this!'

Fang had managed to scratch the ink off part of the map when he had snatched it on the boat.

Not bothering about the camera now because I wanted Fang's dirty tricks to be known, I asked Desmond why he hadn't said anything.

'It's not my style,' he replied.

I knew what he meant. Complaining isn't worth it. It's like the time I flicked cake batter at Summer in food tech. I got into trouble and had to do a litter pick at break AND lunch time. I could have explained that I had had enough of Summer and Holly saying my food looked like sick or poison or dog poo week after week, but I didn't. I might not have been in trouble at all if I had said that I'd finally cracked because when I tasted my cake mixture I realised they'd swapped my cocoa for gravy powder. But we all know how that ends. Holly and Summer deny everything or worse still say 'it was only a joke, Mr. Tresspot.' The 'only a joke' defence is what they try when everything else has failed. They know it's rubbish and I know it's rubbish but somehow Summer and Holly get away with it. So what's the point? Even if Mr. Tresspot had listened to me, I would have to spend the rest of the day hearing, 'Cid can't even take a joke. Pathetic!'

So I couldn't blame Desmond for saying nothing. Unfortunately, however, there was more at stake than a lunchtime detention.

'What do we do now?' I asked.

'We keep on until we find the right path.'

'But if you don't find the treasure by sunset, we lose the £10,000.'

Desmond shrugged. 'What do you suggest?'

Before I could tell him I had absolutely no idea, Shuggy called out, 'Has anyone seen Prendergast?'

We all looked around, but the only parrots to be seen were a couple of local ones who didn't like 'tourists' and refused to have anything to do with us. We all started shouting 'Prendergast!' Shuggy even climbed up a tree, but his nose began to bleed so he had to come down.

Before long Prendergast returned. For once we were all glad to see him, especially when we realised why he was squawking, 'Two o'clock and all's well' at us.

'It's what he squawks when it's his turn to do night watch,' Desmond said. 'He's very clever'

'He's a blasted nuisance,' said Clayton. 'He can't even get the time right. It's getting on for four o'clock. And all is not well.'

'Ooh, ooh, ooh!' Gruff stuck his hand in the air as far as it would go. 'I've got it!'

'Unlikely,' said Carlos.'

'Actually, I have, but I'm not going to tell now.' Gruff started sulking. It was like being back in year 2 again.

'We don't have time for overgrown, sulky wusses!' I yelled, then felt embarrassed. After all, I was supposed to be there for moral support. Desmond took charge.

'Cid's right,' he said. 'Let's not lose sight over what's at stake. Gruff, what's your idea.'

Still looking grumpy, and turning his back on Carlos, Gruff said, 'It's what they say on army and cop films. "The enemy is at two o'clock" means they're in the direction of where two on a clock face would be.'

'What if you've got a digital watch?' asked Spud. Everyone groaned.

'And where's twelve?' asked Barry.

Desmond thought for a moment. 'Six would be behind us, and that would be the direction we came from.'

'My brain hurts,' said Clayton.

'That's because it's bruised from rattling round inside your thick skull,' said someone who wouldn't own up but who sounded like Gruff.

'Points for teamwork!' I reminded them.

'Six o'clock must be over there,' said Carlos, pointing to his left.

Shuggy disagreed. 'I think that's more like seven o'clock.'

'Why don't we toss a coin for it?' suggested Spud.

There was more squawking.

'Or maybe,' I said, 'Prendergast is pointing out the direction you should go. Where he's circling over the trees.'

'Seriously?' asked Barry. 'You think a parrot can read a map?'

'Never underestimate a parrot,' said Desmond. 'It's a motto to live by.'

Delia paused her camera and beckoned me and Desmond over.

'I shouldn't be telling you this, but according to what I'm hearing on my headset, Putrid Pete's crew has already found their treasure. Sunset is officially at 6.37 and it's 3.42 so you need to get a move on.'

I followed Prendergast, Desmond and Team *Seahorse* at a quick march through the palm trees and undergrowth. Delia ran around and about, looking for the best camera angles, occasionally asking the pirates to stop for stills and frequently telling them to 'act natural'.

And sure enough, Prendergast *was* right. Before long we arrived at a small, sandy beach with caves and cliffs to the west. I stopped feeling anxious and started feeling excited.

Wednesday 28 July 4.13 p.m.

Desmond stood to his full height, such as it was, and addressed his crew in a voice that I hadn't heard before, even when he was at his most captainly. It was much deeper.

'According to the map, team, this is it!' he said. 'X marks the spot and the spot is somewhere in this cave here. This is…'

Delia interrupted.

'Cid and I will go in so that I can film you and the team entering the cave. Give me a couple of minutes.'

It took longer than to get the camera set up but, luckily, Desmond had plenty to say in the meantime. Finally, Delia called out, 'Switch to night vision. And – action!'

The pirates huddled at the cave entrance and peered in. This is what the camera recorded:

'Will there be spiders?' asked Gruff. 'I don't like spiders.'

'Possibly,' said Spud.

'What sort of spiders?'

'In a cave? Maybe a beach wolf spider. They're big.'

'Wolf? I don't like wolves either, except for Wilbur. He's not that scary. His glasses make his eyes look huge, which is a bit alarming but not frightening'

There was silence for a few moments. Then, 'How big are they?'

'About this size.' And Spud held his arms wide.

There was a shriek, then an 'oof' as Gruff jumped into Spud's arms.

'For goodness sake!' snapped Carlos. 'I thought I heard something.'

'You did,' said Spud. 'Gruff squealing like a big baby.'

'I felt one of those beach wolf spiders,' said Gruff. 'It was crawling up my leg.'

I shuddered. I wished they'd shut up about spiders. Delia had said there were none but...

'Like this?' asked Clayton, laughing and he tickled Gruff's leg with a palm tree frond.

'Stop it and listen! I think someone's in here with us.' Carlos sounded so serious that everyone shut up immediately.

Even Delia and I froze. I could feel my blood pounding in my temples. I was sure Carlos was right. Although the cave was very dark, especially after being out in the bright sunlight, I was sure we weren't alone. I had almost pinpointed the direction it was coming from when ...

'A-a-a-tish-oo!'

Followed by an angry whisper of 'Ouch!' as one pirate elbowed another.

'Well, stop sneezing then!'

'I can't help it. I think I'm allergic to being scared.'

Silence again. I had almost re-focused when there was more 'whispering.'

'Gerroff my foot!'

'I'm not on your foot.'

''Well someone is!'

'Shush!' I recognised that hiss. It was Carlos.

We waited, hardly daring to breathe, but there was nothing. Finally, Desmond decided to take control. He took on his most captainly posture and commanding voice and called out, 'Hello? I know someone's there. Who is it?'

He waited but no one moved. I thought I saw the shadows in the corner of the cave change shape. But, before I could work out exactly what was happening…

'Diddle ling ding, diddle ling ding, diddle ling ding-ding.'

'Ooops. Sorry,' said Barry.

'Turn that thing off!' Carlos's 'whisper' was very loud. 'Now for the last time, SHUSH!'

Silence again.

'It might have been an important call, Barry,' whispered Clayton. Except Clayton didn't really do whispering.

'That's it! I give up!' Carlos cried, standing up and looking at the others. 'You're hopeless. If it's not a mobile going off, then one of you is fidgeting and someone else is afraid of the dark.'

'That was only because this is *very dark* dark,' said Shuggy.

'And Clayton, if you're going to eat a boiled sweet then keep your mouth closed. You were slurping right in my ear!'

The other pirates looked down, shuffling their feet.

'Now, now, Carlos,' said Desmond. 'Getting angry doesn't help anyone, does it? We're all tense, and there's a lot at stake but being a Frenzied Frank won't get the job done.'

'Perhaps not,' grumbled Carlos. 'But there is only so much a true professional like me can take. Pirating is an art form. I am an artist.'

'So true,' said Barry.

'It has been said that I am exceptional,' continued Carlos. 'Unique.'

'You are indeed matchless,' added Barry. 'A one-off.'

'He's certainly unbelievable,' finished Clayton. 'A show off.'

Desmond returned to full captain-mode.

'Gather round, team. Prendergast, stand guard outside the cave. Don't let anyone in or out.'

Prendergast puffed out his feathers and strutted over to the cave entrance.

'Now, according to the map, the treasure is buried ... over there.'

Desmond walked over to the far corner. Next to a big pile of rocks was a mound of sand.

'I'd say this is where Scrope's people buried it. They've not covered their tracks well. Still, I suppose we had to work out the way through the jungle to find it.' He smiled as he looked into the camera. 'The points are in the bag, Miss Fitz. See, Clematis, there was no need to worry.'

I was so relieved that something had at last gone right that I didn't even tell him off for calling me Clematis.

Wednesday 28 July 4.40 p.m.

'Get shovelling, team!' cried Desmond.

Leading by example, he stuck his spade in the sand and started singing one of his own creations. The others joined in. Even Shuggy forgot his fear of the dark in the excitement.

'Glory is not found in treasure,
The real prize is beyond measure,
It's knowing that you met the test,
And proving you have done your best.
You got stuck in and stayed the course,
And that's the victory that is yours!'

By the time the pirates hit something hard I was fed up with the new shanty.

'We've got something!' Barry said as his spade scraped the bottom of a very deep hole. 'Rock.'

'Something isn't right,' Delia whispered to me.

'Can't we turn on the camera lights to help them?' I asked.

Delia shook her head. 'The rules say filming in the cave has to be done in night vision.'

Desmond frowned, jumped down to where Barry was and began

scraping at the bottom of the hole. The sound made my teeth feel itchy but worse than that was the feeling that I had relaxed too soon. I even felt I had somehow jinxed things by being sure everything would go well. (Have you noticed you never think like that when things *do* turn out well?)

'It's not there, Captain!' cried Shuggy, as Desmond stood back and stared at the bare rock.

'I knew it was too easy,' said Gruff. 'Just our luck.'

'Aye,' said Spud. 'Bad luck.'

'I did think that mound of sand was a bit too obvious,' said Desmond. 'But it has to be here. Nowhere else fitted the clues.'

The others gathered round and stared at the map. The camera zoomed in to their puzzled faces.

'This is it all right,' said Gruff.

'I don't get it,' said Clayton. 'It's not fair.' And he threw his shovel down. It hit the pile of rocks and a couple tumbled to the ground. 'We've done everything right. I don't see what else we can do.'

Carlos looked at Clayton. Then he nudged Barry who prodded Shuggy who pushed Gruff who elbowed Spud who poked Desmond – very politely, of course.

'What?' asked Clayton, seeing his team mates looking at him.

'I think you've done it,' said Carlos.

'Says who?' replied Clayton. 'Prove it!' As he stood up to eyeball Carlos, more rocks fell from the pile.

'Well done, Clayton my lad,' beamed Desmond, clapping him on the back. 'We almost failed the test, but for you.' Sure enough, where Clayton had dislodged the rocks, there was the top of a treasure chest poking through. And he pulled at the pile of rocks to reveal the top of a chest.

'Huzzah!' shouted the crew and I joined in too.

Wednesday 28 July 5.05 p.m.

Delia filmed Team *Seahorse* scrabbling at the rocks, moving them away in time to another three choruses of Desmond's song (which weren't nearly so annoying this time). At last, there it was – the treasure chest.

There were high fives all round, including for me, Delia and even Prendergast, who had flown back to join in.

Delia smiled. 'This will make *great* viewing,' she said. 'Mr. Birkwhistle will love it – the highs and lows of reaching the spot, digging down only to find no treasure, Clayton accidently stumbling on the chest.'

'Even if Desmond's team don't win, surely after all this Mr. Birkwhistle will be pleased with them?' I asked, hopefully.

'It's hard to know for sure but... possibly,' said Delia.

'There could even be a new series following the trials and tribulations of various characters at the Miss Fitz Agency as Aunt Fenula gets the business on its feet again. That'd make great realty TV, wouldn't it?'

'Maybe.'

My mind raced ahead. A few quick calculations told me that the agency could be sliding back down the Trouble Scale to 3 or maybe even lower.

'Open it! Open it!' shouted the crew.

'Can we get it back to the beach first, Captain?' asked Gruff.

We all looked at him.

'Spiders,' he explained.

Desmond nodded, Delia carried on filming. Later we watched back what happened next several times, once in slow motion.

'Shuggy, Spud get hold of either end,' said Desmond. 'And remember your health and safety training; back straight, bend the knees, look forwards. '

'Brace yourself,' said Shuggy as he tied back his dreadlocks. Then he assumed The Position as ordered and. 'One, two, three and...'

He and Spud flexed their fingers and huffed and puffed a little.

'Lift!' said Shuggy.

The next thing we heard was 'Heeeelp!' as Spud disappeared backwards into the deep hole that the pirates had dug earlier. Then:

Thud!!! Spud hit the rock.

Crack!! The chest fell on Spud and splintered.

Flump! Shuggy topped the heap.

Shuggy lay there, blinking in the glare of the camera light and looked up at a line of faces staring at him.

'Geroff!' gasped Spud.

'Is there anything there?' shouted Barry.

'I'm fine, thank you for asking,' snapped Gruff. 'And no! Now, help me out. Shuggy's a lump.'

'He's a Shuggy lump!' shouted Clayton. And he started giggling. Before long we were all helpless with laughter. It wasn't that it was very funny, but if we hadn't laughed we'd probably have cried.

It was only once everyone was back out in daylight that it hit us. There was no treasure, no £10,000 to give to the Miss Fitz Agency, nothing to save us or our friends.

Chapter Fourteen

Wednesday 28 July 5.30 p.m.
Trouble Scale 8 possibly 9

'I'm sure there's been a mix up or something,' Delia said, but I didn't really believe her.

You can tell when someone's trying to cheer you up, and although I knew Delia meant well, I didn't want her to. It's always hard to hold it together when people are nice to you. Not that I want them to shout or be mean or anything, but when I'm blinking back tears I need to really concentrate.

'Delia's right,' Desmond said. 'Mr. Scrope is very rich. To him £10,000 is like loose change. He probably forgot to put it in the chest.'

I know he was trying to keep up our spirits, but it wasn't working. There was no chatter on the way back to the shore, not even grumbling. There was only the relentless schlump-schlump-schlump of tired pirate boots being dragged along the ground. Relentless always sounds like a long, angry, weary word to me and it fits how we were all feeling. Even Delia kept the filming to a minimum.

Wednesday 28 July 7.15 p.m.

Thankfully, the walk back to the beach where we had been dropped off was much faster without all the kerfuffle of the walk to the caves. When we arrived, there was still nearly an hour to go before the launch was due to pick us up. Sunset had come. Daylight was starting to fade as dusk began seeping across the sky like ink on wet paper. Desmond looked at his pirates, flopped on the sand and then scurried over to the hamper. It had been in the shade of the sun umbrella all day, so when Desmond undid the enormous picnic hamper and poured out large glasses of lemonade, it was still slightly cool.

'I think a little cheering up is in order,' he said. 'Come on, Team *Seahorse*, Cid, Delia. Drink up. Then you can have slices of cold pizza. I won't even make you eat any salad with it.'

I smiled. Sometimes Desmond got things just right.

'Then,' he continued, 'we'll tuck into this.' And he held up an enormous, three tiered chocolate fudge cake. It was dripping and slipping in places, but that made it look all the more chocolatey and delicious.

'Maybe,' Gruff reasoned, 'Mr. Scrope decided not to put the £10,000 in the chest. It's a lot of money to bury. You never know what might happen to it. There are thieves and robbers everywhere, you know.'

'Indeed, Gruff,' said Desmond. 'And Mr. Scrope is, I am sure, a man of his word. He wouldn't try to swindle us. In any case, we can still win the contest and the £10,000 bonus for the Miss Fitz Agency.'

I didn't have the heart to burst his bubble.

'And if Scrope *does* try to wriggle out of it,' Shuggy said, 'we'll kick up such a big fuss on camera that it'll go viral and everyone will know what an old fraudy-cheat he is.'

Desmond sidled up to Delia and me and whispered. 'Can you make sure that last bit is deleted?' Then he got out the accordion. 'Barry, if you play a tune, we'll do a jig or two.'

By the time the launch arrived to pick us up we were all full of cake, singing sea shanties and dizzy from dancing jigs. Desmond was especially pleased. He had managed to use his full list of dance moves, including a daring leap that would have ended in disaster but for Clayton being a nice, soft place to land. Better yet, Delia had caught it all on camera.

'Stardom beckons, Cid,' he told me as we climbed on the boat 'Stardom beckons!'

Wednesday 28 July 8.45 p.m.

I went to find Aunt Fenula as soon as we returned from the island to see if she had any idea what had happened to the £10,000 of gold coins. She had seen everything on the live feeds, of course and I had been worrying about what state I would find her in all the way back to the mainland.

Neither of us had slept well after the 'visit' from Nudgebuster & Co. and the thought of having £10,000 towards what the agency owed had really cheered her up.

I found Aunt Fenula and Rory sitting in one of the outside broadcast vans. From the outside it looked like a ginormous, white horse box with a satellite dish on top. Inside it was like a top secret surveillance control room, very dark with banks of glowing screens and switches.

'Did you see what happened?' I asked. 'Where did the gold go? What's Scrope playing at?'

'Yes, I saw,' replied Aunt Fenula. 'Scrope isn't playing at anything. Let me show you something. Rory?'

'Yes, Miss Fitz?'

'Show Cid the footage from the hidden cameras.'

'Hidden cameras?' asked Cid.

'Of course,' said Rory. 'They all play up to the camera they can see – especially Carlos, Barry and Clayton. Putrid Pete can be as bad. So we have hidden cameras to catch their more "natural" moments. Now, take a look at this.'

I watched me and Delia enter the cave where the treasure was hidden, followed by Desmond and his crew. I could make out some of the louder noises:

The cry of, 'This is it, team! X marks the spot…'

The shriek as Gruff jumped into Shuggy's arms.

Carlos snapping at Gruff and Shuggy.

The loud sneeze.

Then Desmond, taking control. 'Hello? I know someone's there. Who is it?'

Then the mobile phone ringing – and that's when I saw it. Carlos had been right, which is not something that often happens. It was only a couple of seconds in the top left corner of the screen but that was enough. The shadows had changed shape. Then, moments later, Fang's ankle ring glinted as he reached the mouth of the cave.

As Rory switched feeds to a camera in the trees opposite the cave, I saw Scurvy Sam sneaking out into the sunlight with a large bag, presumably full of gold.

'Well done, Fang,' I heard Scurvy Sam say. 'Now, fly up and guide us back to Captain Pukebreath.'

I was furious. Raging, in fact. Fuming. Livid.

'The cheating…' I began, but changed what I had been going to call them to 'what's-its' because Aunt Fenula wasn't in a fit state for more shocks. I let out a long breath then said, more calmly,

'But that still doesn't explain how they knew.'

'Your aunt and I have been analysing the footage, Cid. We think it happened in the boat.'

He slowed down the film of the fight on the way to the island.

'Watch Fang.'

I watched closely. As Putrid Pete kicked at Prendergast, he stumbled into Desmond – who dropped his map. Fang took it to the stern. I watched, but I couldn't quite believe what I was seeing. Fang unfurled the map with his claws and seemed to be… studying it?

'Am I imagining it or is…' I began.

'… Fang reading the map?' Rory finished. 'It sounds crazy but it certainly seems like it.'

'In my line of work, young man,' said Aunt Fenula in her best 'wise old woman' voice, 'you meet all sorts. Cockatiels who can conduct symphony orchestras, juggling snakes, flea circuses…'

'Flea circuses?' Rory asked. 'How do they work?'

'Focus!' I told the pair of them. We turned back to the screen.

As we watched, Scurvy Sam glanced quickly at the map before nodding at Fang who began scratching it.

'Well,' said Aunt Fenula, 'Scurvy Sam certainly had a quick look. Enough to know the treasure was in a cave. Either she has a photographic memory or Fang must have memorised the map. She was definitely relying on him to guide them back across the island with the gold.'

'Watch the rest of the clip,' said Rory. We saw Putrid Pete yelling at his parrot.

'Fang! Get back 'ere, you naughty bird. And give the nice gentleman his map back.'

Then we noticed Putrid Pete winking at Fang before glancing at Scurvy Sam, who gave him a quick thumbs up.

'So, that's how they did it,' said Rory, stopping the video.

The rage inside me felt uncontrollable, like dodgems racing and crashing around my stomach. I'd been holding it in for long enough and now it all came out in a rush. 'They cheated! They stole the money that was meant for us, money that could have saved the agency.'

Aunt Fenula nodded. 'Yes, but surely that's a good thing?'

I exploded again, not because I was angry with Aunt Fenula but because it was so frustrating. Luckily Aunt Fenula understands that sort of thing. She has to; some of the clients on her books are trying, to say the least.

'A good thing? How on *earth* is that *good*?' I cried.

'We'll take it to the judges,' Aunt Fenula replied.

I was suddenly calm. Perhaps our luck was finally going in the right direction after all?

Wednesday 28 July 9.42 p.m.

Half an hour later, Aunt Fenula was still trying to persuade the judges.

'But you saw the evidence! Putrid Pete stole Team *Seahorse*'s treasure.'

'Stole?' snorted Nifty Nikolai. 'Hello! They're pirates! Of *course* they stole it. It's what pirates *do*.'

Everyone else round the table was silent. Rory, Byron Birkwhistle, Graffham H. Scrope IV and Gloria Golightly had also watched the video of Scurvy Sam leaving the cave with Team *Seahorse*'s treasure.

I'm not sure why I thought I could persuade Nifty Nikolai to change his mind, however it was out of my mouth before I even realised. 'But … they *cheated*!'

Then Gloria Golightly joined in. She'd been looking in her copy of the *Premier Pirate Knockout* rules. 'They haven't broken any rules. It says here that cheating is (a) tampering with the other team's equipment; (b) deliberately misleading the other crew; or (c) not following competition procedures. There's nothing to stop them… how shall I put it … using their initiative.'

'However,' Mr. Scrope cut in, chewing furiously, 'Team *Screaming Skull* will forfeit *all* their money for this…'

He nodded at Rory, who clicked <PLAY>.

While Team *Seahorse* had been comforting themselves with cold pizza and chocolate cake, things had become very 'lively' on the east side of the island.

Having returned with their treasure, Putrid Pete had cracked open the rum. After the first barrel, there was a lot of joking and laughing. By the end of the second barrel, there was a lot more shouting and very little laughing. Half way through the third barrel, a fight had broken out as the pirates argued about what they were going to do with the treasure and who was going to get how much.

It had all started when someone had said 'I don't see why Scurvy Sam and Fang should get anything. They didn't help with the digging and lugging.'

'Pieces of eight!' squawked Fang.

'Why does that stupid bird go on about "pieces of eight"?' snarled another, whose name was Vicious Vince. 'We don't even have them anymore.'

Fang flew in for the attack, but Vince dodged and Fang smacked into a nearby palm tree with a flurry of feathers.

'Stop your whinging!' yelled Putrid Pete. 'Sam, show us what you and Fang were busy doing today.'

Sam held up Team *Seahorse*'s bag of £10,000 gold coins.

'It seems we've got £20,000, me hearties,' roared Pete, showering gold coins onto the sand. And that's when things turned really nasty, as Team *Screaming Skull* bundled on top of each other in a massive free-for-all, fists, hooks and peg legs everywhere. By the time the launch arrived to take them back to the mainland, the only one left standing was Fang, although he looked dazed.

'Appalling scenes' said Mr. Scrope after the playback was over. 'This is supposed to be a family show with family values. I'll not stand for such disgraceful behaviour.'

'That seems most fair, Mr. Scrope,' said Gloria Golightly, trying to calm things down. 'Now, shall we announce the results to the teams?'

The fact that Team *Screaming Skull* were losing all the £20,000 of gold coins they thought they'd won made me feel quite smug. Being smug isn't popular, I know, but for this one time it was *extremely* satisfying.

It had cheered Aunt Fenula up as well. 'I can't wait to see Putrid Pete's face, can you?' she whispered we went out to the dockside. 'It'll almost be worth £10,000.'

That brought me down again. I'd prefer that we had our gold coins to seeing Team *Screaming Skull* lose theirs. Still, it was better than nothing and, like Aunt Fenula, I wanted to see Putrid Pete's smirk wiped off his face. Sure enough, when the decision was announced, Putrid Pete's crew shouted, cursed and started blaming each other for what had happened. Fang circled overhead, squawking and Gloria Golightly felt something warm oozing in her hair: parrot droppings – although as Putrid Pete pointed out later, it could not be proved that it was Fang who had done the dirty deed. Nevertheless, Gloria had a further announcement to make.

'Team *Screaming Skull* can keep the five points for finding the treasure, but the five awarded for team work are being deducted.'

While everyone else was caught up in the continuing *Screaming Skull* commotion, I saw Putrid Pete slide over to Nifty Nikolai. I couldn't make out what was going on, but Putrid Pete looked much happier afterwards.

As for me, I wasn't happy at all. Something was definitely up.

It took a few minutes, but finally Putrid Pete's pirates were under control.

'Now for Team *Seahorse*,' said Nifty Nikolai. 'As they did not complete the task, they can't be awarded any points. Furthermore, for such poor pirating that their treasure was stolen from them before they had even found it, we are deducting ten points.' Nifty Nikolai did a quick calculation on his fingers. 'That means they go into the grand finale with 1 point.'

There was a gasp.

'I detect the stench of corruption!' declared Carlos.

'I sense the whiff of injustice!' added Barry.

'It stinks rotten!' finished Clayton. 'I don't want to play anymore.' And with that he turned his back on everyone and sat down on the ground in a huff.

Even through my glasses my vision was blurry. I tipped my head back to stop unshed tears and dribbly snot from trickling down my face.

I tried to speak but the words couldn't find their way over the lump in my throat.

'I know this is bad, Cid,' Aunt Fenula said. 'But let me speak to Nudgebuster & Co. If we can give them the £10,000 fee we receive for Desmond's crew taking part in *Premiership Pirate Knockout*, perhaps we can work out a plan to pay back the rest in instalments.'

That's my Aunt Fenula. Never giving up, even when the famous fat lady (whoever she is) has started to sing. Both she and I knew it was never going to happen, but she pretended that everything would be all right and I pretended to feel better.

As I watched her hurry off, I had another one of those bucket of cold sick moments. Hadn't Putrid Pete mentioned Nudgebuster & Co. that morning on the way to the island? Something about them telling him all about the Miss Fitz Character Agency. I wondered what the connection could be between the two – given what I knew about them both, it couldn't be good. I guessed it was Putrid Pete who told them about Desmond's dismal day one. Nudgebuster & Co. seemed desperate to get their hands on the agency, which must mean they were set on Desmond losing. Today had proved that what we called cheating, Putrid Pete and Nifty Nikolai called "good" pirating. If Putrid Pete was helping Nudgebuster & Co., it made our task even harder that it was already.

Far from slipping down the Trouble Scale, if my suspicions were right, point 10 was less than a day away.

Chapter Fifteen

Wednesday 28 July 11.50 p.m.

It was very late when Aunt Fenula returned. Of course she got nowhere with Nudgebuster & Co. Mr. Nudgebuster told her to expect them at any time in the next three days to inspect their property, but didn't say when. '"Their" property? How dare they!' I still wasn't sure what my dander was, or where I might find it, but it was definitely up.

'They're trying to keep us on edge, unsettle us so that Desmond and Team *Seahorse* can't focus and they lose the final battle,' said Aunt Fenula. 'That way they get their hands on our property. I don't know why they are bothering.'

This wasn't good. Aunt Fenula was always so positive. 'Let's face it, Cid, this was a stupid idea from the start. There was never any realistic hope of us winning. I've always believed in miracles, but... Today was our best chance of getting some of the £20,000 we need and now we have nothing – not even the points Desmond earned.'

I knew that Nudgebuster & Co. seemed to be working with Putrid Pete, who was in cahoots with Nifty Nikolai, but I didn't want to tell Aunt Fenula that. Better that she keep believing. She was very tired now, but we needed her to carry on leading the fight – we'd come too far for her not to. I was still running on "dander" power, so I tried to cheer her up.

'Doesn't the fact that they've cheated show they are worried about Desmond?' By now I was scraping the bottom of the barrel of positive thinking. 'Anyway, Mr. Birkwhistle might still be won over by him. Delia thinks Desmond and his crew are very funny and will be popular with viewers. If she's right, Mr. Scrope might even still buy *Premiership Pirate Knockout.*'

Aunt Fenula pulled up a smile from somewhere. 'True,' she said. She even managed one of her sayings. 'I suppose stranger things happen at sea, Cid.'

Unfortunately, I couldn't think of anything 'stranger at sea', than Desmond and the crew of the *Seahorse*.

Thursday 29 July 10.15 a.m.

Aunt Fenula was still sleeping the next morning when I went to the BUMP studios to find Rory. Thursday and Friday were non-filming days as everyone was supposed to be getting ready for the grand finale. I wanted to tell him my suspicions that Putrid Pete was working with Nudgebuster & Co. and that Nifty Nikolai seemed to be in on it too. And then I wanted to know what he was going to do about it.

I found Rory sitting alone in his dad's office. He looked as tired as I felt. Unfortunately, I was so shattered that I didn't do a very good job of explaining my concerns. I am not known for being tactful at the best of times, which this wasn't. I didn't even begin gently with a 'how's it going?' or anything. Instead I blurted out,

'Do you mind telling me what's going on with Nifty Nikolai, Putrid Pete and Nudgebuster & Co. There's something dodgy happening and I demand to know what it is.'

For a pale boy, Rory can certainly go an impressive shade of red. I looked at a colour chart later and matched him to 'Volcano Burst.' It wasn't only Rory's face that went 'Volcano Burst.' He erupted.

'How DARE you! The only DODGY thing around here is you and your aunt and those RIDICULOUS pirates you sent us. Why don't we get to the bottom of that, hmm? I'd say you're guilty of fraud! How's that for DODGY?'

According to the same colour chart, I went 'Frosted Moon'. I couldn't deny that we had, at the very least, fibbed a bit, but fraud? Rory wasn't finished yet.

'What? Have you run out of things to say? Or are you "method acting"?'

'That really is an Actual Thing,' I said.

'Only Carlos, Barry and Clayton WEREN'T method acting, were they? They were telling the truth. It really IS Dazzling Desmond de'Ath, isn't it?'

'Who told you?'

Not only was it the wrong thing to say, but it came out like I was accusing Rory of something. Big mistake.

'Ha! So you admit it? Whoever told me, it certainly wasn't YOU! You were happy to carry on lying.'

Rory had pushed back his floppy fringe. Sweat held it in place. He had run out of shout, and now sounded weary.

'Look, you don't understand...' Before I could explain about PJ, Arthur, Wilbur and the others, Rory interrupted.

'Drop it. The contract is off, Cid. There is no way Desmond's Drop Outs can win. My father is trying to persuade Mr. Scrope to give us more time so we can find another pirate crew to go up against Putrid Pete.'

I felt sick and shaky.

'What ... what's your dad telling Mr. Scrope?'

'Don't worry. Dad went along with your story about method acting to lull Putrid Pete's crew into a "false sense of security". He doesn't want to look like he was taken in by such an obvious trick.'

That was something at least.

'He's saying there are too many "artistic differences" that can't be sorted out.'

'What does that mean, "artistic differences"?'

'Whatever you want, I guess,' said Rory, shrugging.

And he went back into the editing suite, leaving me wondering how I was going to break the news to Aunt Fenula and everyone back at the Miss Fitz Agency. My face was now 'Ghostly Grey' and that was exactly how I felt. What would happen when school started again? I could see Summer and Holly pointing beautifully filed and painted finger nails at me while laughing about what a loser I am. Of course, they'd be extra nice to Rory. The thought of them making fun of Desmond was bad enough but what if they started on Aunt Fenula? I felt sick. I'd need to work out new strategies for next term, but right now I was too tired.

Thursday 29 July about lunch time

The Miss Fitz Agency felt rather flat when I returned, but not as flat as I was feeling. Things were quiet in the office. Aunt Fenula was sitting on her swivel chair, facing away from her desk and tapping her teeth with a biro. She didn't look up until I said, 'Hello.'

'I've been thinking, Cid. The other evening Nudgebuster and Big Ma kept asking us where "it" is.'

'I remember.'

'So they clearly think there's something hidden somewhere in or around here. And as they seemed desperate, they must think it's valuable.'

'That had occurred to me too,' I said.

I didn't go any further. If Aunt Fenula hadn't realised that we were in danger because Nudgebuster & Co. knew that we now knew there was something valuable hidden in the agency, I wasn't going to tell her. I had enough bad news to deliver.

'So if we can find it before they do, it might make up for Putrid Pete taking our treasure yesterday. Or maybe we could trade whatever it is in return for Nudgebuster & Co. ripping up the agreement I signed.'

Desmond walked in to the back office from the courtyard.

'You wanted to see me, Miss Fitz?'

'Yes. I was thinking that you might organise a search of our premises for whatever it is that Nudgebuster & Co. wanted the other evening, Desmond. I know yesterday was disappointing, but you're still the best treasure hunter we've got.'

I listened as Desmond talked about drawing up a grid search pattern, how many shovels, pickaxes and buckets we'd need, what to do with the rubble and soil we dug up and so on, but his words ran into each other. Scenes of what might happen at school were running through my head instead.

'Isn't that right, Cid?'

I realised that Aunt Fenula and Desmond were looking at me.

'Er, yes.' I paused. They were looking at me like they were expecting me to say something else. It was now or never.

'The thing is, we really need to find whatever it is Nudgebuster & Co. think they're going to find here because... because... I went to see Rory and Mr. Birkwhistle is cancelling the contract.'

Aunt Fenula froze. She looked like a fish staring out from a tank, glassy eyed and open mouthed. Desmond shifted from one foot to the other and fiddled with his ruffles. I didn't know what to say or do for the best, so I carried on.

'He's asking Mr. Scrope for more time so BUMP can find another pirate crew to go up against Putrid Pete.'

'Good luck with that,' Desmond snorted.

Aunt Fenula finally spoke. 'Good luck? Desmond, what are you on about?'

'BUMP won't find another pirate crew to take on Captain Pukebreath.'

'What do you mean?' I asked.

'They all think the show has been cursed by Blind Hugh.'

'Who's Blind Hugh?'

'I don't know exactly, but he's supposed to curse pirates and pirate ships.'

'Why?'

Desmond shrugged. 'Does he need a reason?'

He reached over to Aunt Fenula's keyboard and did an Internet search on 'PIRATE KNOCKOUT CURSE OF BLIND HUGH'. He clicked on a website called Pirate Prattle, which had the slogan, *The News From Inside Where It's Made* and clicked on a *Premiership Pirate Knockout* link.

'The latest casualty from *Premiership Pirate Knockout* is, we hear, Fearsome Finbar Frizzbeard. He's the fifth to have met with a mysterious accident on set. He's the only contestant who's been willing to talk about it. These are his own views and not necessarily those of Pirate Prattle.'

"It's the curse of Blind Hugh. The other crews are too scared to admit it – there are those as reckon even saying his name can bring bad luck. But someone has to say what we're all thinking. Look at what's happened so far. I'm in no doubt that something weird is going on."

There was a short video clip. Desmond clicked <PLAY>.

There was Finbar, cannon firing coconuts at him from all sides, but he certainly was not afraid. He was swinging over the *Screaming Skull* and had reached the poop deck when his rope gave out.

S P L A T !

'Ooof!'

CRACK!

'Ow!'

His face was covered in splinters, his two front teeth were lodged in the deck and his parrot, which had been sitting on his shoulder, was too dazed to carry on.

According to the website the contest was stopped because Finbar's crew was too scared of the Curse of Blind Hugh to carry on.

'Putrid Pete's opponents in the other episodes met with nasty accidents too,' said Desmond. 'Bodley Bones, Winnie Wolfsbeard, Lanky Louis and Ruby Redblood, all of them.'

'And yet nothing has happened to Putrid Pete,' I said. 'That's a bit suspicious.'

'I know what you're thinking,' Desmond said. 'But Winnie's raft was attacked by a shark. How could anyone organise that? It was only thanks to Delia, who was filming overhead from a helicopter, that they were winched to safety. And Lanky Louis and his crew caught a bad case of Pirate Pox and are still in quarantine. The only thing I can think of to explain Captain Pukebreath, is that he doesn't believe in curses.'

'You mean the others believed in the curse and that's why they met with accidents?' asked Aunt Fenula. 'It's a bit far-fetched.'

'Fear makes people jittery. Jittery people make mistakes.'

'But what about the shark? And the Pirate Pox?' I asked.

'Lots of animals can sense fear, why not sharks? Maybe fear weakens the immune system and makes it more likely you'll get ill?'

'And because Putrid Pete isn't frightened, he's not affected?' I said. It made as much sense as Blind Hugh's curse.

'Or maybe he's next,' said Aunt Fenula, who had suddenly perked up and bounced back. 'Serve him right, too.'

Desmond was shocked. 'I could never wish harm on anyone, Miss Fitz, even Putrid Pete!'

And he meant it.

'If there is a curse,' I said, 'he can't go on beating the odds, surely?'

Aunt Fenula smiled. 'Cid's right! Things could go our way after all.'

Desmond looked at us. He went very captainly. 'That's not how I want to win. Preparation is what's needed. Battle Plans!'

'You have battle plans?' I asked, suddenly feeling as if we might yet pull off a famous victory.

'Ah,' said Desmond, 'we've...we've errr...not quite...well, we're working on them. Plans that is. Or we will be. And... don't worry... I'm sure we will... by Saturday.'

I groaned. Having my hopes raised and squashed in under a minute was some kind of record. At least I had a few plans buzzing around my head. First, was to go back to BUMP to ask Rory if he knew about Blind Hugh's curse. If not, that changed things.

Chapter Sixteen

Thursday 29 July 2.22 p.m.

It took me a while to find Rory at BUMP Studios. It was quite a large place, with two warehouses fitted out as studios and a third where they kept sets, props and costumes. In the main building were smaller studios, editing suites, the make-up department, a special effects room and offices of people working away at computers.

Even walking around BUMP studios was exciting. I began daydreaming. If the Miss Fitz Agency could persuade Byron Birkwhistle to go with Desmond whatever the outcome of the final battle, it could really help the agency and not only in films needing werewolves, vampires and stunt princesses. I was sure we could sell Mr. Birkwhistle the idea of a reality show following some of the Miss Fitz characters.

Then again, maybe we could pitch it to Graffham H. Scrope IV instead? If we could break into the American market, we'd be made. I could see Summer's face as I turned up to school in a limo wearing all the latest designer label gear. My braces, stick legs and potato shaped knees wouldn't matter and my glasses would be designer with tiny real diamonds down the arms. I'd have a horse called Shooting Star and a special garden made for my stick insects. And nobody would think I was weird or a loser because I'd be rich.

I was so busy imagining how Summer, Holly and Rory would all be desperate to be my friends and how gracious I would be about it, that I almost tripped over Rory. Mind you, he was crouching down with his ear against a crack in the door to a conference room. Not that he needed to; anyone could hear Graffham H. Scrope IV whether they wanted to or not. Mr. Birkwhistle's voice was also growing louder, the more desperate he became.

I joined Rory and listened in.

'What are these "artistic differences", Byron?'

'Oh, err, well, Mr. Scrope … there are…'

But Mr. Scrope was not listening.

'You'd better sort them out ASAP. I like that Death fellow and his crew and their plan is genius. Whatever "method acting" is, it's working. They are the perfect bunch of losers – even I'm feeling sorry for them. TV audiences will be 110% behind them.'

'But it's not possible to carry on, Mr. Scrope…'

Graffham H. Scrope IV was clearly having difficulty being expected to listen as well as talk. It took a while for what Mr. Birkwhistle was saying to filter through.

'Their victory is going to be sweet, Byron. Sweet! I can't … Wait. What did you say? What's not possible? "Not possible" is something I don't believe in.'

Rory winced as he heard his dad trying to wriggle off the hook.

'The artistic differences. The two parrots can't get on for a start and they're making a mess of things. Literally. And lots of technical stuff too, like the mise en scènes, swish pans…'

He reeled off a few more strange words.

'What do all those things mean?' I whispered to Rory. 'I've heard no complaints about "swish pans" or anything else.'

'They're technical terms, nothing to do with anything. But Mr. Scrope doesn't know that.'

I might only be twelve but I've been around long enough to know when someone is making it up as they go along. Let's face it, anyone with parents, guardians, older siblings, teachers and so on knows they do it all the time. Like when my mum says, 'Why can't you be like Silvia, next door? She bakes cakes every Sunday, cleans out her guinea pigs without being asked and has never been late with a piece of homework.'

So I say, 'But I'm not Silvia, I'm me and being me means I don't like baking or homework and I haven't got a guinea pig.'

Except I only say it in my head because I know I'd be grounded or made to clean the loos or something.

But when I say, 'Why can't I see "Alien Zombie Bloodfest Apocalypse" like Silvia?'

Mum says, 'You're not Silvia.'

And I say, 'I know, but why can't I go if she's allowed to?'

And Mum comes back with the classic, 'For all sorts of reasons. You'll understand when you're a parent.'

The way I see it, there's no consistency to what Mum is saying and she's making it up as she goes along to suit herself. Not that I would point that out to her, because she is the one who pays for my mobile and I'm not that stupid.

Anyway, back to the crack in the conference room door.

After Mr. Birkwhistle had finished saying lots more words that didn't mean very much but that bamboozled (I love that word) Mr. Scrope, he began begging. Rory winced even more.

'We can't go ahead with Desmond and the Miss Fitz Agency. All we need is time to find another pirate crew to replace them.'

'Time is money, Byron. And I've got business back in the US to see to.'

I tapped Rory on the shoulder.

'What?' he snapped.

'There's something you ought to know.'

'What? The truth about Desmond? Don't bother.'

'There's something else.'

'Something else? What more could there possibly be? I'm through listening to you and your mad aunt. My dad's in there, pleading for our future, and it's all your fault.'

'Our fault? You came to us. You were desperate for pirates. We gave you some. In fact, you got the only pirates available.'

Rory laughed, but not in a nice way.

'It's true,' I said.

Rory ignored me so I turned to go.

'Good luck finding anyone to take Desmond's place.'

'What do you mean?'

'I thought you were done listening to me?' I snapped.

Judging by the look on Rory's face, that was not the best thing I could have said. He looked furious and his eyes were shining, though it was hard to tell if it was anger or tears. I sighed.

'All right, I'm sorry,' I said. 'We thought you'd like Desmond and his crew. They do kind of grow on you, you know. But you won't find any other pirates to go up against Putrid Pete. They all think the show is cursed by Blind Hugh.'

Rory's face changed, like traffic lights, from red (Shut up and go away) to amber (I'm ready to hear what's coming next). I pulled out my phone and showed him the Pirate Prattle website. Then I explained that Desmond was the only captain there was who knew of the curse and yet was prepared to volunteer anyway. He groaned.

'This is a disaster.'

'Maybe,' I said, 'maybe not. Mr. Scrope still thinks Desmond is a good bet. We could tell him the "artistic differences" have been settled.'

'If Scrope thinks my dad lied to him about anything, he'll pull out of the deal for sure and we lose everything.'

I could still hear Mr. Birkwhistle pleading with Mr. Scrope. I wanted to cheer Rory up.

'Okay, so suppose Mr. Scrope doesn't buy *Premiership Pirate Knockout*. It's not the end of the world. Delia thinks people will love Desmond and his crew because they're so funny.'

Then I hesitated. I wasn't sure that Rory would want to hear what I was going to say next, but my dreams were disappearing faster than puddles in a heatwave. He was already angry so I had nothing else to lose.

'And I've been working on a couple of ideas for reality TV shows. The Miss Fitz Agency would make a great...'

Rory cut me off.

'You don't get it, do you? Without Mr. Scrope's deal there won't be any more BUMP, or *Premiership Pirate Knockout* or anything. No more house, no more help for Mum, nothing. You're not the only one with problems.'

And then it clicked. A key turned a lock somewhere in my head and things fell into place. Unfortunately, it meant that we were heading for point 10 on the Trouble Scale and from there probably out of business.

'Don't tell me. Your dad is in debt too? That's why he's so desperate to please Mr. Scrope?'

Rory nodded, slid down the wall and sat slumped against it.

'Dad put everything into the show, all the money we had. When I say "everything", I mean it. He even mortgaged our house to

Nudgebuster & Co. If Mr. Scrope doesn't buy the show for the States, we'll be homeless. Nudgebuster & Co will take the lot. We won't even have enough to pay you £10, let alone £10,000.'

'So, you lied to us, too.'

Rory nodded. I should have been furious with him, but it was far too late to be angry. And besides, I knew what he felt like. Instead I said,

'Better get in there and stop your dad from ditching Desmond. It looks like all our hopes are depending on him beating Putrid Pete.'

I stayed where I was and watched from the crack in the door.

Rory said something about an urgent message from Delia. His dad excused himself and they turned around, talking in whispers. I could see both their faces, although I couldn't hear anything. Rory showed his dad the Pirate Prattle website on my phone. Mr. Birkwhistle shut his eyes, swallowed and looked up at the ceiling before giving Rory a sort of half smile.

Rory came back out and sighed. Although his face was 'Frosted Moon' his eyes were red rimmed. We listened to what happened next.

'Wonderful news, Mr. Scrope. Rory came to tell me that all the artistic differences have been sorted out.'

'Excellent, Byron. I love those Dezzy Death guys.'

'I was wondering, Mr. Scrope,' Byron Birkwhistle continued, 'suppose – just suppose – that something went wrong with Dezzy's plan in the finale. Would it really matter – I mean, to your American audience? If he didn't win, that is.'

'Matter?' Graffham H. Scrope looked aghast. 'Aghast' is exactly the right word, because this was most definitely a ghastly situation. '*Matter*? OF COURSE it'll matter! It's a family channel. All our sponsors and advertisers are family companies with family values, Birkwhistle. Yes, they love pirates, *I* love pirates – who doesn't? But the finale has *got* to be about goodies versus baddies.'

'Of course, I see your point, but…'

'But nothing, Birkwhistle! You told me you could deliver. All the weeks Putrid Pete Pukey-thing has been winning, you said it was about making his crew the one everyone loves to hate. You said the finale would be his comeuppance. That's what's kept me hooked – that's what'll keep my sponsors happy and my audiences tuned in. If that Dezzy doesn't win tomorrow, it's no deal. The whole thing's off.'

'It's just that…'

'Off, Birkwhistle, off!'

Rory looked at me and held out his hand. I shook it. We were in this together now. We both needed Desmond and Team *Seahorse* to defeat Putrid Pete Pukebreath and Team *Screaming Skull* or else.

'Looks like we've hit 10,' I said.

Rory looked puzzled.

'On my patented 10 Point Trouble Scale. Point 9 is "catastrophe" and point 10 is "as serious as it gets". Actually, there is a fall-back position too. Point eleven.'

'Which is?'

'Which is "It's Nothing To Do With Me. I wasn't even there. Honest." But that's not an option. There's too much at stake and we've got less than forty-eight hours to come up with a plan.'

Chapter Seventeen

Thursday 29 July 7.10 p.m.

That evening it was as gloomy as a damp classroom on a Monday afternoon after wet lunch AND break in the FFAFA studio. Even Dusty didn't have the energy to hold himself together any longer and had folded himself into a neat pile of bones under the table. I felt like a squashed chip on the kitchen floor after the party's over. What was worse, even Aunt Fenula looked smaller and sort of shrivelled. The only one with any oomph was PJ. She was pacing the room, trying to energise us.

'There has to be a way out of this. Come on, people. It's like the man said, the finale must be about goodies versus baddies. It always is.'

I thought about it. PJ was right. All the sorts of stories our characters came from ended with goodies defeating baddies, right overcoming wrong.

'PJ has a point,' said Aunt Fenula, 'but I can't think of any story with goodies quite like ours. No offence, Desmond.'

'None taken, Miss Fitz,' Desmond replied. 'I am proud of my crew. Nothing will make me do things Putrid Pete's way, especially not him!'

Aunt Fenula decided to drop in one of her favourite Old Sayings. 'As my old mum used to say, Desmond, always be true to yourself.'

'Fancy her saying, "Desmond, always be true to yourself." How wonderful. It's like she had a premonition. I can't believe she really said that.'

'No, Desmond, of course she didn't. She used to say "*Fenula*, always be true to yourself." Obviously!' For Aunt Fenula to snap at someone showed how anxious she was.

Desmond blushed a shade of red that I like to call 'Tongue Tied Tomato'. It's the one where you feel so hot it's like your neck has swollen and is choking you, trapping the best-ever come-back in your throat.

'If Desmond stays true to himself, we're doomed,' Vlad wailed. Then he added, 'No offence, Desmond.'

'Dusty will be all right,' said Arthur, who was now the Invisible Man. 'He can fit in a box. And he doesn't eat or drink.'

'You'll be OK, Arfur,' replied Wilbur. 'You can go invizhible and hide somewhere cosy.'

'Not smelling like he does,' chuckled Spud.

'It is indeed a most noxious odour,' said Carlos, 'like a steaming bowl of sewage soup.'

'It is a most offensive stench,' agreed Barry, 'like a squidgy bag of mouldy mushrooms.'

'It's a nasty niff all right,' finished Clayton, 'like a wet ferret's fart.'

'Clayton!' cried Desmond.

'Well it is,' Clayton added. 'I could have said it's like an elephant's…'

'Clayton!' we all shouted.

'That is *enough*!' PJ's yell brought everyone back together. 'Focus, people! We need a Good Old Fashioned Happy Ending. Think!'

And that's when everything fell into place – again. Twice in one day was a record for me. Of course, a traditional ending! That was it. I was so excited, the words couldn't come out fast enough.

'PJ is EXACTLY right. That's the answer. We go traditional!'

I was being stared at by a bunch of blank faces.

'What always happens in films,' I said, 'where the evil villain has won, captured the heroes and is about to blow up the world?'

Heads tilted this way and that and eyebrows went up and down until, 'Ooh, ooh, I know the answer to this one.'

'It's OK, Gruff,' I said. 'You don't need to put up your hand.'

'The villain starts going on about where the hero went wrong and how he, the villain that is, is the greatest evil genius ever and all that sort of stuff.'

'Exactly,' I said. 'Villains always get cocky, think they've won and take their eyes off the ball. That's when heroes finally come through and save the day.'

Aunt Fenula seemed to be re-inflating to her usual size. 'Yes! And that's the mistake Putrid Pete is making.' Then she stopped. 'Except, if we're still being true to ourselves, he's not underestimated Desmond, has he? No offence, Desmond.'

I jumped in before Desmond actually did take offence.

'That is the other part of the answer,' I said.

Blank faces all round again.

'Desmond and Team *Seahorse* must be true to themselves. They shouldn't change a thing.'

Still nothing. Not to worry. I could feel excitement spreading over me faster than butter on hot toast. I had to get started immediately.

'Leave it with me,' I cried as I left the room. 'I've a lot to work out.'

Friday 30 July 8.55 a.m.

The next day, I was in a grump. I had not finalised my battle plans until after two that morning and then had been too excited to sleep. My brain felt scrambled, like the pile of leads and chargers Aunt Fenula has next to the socket in the corner of her sitting room. My thoughts couldn't untangle themselves. What had seemed like a brilliant scheme in the middle of the night was starting to seem really lame. And it still relied on Desmond's crew. As I drank the milk left over from my Nutty-Oaty-Choco-Crunch cereal, I watched them in the courtyard.

Desmond was trying to teach his Dancing Desperados a new dance for their sea shanty, but Shuggy was mimicking Carlos who had just caught on and was now sulking. Meanwhile Prendergast (who had insisted on a starring role) was flapping around and squawking something about 'losers'. I was more convinced than ever that my idea was stupid.

Suddenly, there was a thud and the door to Aunt Fenula's portacabin home shuddered as Rory flung it open saying,

'I think our troubles are over! Check your emails!'

Sure enough, there was one from Rory with several video files attached. It had been sent at 01.47 am and the subject line read: 'I've cracked it!?!' but there was no message. Before I could say anything, Rory had come over, opened the first file and was already explaining.

'I asked Delia to send me the unedited videos of the other episodes yesterday. I thought I'd look through, see if Putrid Pete had any weaknesses we could use to help Desmond.'

'And?' I asked, with my fingers, toes, eyes and eyebrows crossed. If he was right, my so-called Master Plan need never be known. I closed my tablet cover.

'And I think we might have solved our problem. All the weird stuff that happened to the other pirates – Bodley Bones, Winnie Wolfsbeard, Lanky Louis, Ruby Redblood and Finbar Frizzbeard – turned out to be well planned. There is no curse!'

'So it was all skulduggery!' I said. I was very pleased because I had been waiting for a chance to use that word. It's better than simply saying they cheated because skulduggery sounds like the skull and crossbones and digging up treasure all rolled into one. It's a totally pirate-y word. Rory didn't seem so impressed. He stared at me for a moment and then hit <PLAY>.

'Pay attention – I had to look really carefully. I've tried to zoom in but it's a bit fuzzy in places.'

Sure enough, there was Brazen Bodley Bones of the pirate ship *Scrabster* meeting with a nasty accident in episode one. He had just opened the hatch to the ship's hold when …

B$_O$O$_M$!

There was an enormous explosion. As the smoke cleared there were his boots standing all alone, nothing and no one inside them.

'That was all that was left of him,' said Rory, 'His eyebrows washed ashore a few days later. I've still got them somewhere. Do you want to see?' And he took a match box from his pocket.

It was one of those times when your stomach says 'NO!' but your brain says 'YES!' Anyway, they were gross (stupid brain – now it can't get rid of the image).

'Why didn't they cancel the *Premiership Pirate Knockout* then?' I asked.

'If we had, BUMP would have folded straight away. Plus, all the pirates signed an agreement that they wouldn't sue BUMP if any accidents happened. Anyway, it was great for viewing figures. Mr. Scrope was very happy, you can't buy that kind of publicity. And as his crew carried on without him, no one was surprised when Putrid Pete won.'

'I suppose if *Premiership Pirate Knockout* had ended with episode one, we'd have been out of business by now too,' I said.

'Now look at what was left out from the final edit,' Rory continued. 'It comes from the CCTV cameras that are around the ships, to catch the crews' off guard moments. They're vital for reality TV.'

There was a blurry Scurvy Sam climbing out from the *Scrabster's* hold, then bending over the hatch. A few moments later, she stood up, and climbed over the side of the ship.

'So?'

'Don't you see?' Rory said. 'Scurvy Sam is doing something at the very hatch that later explodes and blows Brazen Bodley Bones sky-high.' Rory clicked on another video file. 'Now look at this from right before a raft race that was one of the rounds in episode two. The two crews had to race to a treasure chest, winner takes all.'

Wicked Winnie Wolfsbeard and her crew were definitely leading the race when suddenly a huge shark surfaced. It had that creepy, gormless look that sharks have – staring dead ahead with no expression as their razor teeth loom in for the 'CRUNCH'.

The shark fell on Wolfsbeard's raft and bit it in two. Luckily, Delia was filming above from a helicopter.

'All were winched to safety except Winnie's parrot, Graham,' said Rory. 'He was buried at sea with full pirate honours. It was actually quite sad. The coffin was small, even for a parrot, but then all that was left of him was a drumstick, some feathers and his beak. I kept the beak. Want a look?'

My brain took control over my stomach again. It wasn't a Yuck Moment like the eyebrows, but the beak was frozen, mid-squawk and looked quite scary. I was beginning to wonder about Rory. Collecting souvenirs is one thing but this was all rather gruesome. As if he knew what I was thinking he butted into my thoughts.

'I'm going to open a showbiz museum one day. Artefacts like these will pull in the crowds.'

Again we watched the out-takes. A figure could be made out, under the water's surface, tying a huge joint of meat to Wolfsbeard's raft. So, that explained the shark.

'After such a shock, no one was surprised when Putrid Pete won, especially as Winnie was very upset over Graham.'

Rory clicked open a third file. 'We never finished filming episode three,' he said. 'Lanky Louis Longbeard's crew woke up on the last day with Pirate Pox.'

'Never heard of it!'

'Me neither, but my dad's doctor said that was what it was. Very catching and highly infectious. In fact, the doctor was very pale and sweaty too.'

Rory slowed down the video. 'Now, look at this footage from the dockyard's CCTV. Once I realised Putrid Pete had cheated on the first two episodes, I knew there was no way he hadn't cheated in the third.'

It was hard to make out, but I would bet my birthday money on it being Scurvy Sam and Vicious Vince tiptoeing up the gangplank. Sam carried a large box.

'I reckon that's the show's make-up case they've got. I think they stuck false spots on the Lanky's crew as they slept, then painted over them,' said Rory. 'Easy to do and almost impossible to get off. I've heard Lanky Louis thinks they're still sick. Anyway, we made a programme using the first two days' contests. Putrid Pete was ahead by one point, so he won.'

'But the doctor wouldn't have been fooled by stage make-up, would he? I asked. 'And he said it was Pirate Pox.'

'Putrid Pete must have got to him somehow,' replied Rory. 'That's how he does most things, threats and bullying.'

That was true, just like it was also true that Putrid Pete's opponents weren't suffering from a curse or even bad luck.

'What about episode four?' I asked.

In episode four, Team *Screaming Skull* had been up against Rancid Ruby Redblood.

'This took me a long time to find,' said Rory. 'At first it looked like an accident, but I went back through all the footage from the CCTV cameras on-board ship and eventually I realised what was going on. You'll need to listen very carefully.'

At first I couldn't hear anything other than some snoring and snorting from one or two of the hammocks swinging gently over the gun deck. But then the tapping started and there was the sound of fingernails being scraped down wood (another Yuck Moment). Finally, the ringing of the ship's bell when no one was there. On the second night the tapping became banging, and there were blood-curdling screams and screeches in the dead of night. The crew rolled out of their hammocks, ran down the gangplank and refused to go back, even in daylight. Not Ruby, though. Nothing scared her.

I watched as she strode across the main deck roaring, 'Watch me, you lily-livered, dung-breathed, whimpering wusses!

I liked her style.

'See?' she shouted.

Unfortunately, she didn't. If she had, she might have jumped out of the way before it fell from the main mast and knocked her out.

Ruby's crew had already decided the ship was haunted, so as far as they were concerned the accident proved that not only the ship but the whole show was cursed. Nothing could persuade them otherwise.

'I hate to say it,' said Rory, 'but if I'm right, this was quite clever. I had to go right back to the CCTV footage of the pirates preparing their ships.'

I stared at the screen. 'What am I supposed to be looking for? So far Rancid Ruby's crew is all I can see.'

Rory pointed to some shadows. 'Look, if I zoom in on the dockyard's CCTV footage you can make out someone hiding things in amongst the supplies. Now look at the footage from the quayside CCTV. Someone is tampering with Ruby's crew's duffle bags.'

It was dusk, so it was hard to make out what was going on, but there were two pirate-shaped blobs moving around the ship and another on the quay. I couldn't see what they were up to, though.

'What are they doing?'

Rory grinned, which was good to see after all that had happened the day before.

'I think Putrid Pete's pirates were hiding tiny transceivers, like you see on the films where undercover police wear wires to record conversations and talk with whoever is monitoring them. Then Putrid Pete could play ghostly noises all around the ship at night to frighten Rancid Ruby's crew.'

'Are you sure?'

'Well, I think so, but the problem is we can't see exactly what is being done to their stuff.'

I nodded. 'OK, so what about episode five, Finbar's crew?'

'They were nervous before filming even started. I'd never seen jittery pirates before. It was kind of strange. Anyway, when Finbar met with his "accident", (here Rory did that thing with his fingers to make speech mark signs) 'his crew refused to carry on.'

'What have you found out about Finbar's accident?' I asked.

'I've not found anything yet,' Rory said, 'but I doubt it was a genuine accident.'

I had to agree. Although if it had been genuine, the rumours of the curse of Blind Hugh would have probably scared them off as it had every other pirate captain and crew. Except Desmond.

'So what do you think?' asked Rory. 'According to what Gloria Golightly said yesterday, this has to count as tampering with the other crew's equipment. And that's cheating. We have to go to the judges with this. There's no way Putrid Pete can win now.'

I thought for a moment. Some of the footage was difficult to make out. Also, I couldn't see Putrid Pete admitting to anything. But there was another, more important factor to consider.

'Would Mr. Scrope buy *Premier Pirate Knockout* if all those other episodes were won by cheating?' I asked. 'And what about everyone who's been following it so far in this country? They'll think the whole series has been a fake. No one will watch the grand finale.'

Rory frowned, banged his fist on the table and yelled some things that I'm not going to repeat.

'I know how you feel,' I said, 'but there's too much at stake. If we unmask Putrid Pete, we're all out of business. And you're homeless, and so is my aunt and all the other agency characters. We have to keep this secret. If the cheating leaks out, that's an end to everything.'

Rory looked at me. 'Okay, but if Putrid Pete's crew so much as sneezes on Team *Seahorse*, I'll take it to the judges and insist they dock points. Mr. Scrope wants Team *Screaming Skull* to lose, so they'll be under pressure to do it this time.'

I nodded. That at least could work in our favour and help Desmond win. It was fifty points for winning the battle and a score of fifty-one would be enough for Team *Seahorse* to win the finale of *Premiership Pirate Knockout*.

'So we're agreed?' I said. 'Keep the cheating Top Secret?'

'Yes. Let's take a spit oath.'

A spit oath is like a blood oath, but you don't have to shed any blood. It's not very pleasant. If you think about the germs that must live in spit, it's at least as dangerous as blood, so that makes it as solemn an oath as I can think of.

'So, we're left with your plan,' said Rory. 'What is it? Unless it's to convince Mr. Scrope to turn the finale into some kind of dance competition, I don't feel very confident. No offence to the Miss Fitz Agency or anything, but let's be honest, whether it's Dazzling Desmond or Dastardly Dezzy Death, his crew is pathetic.'

'I know,' I said. 'But they do grow on you. They are rather sweet.' Rory rolled his eyes.

I opened my notebook. What had seemed so brilliant in the middle of the night now seemed ridiculous, even if we could pull it off. On the other hand, there was no other plan and we had just over twenty-four hours until the grand finale was due to begin. I tried to sound as convincing as possible, and not only for Rory.

'I've been going over the footage of the competition so far as well, looking for the strengths and weaknesses of the two teams.'

'Putrid's strength is cheating,' said Rory. 'And Desmond's crew, their only strength is getting it wrong.'

'Exactly!' I said. 'Come with me. I want you to meet someone.'

Friday 30 July 10.45 a.m.

In the FFAFA Rehearsal Studio everything was quiet, except for Arthur and Wilbur. Arthur was still working out a few glitches in his new-found invisibility skill and was currently stuck at hazy. Wilbur, meanwhile, was gumming away at a piece of soggy sausage.

PJ took off her headphones when we came in. 'Are you looking for Desmond? He's doing his ballet-robics class with the crew. Something about getting them "match fit" for the grand finale?'

Rory's eyes widened. 'Ballet-robics? Is that an Actual Thing?'

I ignored him because if I hesitated for even a moment I knew I'd give up. My idea was seeming more preposterous by the minute. 'Preposterous' was definitely the word. It sounds like what it means – silly. It's basically a mouthful of letters bumbling around and bumping into each other. The more I thought about it, the more preposterous seemed to fit Team *Seahorse*.

'We need you, PJ. Rory and I have hit point 10 on the Trouble Scale.'

'What about point eleven?' PJ asked.

'Not an option,' I said. 'Desmond and his crew have got to win the grand finale of *Premier Pirate Knock-Out* or a lot of people lose everything.'

This wasn't me being dramatic, it was true. Nudgebuster & Co are what is known as lenders of last resort. That means you only go to them if you are desperate. And you'd have to be desperate because, if you couldn't pay back what you'd borrowed, well... the rumours aren't pleasant, so I'll leave it there.

'Blimey,' said PJ. 'But what can I do to help?'

I went through my plan.

'What do you think?' I asked, when I had finished. 'Will it work?'

'So let me get this right,' said PJ. 'Basically, Desmond's crew will beat Putrid Pete in battle by doing the things they did on day one?'

I nodded.

'When they lost every competition?'

I nodded again. 'Putrid Pete is used to fighting pirates who do things in the same old way and he's sabotaged every crew he's gone up against. He's feeling cocky, certain he'll win. The last thing he'll be expecting is for Desmond's crew to sabotage themselves. Once he and Team *Screaming Skull* are lured onto the *Seahorse,* Rory and I will make sure all ways off the ship are blocked, cut, torn down, whatever it takes.'

PJ looked thoughtful and, to be honest, I was starting to think that the best thing to do would be to pack up and run somewhere – anywhere, as long as we ran fast. Then she grinned.

'I think it might work. I can help you prepare the *Seahorse* and put Desmond and his crew through their paces. I like a challenge!'

Rory, who'd been looking as if someone had dropped cold custard down his neck and then slapped him on the back, also started to look a little happier, but not much.

'It'll be a finale like no other, whatever happens,' he said. 'No one's going to know what's hit them.'

Chapter Eighteen

Friday 30 July 2.00 p.m.

PJ, Rory and I gathered the pirates together on the *Seahorse* that afternoon. We had submitted battle plans to the judges and camera crew. They were needed for filming, but only because of technicalities like where the judges wanted to be for the best view, camera angles, lighting and so on. There was no rule that you had to stick by them. It wouldn't have made sense because even the best laid battle plans can go wrong and the pirates needed to react to the battle as it unfolded. However, I didn't submit the real plans. For a start, I didn't trust Nifty Nikolai. He seemed too friendly with Putrid Pete.

As for the real plan, we made Desmond and his Desperadoes memorise it. I wasn't taking any chances after the incident with Fang on day two of the competition. It took a while...

'So we pelt them with rotting fish and then the captain greases the deck?' asked Gruff.

'No,' I said, through gritted teeth. This was my fourth time of going over the plan and I was ready to shout it at them. PJ stepped in and took over. The pirates were more than a little bit scared of her. First she made them sit up straight and put their fingers on their lips.

'Before I begin,' she said sternly, 'if you've got any questions, put up your hand. Is that clear?'

They nodded hard and, because they had their fingers on their lips, Gruff's went up his nose by accident. At least that's what he claimed happened.

As PJ ran through the battle plan, Team *Seahorse* all sat still and very upright like a class that misbehaved with a cover teacher and was now being threatened with lunchtime detention by the head.

'The *Seahorse* will sit in Bilgewater Bay, looking quiet and deserted,' she explained. 'Prendergast will fly over the *Screaming Skull* squawking that you've all left the ship. Putrid Pete will think you've bottled it.'

Desmond stood up and puffed out his chest. 'I must make it clear,' he said, 'that we're not cowards. We're afraid of nothing.'

'Except the dark,' Shuggy reminded him.

'And fish,' said Spud.

'And spiders,' added Gruff.

'Shush,' said PJ. 'It's all part of the plan. And hands up if you've something to say.' Then she continued, 'So, thinking the ship is deserted, the enemy will board quickly. Desmond, you will be hiding behind the main mast. Once the crew of the *Screaming Skull* is on board, make sure you are seen running down to the gun deck. They'll follow you. As soon as they are there, the others will fire the cannons, just like the other day.'

Desmond put up his hand. 'But we didn't hit anything. All we did was make thick, smelly smoke.'

'Exactly!' said PJ. 'A smokescreen!'

I interrupted. 'Yes, so make sure you all wear wet neckerchiefs tomorrow.'

Carlos put up his hand. 'That's hardly the image for a dashing pirate,' he said.

'Nor is choking and weeping with the smoke,' PJ replied. 'While Putrid Pete's crew are trying to see what's going on, you'll all be back up on deck preparing the next part of the plan. Grease!'

There was a lot of shrugging and face pulling as the pirates gawped at each other and then us.

'Don't you get it?' Rory asked.

'Nope, not at all,' said Gruff. 'Oops. Sorry,' he said, and his hand shot into the air.

I sighed and tried to explain. 'Covering the main deck in grease – slops, chip fat, oil, whatever you can find – will make it hard for Team *Screaming Skull*. They'll be all over the place, just like you were when you fell into the slops.'

The crew of the *Seahorse* began grinning.

'I think I see what you're up to, Cid,' chuckled Shuggy.

'You are without doubt a genius,' said Carlos.

'You are indeed brilliant,' continued Barry.

'You're a right boffy swot,' finished Clayton. Then he smiled. 'We might just stand a chance!'

PJ had to shout 'fingers on lips' to get them quiet so she could explain the rest of the plan.

'Before Putrid Pete and his gang have managed to get their balance, Carlos, Clayton and Gruff will pelt them with rotten fish from the rigging. While that's going on Spud, Desmond and Shuggy will drop the mainsail onto the enemy.'

Spud shuddered as his hand slowly crept up. 'Fish? *Rotten* fish?'

'Stinky, slimy, effective,' replied PJ. 'Don't be such a wuss. Time to take one for the team. Anyway, you'll be up in the rigging.'

'And I won't come down until the decks are properly swabbed.'

'What about me?' asked Barry. He had been waving his hand in the air for a while.

'You've got the most important job of all,' said PJ. Barry smiled. 'Once they're covered with the sail you're to run a rope around them and tie it tight.'

The crew of the *Seahorse* cheered wildly, grabbing each other's arms and jumping up and down. I looked at Rory and PJ and smiled.

'We might actually pull it off,' said Rory.

'I think we could,' I said. I didn't let him see that I had all my fingers crossed behind my back.

Friday 30 July 5.35 p.m.

We worked Desmond and his crew hard that afternoon. They were hot, sweaty and exhausted, and even worse after the cannon firing. It took a lot of practice to make sure they did things in *exactly* the same way they had on that first day but we got there. They didn't give up. Now I understand why my parents pay so much attention to the effort grades on my school reports. I might even try harder myself next term, although I am against making promises that I can't keep, so I'll wait and see.

Anyway, as I was watching the mainsail drop onto an X drawn on the deck, Desmond sidled up to me.

'I'm still not comfortable with this,' he said. 'I get the plan, and it's very clever, but telling my crew to have confidence in their inability to do basic pirating... It's not helping them to be like all the other pirates.'

'Do you want to be like Putrid Pete? Or Ruby Redblood?' I asked.

'Not really,' Desmond sighed. 'But it's what everyone expects and it's what my parents want. I know they say they love me whatever, but I also know I keep letting them down. Every one of the crew is the same. They all dropped out of pirate school, except Carlos.'

'Well, that's something,' I said.

'He was expelled.'

'Oh.'

'He refused to do anything that made him dirty or messed up his clothes.'

'Well, he's not like that now, at least not too much. You must have done something right.'

Desmond continued, still sounding flat. 'I did a deal with him. I said if he tried to take part in pirate activities, he could be in charge of clothing and costumes. We never have enough to spend on them though, so he's never had the chance.'

'That doesn't matter,' I said. 'It worked and that's the main thing. Carlos is very much one of the team.'

Desmond sighed. 'I suppose. Pay no attention, I'm feeling tired. It's just…'

Desmond paused. I looked into his eyes. They weren't shining like they usually do, but there was something else. It wasn't defeat exactly, and it wasn't quite anger. I realised he was fed up, although not of the exercise.

'… We never get to really be us,' he continued. 'We do love being pirates, sailing our ship and visiting different places, searching for treasure and that sort of thing, but we don't like all the fighting and hassle that goes with it. It's not that we are cowards…'

That was true. I'd seen Desmond stand up to Putrid Pete and the others deal with their fears and phobias (including spiders which I was not about to do).

'… but being that angry all the time takes SO much effort. It's a waste of time and we'd rather be doing other things. We like singing and music and dancing. Clayton, Shuggy and Gruff are quite good actors. I'm not bad either, even if I do say so myself. Although, ballet was my real thing when I was a boy.'

And I realised that Desmond was right – he was a good actor. A great actor. He had to be to put on such a happy front and keep his crew going.

'You got the better of Putrid Pete on day one, remember? After the contests were over? You can do it again. Imagine the look on Putrid Pete's face when he's beaten by all the mishaps he laughed at?'

'It is a very imaginative plan,' said Desmond. 'It's certainly the last thing he'll expect. And we'll give it our best, of course we will, but we'll win by being the worst pirates ever. I can't begin to imagine what my parents will say when they watch *Premiership Pirate Knockout*.'

Okay, so Desmond wasn't keen on my plan and I understood why, but it was all we had. Still, if he didn't have confidence, beating Putrid Pete would be even harder for him and his crew. Luckily, Aunt Fenula appeared. She had wandered over with Rory to find out more about my plan.

'Don't forget, you stood up to Putrid Pete, Desmond. That couldn't have been easy,' she said. 'Remember how you felt and channel that.'

As Aunt Fenula smiled at him, Desmond perked up a bit.

'I was actually very angry for once, which helped. And when I saw Putrid Pete flailing around I felt like I was a great pirate captain. And once I started, I couldn't stop. I didn't want to. It felt too good.'

Desmond smiled, at last looking like himself again.

'Not that I believe in laughing at other people's misfortunes,' he added, hurriedly.

And then it came to me. We needed Desmond to have something he really believed in to fight for. When Pete had insulted his ballet, he had stood up to him. Standing up for what he believed in was what seemed to give him courage. And if there was one thing he believed in more than even ballet, it was his own personal code.

'There's something else,' I said. 'If Putrid Pete is such a great pirate, why couldn't he defeat any of the other crews?'

'The Curse of Blind Hugh, I suppose.'

'What if I told you there was no curse?'

Rory's eyes widened. He stared a warning at me not to let Desmond know about the cheating. After all, we had only made the spit oath that morning. I ignored him. Instead I asked Aunt Fenula and PJ to round up

Team *Seahorse*. I had to make sure they were out of earshot. PJ could easily let the truth out if she were angry enough and Aunt Fenula would have marched right up to Putrid Pete and told him exactly what she thought of him.

'Cid, if you're going to say what I think you're going to say...' whispered Rory.

I ignored him again.

'Putrid Pete's a cheat, Desmond. Not only is there nothing supernatural going on, but those weren't accidents at all. Rory's got the proof on film, haven't you, Rory?'

Rory was furious. 'Cid! We agreed! If this gets out...'

Desmond was still processing what I had said.

'What about the Pirate Pox?' he said.

'Good make-up and a terrified doctor,' I said. 'Pete threatened him with a "good sorting out" if he blabbed.'

'And the shark?'

'Bait tied under Winnie Wolfsbeard's raft.'

Desmond's sense of honour was kicking in as I knew it would. This was what he needed to lift his spirits, an injustice to fight. He seemed to swell and grow before our eyes. He was outraged.

'He must not be allowed to get away with such despicable behaviour!' he cried. 'Honour amongst pirates is the most important rule of the Modern Pirate Code. He must be reported at once!'

'So much for keeping it top secret,' hissed Rory.

But Desmond's sense of honour meant he could be trusted. I explained the situation to him and added, 'So, if any of this gets out, Mr. Scrope's deal is off for sure and we're all out of business and on the streets. You must promise, upon your honour, not to breathe a word.'

'You can trust me, Cid,' Desmond replied.

Now when I looked into his eyes, I could see that there was a possibility that things might work out.

'I hope you're right, Cid,' said Rory as we headed back to the ship.

'Now his sense of honour has kicked in he'll do his best to make the plan work,' I said. 'That's the only chance we have.'

Chapter Nineteen

Friday 30 July 6.35 p.m.

At last I was feeling a little more positive. At least if we lost, we would go down fighting, thanks to Desmond. In fact, I felt the best I had since Nudgebuster & Co. had walked into the office a week ago demanding £20,000 – which was just as well because when we reached the ship, it was business as usual among the crew. They were moaning about how hard PJ had been working them.

'I am fading fast,' said Carlos, 'like the dawn mist as the midsummer sun kisses the dewy grass.'

'I'm shattered,' continued Barry, 'like a fine crystal vase dropped on a marble floor.'

'I'm pooped,' finished Clayton, 'like a big poopy thing.'

Thankfully he didn't explain any further.

'Are they ready?' I asked.

'As they'll ever be,' said PJ.

'Do they know the plan thoroughly?'

'Inside out and back to front.'

Aunt Fenula smiled. 'I knew you'd come up with something, Cid. You always do.'

Friday 30 July 8.20 p.m.

Later that evening, Rory, PJ and I were discussing strategy, eating ice cream and watching television when there was a kerfuffle from the courtyard. I looked out. Aunt Fenula was at the centre of things, standing next to a pile of large, sparkly pom-poms. Arthur had picked one up and was chasing Dusty around, trying to tickle him. Every time he succeeded, Dusty started laughing and collapsed into a heap.

'It's not funny!' Vlad was saying as he ducked a couple of flying ribs, which can be quite sharp. I think I saw Wilbur lick his lips as one of them hit the ground and bounced in his direction, but thankfully he didn't have his teeth in.

'Is it usually like this?' asked Rory.

'Pretty much,' I said. 'Except for the pom-poms.'

I saw Rory bite his lip. It was like I could read his mind. Pound to a penny he was thinking, 'What have we got ourselves into with the Miss Fitz Agency?'

It was probably good that BUMP was in a seriously bad way too, otherwise I think he might have said, 'Thanks, but no thanks, we're not that desperate.'

But they were, so that was that.

Suddenly there was a green glow as Desmond appeared from the FFAFA studio in legwarmers, carrying a small but powerful speaker booming out some music with a deep bass beat.

'What *are* they up to?' I wasn't sure if Rory was actually asking a question, but PJ answered.

'Cheerleading. It's Miss Fitz's idea. They're coming down to support Team *Seahorse* tomorrow. They'll cheer on Desmond's lot and advertise the agency at the same time.'

It was actually my idea, but I kept quiet. Aunt Fenula was desperate for ideas to promote the agency and as far as desperate ideas were concerned, this was the most desperate one I had ever had.

Desmond managed to get everyone into some sort of a line (even Aunt Fenula) and took them through some basic steps. Before long they were marching on the spot, turning, leg-kicking and raising their arms more or less in time with each other. Well, less to be honest. To be fair, it wasn't easy. They had to dodge little piles of dirt and cobblestones where small holes had been dug in an effort to find whatever it was that Nudgebuster & Co. wanted so badly.

Then they added pom-poms, making the cheer leading look like a box of exploding fireworks, and not in a good way. Eventually, they worked out the spacing and the moves so that Dusty was safe from being tickled and losing control. Perhaps it's just me, but one of the dancers falling into a heap of bones every time a pom-pom is waved his way spoils the effect.

After a great deal of practice and a slight improvement, Desmond smiled.

'Well done, team! Especially you, Miss Fitz. I saw some definite progress. If one of you makes a mistake tomorrow, all do your own thing and we'll call it free-form. The main thing is to have fun.'

The evening should have left me feeling happier and more determined, but something was unsettling me. All the while we were in the courtyard I had the feeling we were being watched and it was the outside loo that was making me most nervous. The outside loo is a place I like to avoid, mainly because of spiders. I suppose it could have been the spiders that were the problem because they have eight eyes, so being watched by three spiders involves as many eyes as twelve people have. But why would spiders be interested in cheer leading? No, it was someone, or something, else.

I moved as near to the loo as I dared, which wasn't very far, and peered at the dark spaces that were the window and door. I thought I saw something shimmer, but it could have been a ray from the setting sun catching the gnats that like to gather there.

'You're imagining things,' Rory said when I told him that I felt as if we were being watched.

'What if it's Nudgebuster, Big Ma and the Lads?' I asked. 'Or maybe Putrid Pete has sent a spy?'

Rory agreed to take a look but he only got as far as the door when Aunt Fenula called us back to watch the cheerleaders perform their final routine.

'I didn't see anything, Cid,' he said. 'You're probably tired or being a bit... you know.'

'No, I don't know,' I replied. 'What?'

'A bit...weird.'

I frowned at him.

'No offence, I quite like it. But you have a farm for your stick insects, use words like "kerfuffle" and you fit right in with your aunt and her "characters".' Rory looked over towards Desmond, the pirates and their cheerleaders. 'Somehow I don't think you don't see the world like the rest of us.'

I was taken aback and even more so when Rory smiled at me. It was a genuine smile, not the sneery kind I get at school. So instead of ranting as I had planned, I smiled back.

'Perhaps,' I said. 'But the world's more fun if you look at it my way. You ought to try it some time.'

I still felt uneasy as I went to bed in Aunt Fenula's flat that night. I looked over the courtyard. Suddenly the gate squeaked and swung shut.

'Odd,' I thought. 'I could have sworn Aunt Fenula locked it when we came in for the night.'

Chapter Twenty

Next morning, we got up early and headed straight for the dockyard to prepare the *Seahorse*. Although the *Screaming Skull* was at anchor around the headland, Fang was circling above, squawking and splatting anyone he could. I wondered if he was spying for Putrid Pete. Prendergast, who you have probably realised is a bit of a prima donna, refused to chase him away. ("Prima donna" is a phrase I learned from Delia. It describes someone who thinks they are far more important than everyone else and has a hissy fit at the slightest thing.) Instead, Prendergast strutted along the poop deck rail, sunning himself, until Fang splatted him. He cheered up a little after Rory promised to "floof up" the feathers on his head for the filming that afternoon.

Finally, we were ready. I gathered everyone together.

'Sit still and stop fidgeting. It's time to focus. Each of you has an important part to play.'

'Try to forget about being on TV,' said Rory. 'Today's filming will be done with cameras set up round the ship. It's too dangerous to have a film crew getting under your feet.'

'I'm a-quiver with anxiety,' said Carlos. 'I think I've got stage fright.'

'I'm all jittery with the collywobbles,' added Barry. 'I think I've got a bad case of nerves.'

'I've got a squirty tummy and a burbly bottom,' finished Clayton. 'I think I've got to apologise.'

The other pirates shuffled as far away from him as possible.

Then the gun fired.

Someone shouted, 'Pirates – to your posts!' through a megaphone.

The final battle was about to begin.

Saturday 31 July 12.01 p.m.

When we heard that the *Screaming Skull* had weighed anchor, it was time for me to join Team *Seahorse* below decks. The *Seahorse* was to stay anchored in the bay itself. I knew that this would puzzle Putrid Pete and that he'd have his telescope on us. He might even send Fang to fly overhead and reccy the situation. ('Reconnoitre' is the proper technical term according to Princess PJ and Desmond, but on all the films they say 'reccy' and it sounds much more exciting.)

Once I was below decks, I warned Team *Seahorse* to do a much better job of keeping quiet than they had in the cave on Day 2. It didn't go well. Spud got the giggles, and the others fell about laughing, one by one, like toppling dominoes. If you've ever sat in class or assembly trying not to laugh, you'll know how hard it is to stop once you've started. You'll also know that teachers don't find it at all funny and I was beginning to see why.

'If you don't stop,' I hissed, 'I'll tape your lips together.'

There was a moment of silence and then Clayton's burbly bottom squeezed out something that sounded like a dying duck and didn't smell much better. The roar of laughter that followed it stopped abruptly as the stink filtered through and the groaning started.

As Clayton explained what he had been eating, Prendergast swooped in through the hatch long enough to squawk 'Ship ahoy!' and then flapped back up to the crow's nest.

'Right, this is SERIOUS!' I whisper-shouted. 'If you lot don't get a grip, we're all stuffed like...'

'... a Christmas turkey,' suggested Shuggy.

'Then our goose really will be cooked,' continued Gruff, wisely.

Before more poultry-related sayings got underway (and believe me, there are a lot of them) Desmond took control and, I have to say, saved the situation.

'Now chaps. Remember what we do in yoga to calm down. Breathing exercises.'

And he made them close their eyes as he counted their breaths: in, two, three – hold, two three – out, two three. It was like magic. After a minute or so peace and calm was restored.

'Breathing's an important part of ballet,' he whispered to me once the crew was in a steady rhythm. 'Yoga really helps.'

I nodded. I didn't care what they did as long as it worked.

Moments stretched into minutes but at last the *Screaming Skull* came alongside the *Seahorse*, jeering and shouting insults. I saw Desmond's fists clench. Prendergast took his role very seriously. He flew over the heads of Team *Screaming Skull* squawking,

'Gone! Gone! Help!'

Later, he claimed that the entire plan would have failed without him setting the right tone.

There was a loud thud. Wood ground against wood as Putrid Pete prepared to board.

I nudged Desmond. 'You're on. It's the role of your life, no second takes, so give it all you've got.'

He nodded and crept up on deck to hide behind the main mast.

Saturday 31 July 12.20 p.m.

'Sorry, me hearties,' we heard Putrid Pete shout. 'No fight today. The yellow-bellies have run home to their mummies. But let's claim our prize!'

I can still hear the thunder of their trundling boots as they boarded the *Seahorse*. What happened next I only saw when I watched the video footage.

As soon as Putrid Pete, Scurvy Sam and the rest boarded the *Seahorse*, Desmond sprang out from behind the main mast.

'Ahoy there!' he shouted, adding a quick entrechat jump in excitement.

'After him,' yelled Putrid Pete, waving his cutlass.

Desmond ran to the ladder leading below decks and slid down it. Putrid Pete was not as nimble, and landed on the gun deck with a thud.

'Where's he gone, the snivelling little worm?' he hissed, as the rest of his crew bundled in after him.

If Team *Screaming Skull* had bothered to look behind the ladder they'd just run down, they would have seen Desmond hiding there, but they were too busy pushing and cursing at each other.

'Disorganised rabble!' was all PJ said when she watched it later.

'Silence, you swabs!' Putrid Pete roared at his crew. 'I can't hear myself...'

Right on cue came the cannon fire. So far, so good.

BOOM-BOOM-BOOM-BOOM

Smoke filled the gun deck. If anything, it was worse than before.

While Putrid Pete's crew was coughing, choking and trying to see through their own tears and the thick fog from the cannon, Desmond and his team ran back up on the main deck, their damp neckerchiefs protecting them from the smoke. Hurriedly they spread fat, oil, slops and grease across the deck before taking their places for phase two.

The smoke was far more effective than we could have hoped for. It took Putrid Pete and his crew a good couple of minutes to realise what had happened. That might not sound long but it was more than enough for Team *Seahorse* to get ready.

Desmond, Spud and Shuggy climbed up to the mainsail, only missing the rope rungs occasionally. Meanwhile Carlos, Clayton and Gruff grabbed buckets of rotting fish and kitchen waste and scrambled up the shrouds rigging at the side of the ship. Even Barry managed to gather the rope and hide without any mishaps.

Putrid Pete's crew came charging up from below, Vicious Vince leading the way.

All this happened very quickly. PJ had clearly trained Team *Seahorse* thoroughly, although she later said she'd threatened them with dire consequences if they messed up. One thing was for sure, we all understood what losing would mean for each other.

Thump! Vicious Vince hit the grease and spiralled up into the air, landing flat on his back.

Whump... whump... whump... whump! Putrid Pete and the rest of his crew skidded into him, falling this way and that until all that could be seen of Vince were wriggling limbs from beneath a massive muddle of flustered pirates. I have to say that this gave me a warm glow – when I stopped laughing.

We could make out Putrid Pete crying 'Up and at 'em!' from the middle of the pile.

To be fair, (although I'm not sure why I should) the *Screaming Skull* crew tried their best. They slipped and slid and shouted and snarled as they tried to stand up. Legs went one way, arms another as they grabbed hold of anything they could find to steady themselves – beards, noses, earrings, even eye patches. Vicious Vince managed to get his hook caught in Mouldy Malcolm's belt. Every time Mouldy Malcolm stood up, Vince pulled him back down.

Thwack! Splat! Plop! Repeat.

As Desmond later said, ballet training strengthens the core and improves the balance. I seem to remember him offering Putrid Pete a 'Free introduction to ballet, with Dazzling Desmond de'Ath and his Dancing Desperadoes' after the battle. I cannot repeat what Putrid said, mainly because when I tried typing it in, the spellcheck went crazy and froze my laptop.

Finally, Putrid Pete's exhausted crew managed to separate themselves from each other and regain their balance. They immediately came under attack from rotten fish and stinking gunk flung from above. The timing was brilliant. Soon they were back in the heap where they had started.

'It's like ten pin bowling,' laughed Clayton.

'Strike!' yelled Gruff, as a well-aimed haddock smacked Putrid Pete in the face. He wobbled backwards, he wobbled forwards, then he toppled over and brought his crew down with him. Again. The outtakes alone are guaranteed to go viral. I reckon the cheerleading will, too. At least the pom-poms were smaller than the evening before. Later, Aunt Fenula told me they had been washed and blow dried that morning, along with Wilbur.

Barry gave Desmond, Spud and Shuggy the signal to loose the mainsail. He was a bit theatrical about it and taking a bow was definitely over the top, but he did his job well. Before the enemy knew what had hit them this time, they were covered with canvas and Barry ran round and round the heaving mound with the rope. Only when there was not much left did he tie a knobbly knot to secure it. Finally, he added a small padlock.

'Just to make quite sure,' he said.

There was one particularly big, angry lump cursing from under the mainsail: Putrid Pete himself.

'I think,' said Desmond, climbing down from the rigging, 'that he's asking to be let out.'

Shuggy led the rest of the crew in chanting 'We are the champions' as Desmond cut a hole in the canvas so that Putrid Pete's head could poke through. He was furious.

Saturday 31 July 12.58 p.m.
Trouble Scale falling rapidly, heading for 0

'Cut!' shouted Rory. Delia stopped the filming. It was the perfect end to the grand finale. A worried-looking Mr. Birkwhistle glanced at Graffham H. Scrope IV.

'Well done, Birkwhistle. Good family entertainment, although we'll have to bleep out some of what Pukey Putrid Thingummy came out with. It's not what I was expecting, but I like their style. And what's more, it'll be uploaded, downloaded and reloaded around the globe.'

Things had been going so well up until that point. Then, 'But he CHEATED!'

Chapter Twenty-one

Saturday 31 July 1.03 p.m.
Trouble Scale rising rapidly

Have you ever had one of those moments when everyone and everything else goes quiet except for the one voice? It's usually yours and you're usually saying something embarrassing like, 'Bleah! Great Aunt Veronica's just picked her nose with that finger!'

But this was worse. It was the one phrase that had the power to smash our victory into tiny little bits, grind it into dust and blow it away. And Graffham H. Scrope had heard every word.

Everyone turned and looked at the two captains.

'It's true!' shouted Putrid Pete. 'Ding-a-ling Desmond and his Dribbling Drips didn't follow the battle plan they handed in. It's not fair!'

Everyone was so busy trying to work out what to do next that nothing happened. They all froze. The only person moving at all was Nifty Nikolai, who was on his phone, hand cupped over his mouth. I gave Desmond a hard stare that, roughly translated, meant 'don't you dare let on what I told you about Putrid Pete's cheating'.

My brain was too fried trying to imagine a flow chart of the possible outcomes of Putrid' Pete's outburst. So far all computations ended in the same answer: BAD

Aunt Fenula broke the silence first. 'How dare you!' she shrieked. It was definitely a shriek; my ear drums' vibrations confirmed it.

Then PJ roared, 'How would you know about our battle plans, Captain Putrid?'

Finally, shouting even louder than PJ, was Scrope. 'BIRKWHISTLE!'

Rory's mouth pulled his face into a strange, elongated shape. Then he doubled over and threw up.

'Elongated' is a good word because it's stretchier than 'long' and that was what Rory's face was doing – stretching longer than long as his mouth opened wider. I put my hand on his shoulder, but I'm not sure it was much help other than to remind him we were in this together. Then he went over to where his father was being buffeted by a full-on Scrope outburst.

It sounds like all this took a long time, and it certainly felt like that, but really it was less than a minute. Then the two captains started name calling and poking each other. I was very glad that Barry had used a padlock, otherwise Desmond would have stood no chance.

I looked at Rory, whose face was whiter than even Dusty's, and went into school caretaker mode again. Mr. Spragg was good at separating pupils when he needed to. And Putrid Pete and Desmond were behaving worse than year 3 during wet break.

'Enough, Desmond! Putrid Pete, you're with me.' I shouted. 'Barry, undo the padlock please.'

And then I grabbed each pirate captain by the elbow and marched them down the gangplank and over to the judges. Even Putrid was too shocked to disobey. I think I could have a great future ahead of me in school caretaking. It's got to be better than teaching – no marking, for a start.

At that moment, as if things weren't complicated enough, a large silver car with blacked out windows arrived. Out got Nudgebuster & Co. I couldn't be doing with them now. I turned to Nifty Nikolai and Gloria Golightly.

'Well?' I asked out loud. 'Who won?'

Then I said in a low voice, 'And more to the point, how did Putrid Pete know about Desmond's battle plans?'

Nifty Nikolai glared at me and whispered back, 'Don't go there, little girl. You're way out of your depth already.'

I think he thought that "little girl" was some kind of insult. To be fair, I don't consider myself little but then he was rather on the large side. And lots of the really awesome people I know are girls – so I really didn't mind.

Out loud he said, 'Team *Seahorse* cheated. I say they are disqualified.'

'And I say they used their initiative,' said Gloria Golightly. 'Battle plans aren't binding. There's nothing in the rules that says they MUST be followed. They're only there for technical details about lighting, sound and cameras. Mr. Pukebreath's crew was outsmarted, like Captain de'Ath's were during the treasure hunt. Team *Seahorse* win the 50 points. And the contest.'

'That's not going to happen. Those shenanigans weren't proper pirating,' cried Nifty Nikolai. 'They should be ashamed of themselves. Slapstick was what that was.'

Gloria shook her head. 'They played to their strengths, Nifty.'

Rory ran over to join us.

'Any news?' I asked. 'We're getting nowhere here.'

'Mr. Scrope isn't looking very happy,' Rory said. 'He's got your aunt talking at him on one side, my father on the other and two lawyers waving paperwork in front of his face. He's not sure what to make of Desmond's performance. He loved it at the time but now there's talk of cheating, his lawyers are warning him that he could get sued in the U.S. if he shows it there. It's chaos.'

Gloria Golightly left Nifty Nikolai shouting at no one in particular to show Mr. Scrope's lawyers the *Premiership Pirate Knockout* rule book. Meanwhile Nudgebuster & Co. were in a huddle with Putrid Pete. They kept staring at me and Rory, then looking at Aunt Fenula, Mr. Birkwhistle and Mr. Scrope and then glancing over at Gloria and the lawyers. Every now and then there was a raised voice or hand. Then suddenly, Putrid Pete, Mr. Nudgebuster and Big Ma began walking over to me and Rory while we were busy trying to pretend that we hadn't noticed them.

'Get your aunt over here or else!' was Putrid Pete's way of starting what Mr. Nudgebuster and Big Ma assured me was going to be a friendly chat.

I beckoned Aunt Fenula over.

'There is something of a problem, dear lady,' said Mr. Nudgebuster. 'Your crew seems to have cheated.'

Nudgebuster's opening line was much nastier than Putrid Pete's because he sounded so smarmy. If you say it right, 'smarmy' sounds oily, like what it means, and creepy, and Nudgebuster was definitely both of those. His smile was basically a row of tiny teeth, and it stopped suddenly at his top lip. At least Putrid Pete couldn't make his face lie.

Once Nudgebuster's words had been processed by Aunt Fenula (whose own face clearly signalled that she couldn't believe what she was hearing) she swivelled round 180 degrees and then swung back fast, the bag in her hand thumping into Mr. Nudgebuster like a rugby ball with a scrum behind it, winding him and sending him flailing into Big Ma's arms. Having been involved with those arms myself, I knew it was an unpleasant experience and I was more than happy to see that Mr. Nudgebuster was finding the same.

As satisfying as Aunt Fenula's approach to negotiating was, violence never solves anything and this was no exception.

'So that's how it is, is it?' asked Big Ma. 'All right, you've asked for it!' And she rolled up her sleeves to reveal tattoos on her forearms. One said 'POW!' and the other 'THWACK!'

'This is getting ugly,' Roy whispered to me. 'And I don't just mean Big Ma's tattoos.'

Aunt Fenula threw her bag to one side and stood, legs apart and fists clenched in front of her face, ready to box. As that's as much as she knows about boxing, I tried to calm things down. Not only did my calculations put the odds against us even if we included Desmond and his crew, but if a fight did break out there was no way that Mr. Scrope would sign the deal. Violence did not make for 'wholesome family values'.

'Everyone, calm down,' I said.

'I said, *calm down*!' I shouted.

'Will you CALM DOWN?!' I yelled.

Big Ma and Aunt Fenula paid no attention. They were too busy walking around each other in tight little circles, each occasionally swinging a fist that the other had – so far – managed to swerve or duck and avoid. Nudgebuster was still winded from the hand-bagging and Putrid Pete was busy whispering to Nifty Nikolai.

There was nothing for it. I stuck my thumb and forefinger in my mouth and whistled. Loudly. Everyone froze. 'Wow,' said Rory. 'Impressive. Where did you learn to do that?'

Before I could say anything, Mr. Nudgebuster spoke (well, wheezed really). 'Tell you what,' he puffed to Aunt Fenula, 'if you agree to sign the Miss Fitz Agency and all its buildings over to me, we'll cancel Birkwhistle's debt with us. He owes us a LOT of money.'

Saturday 31 July 1.45 p.m.

Rory looked at Aunt Fenula, who looked at me.

'Give us a couple of minutes,' I said. Then I pulled out my phone and worked out a quick flow chart.

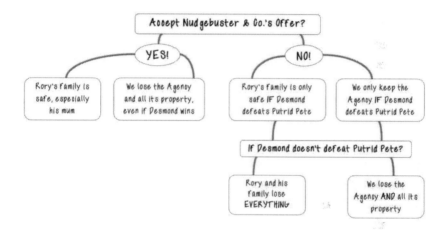

Rory stared at it, then looked at me. I shrugged. The answer wasn't easy, but it was a no-brainer. I looked at Aunt Fenula. She nodded. If she had spoken, the tears in her eyes would have spilled over and I didn't want to give Putrid Pete, Nudgebuster and Big Ma the satisfaction of seeing her cry.

'OK,' I said, 'deal,' and I held out my hand to shake on it.

Before Nudgebuster was able to take my hand, Rory knocked it away.

'Never!' he yelled.

I glared at him.

'Don't be an idiot,' I hissed.

'Rory,' Aunt Fenula said. 'It's all right. Cid and I will bounce back, won't we, Cid?'

I nodded

'I'd listen to the daft old bat if I were you, boy,' snarled Nudgebuster.

Mr. Birkwhistle, having been startled by the yell of 'NEVER!' was already scurrying towards us with Mr. Scrope and his lawyers in tow. Desmond, meanwhile, beat him to it. If Aunt Fenula were in trouble, he had to come to her rescue.

'How dare you, sir, talk to a lady like that?' he declared. 'And how dare you, sir, call me and my teams cheats? We are not the cheats!'

'We've got to stop Desmond, Cid!' Rory whispered. 'He's only one declaration away from letting the cat out of the bag. If Mr. Scrope finds out Putrid cheated all along there's no hope for any of us.'

But Desmond continued. 'How would you know our plan wasn't what we handed in to the judges? By cheating! And why should it matter anyway? Aren't you pirate enough to cope with the unexpected? Especially "Dazzling Desmond de'Ath and his Desperate Dodos" – that's what you called us, isn't it?'

Putrid Pete laughed. 'If it looks like a desperate dodo and it sounds like a desperate dodo then that's exactly what it is, Captain Dodo.'

'You're scared the judges will decide we won.'

Putrid Pete turned to Nifty Nikolai. 'I don't think that's going to happen, do you, Nifty?'

Desmond glared at Putrid Pete and I have to say that even I was unnerved when he said, 'If you were to win, I'd have no option than to demand—'

'NO!' yelled Rory. 'You mustn't!'

'Mustn't what, son?' asked Mr. Birkwhistle.

'Must… not… mustn't… argue. They mustn't argue. If the judges can't decide then it has to be a draw.'

I had been about to say that I would have to demand a second opinion, but a draw would work too. It would at least help the Miss Fitz Agency.

This was sort of good news for us, but definitely not for Rory. Mr. Scrope was not enthusiastic.

'That won't cut it, Birkwhistle. We don't go in for draws in the US. My audience will expect to see a winner. No winner, no deal.'

Rory looked at me. For once I was completely stumped.

176

Putrid Pete pulled Nudgebuster & Co. and his crew into a huddle before making a declaration.

'There's no way I'm agreeing to a draw. I demand satisfaction. In not taking the battle seriously, Captain de'Ath has dishonoured pirating. There must be a duel. Winner takes all, of course.'

Desmond went pale. Aunt Fenula gasped. Nikolai nodded his head. Gloria shook hers. Rory looked at Mr. Birkwhistle who shrugged and we all turned to Graffham H. Scrope IV.

After a pause even longer than before reality TV vote results are announced Mr. Scrope said, 'That's a splendid idea. Could be great for viewing figures. Make it happen, Birkwhistle, and the deal might be back on. But make no mistake, I'm sticking to my guns. If I don't like the outcome, I ain't buying your show.'

'So all Desmond needs to do is win,' Rory whispered to me. 'What are the chances of *that* happening?'

Chapter Twenty-two

Saturday 31 July 2.12 p.m.
Trouble Scale 7+

The duel was arranged for the next morning, less than twenty-four hours away. Rory and I met to plan our next move. We went over to the catering van to grab some breakfast, then sat down on the quayside, away from the tables and chairs where some of the production staff were sitting. We dangled our legs over the water enjoying big mugs of tea and bigger bacon rolls. Tea is great for helping ideas along and we needed all the help we could get because it wasn't only trying to find a way for Desmond to win that was bugging us.

We watched as Mr. Nudgebuster slapped Putrid Pete on the back. We could hear Big Ma's booming voice calling out, 'We'll be back at the end of the day,' as she walked over to the silver car.

'What is going on between Nudgebuster & Co. and Putrid Pete?' I said. 'It's all very suspicious.'

Rory shrugged. 'I don't know but I'd love to be a fly on the wall when they meet.

I thought for a moment.

'What about using transceivers like Putrid Pete had planted on Ruby Redblood's ship? We could use one to bug his dressing-room caravan.' I said. 'That's where he goes after filming, before heading back to his ship. We could hide one in there. We might hear something. The only thing is how do we plant it?'

'Dad's got keys to all the caravans,' Rory said. 'Although we don't want to be seen sneaking around there. Someone's bound to get suspicious. Plus, Putrid Pete has had his own camera put in. It takes photos of everyone coming and going.'

'That means he's either got something to hide or he's afraid of someone,' I said. 'So, how will we get the transceiver in?'

'Arthur?' Rory suggested. 'We've got our own Invisible Man. Let's make the most of him.'

I grimaced. 'But what about his stench?'

'We can blame the drains. Put a few signs around saying "Drain Maintenance. Sorry for the vomit-lurching smell" that sort of thing.'

'"Vomit lurching" is right,' I said. 'One whiff of Arthur trying to go invisible makes my stomach and throat heave like I'm going to be sick.'

I thought for a moment.

'We'll also need a lookout.'

Rory frowned. 'But he's invisible!'

'But he can't control it properly yet,' I said. 'Sometimes he only goes misty or suddenly becomes visible again, especially if he loses concentration. If he hiccups, for example.'

'What about Vlad? He can turn into a bat,' suggested Rory.

'Not in full daylight.'

'What are you two cooking up?'

I jumped and slopped my hot tea on my jeans. 'Ouch!'

It was Aunt Fenula and PJ.

'They're definitely up to something, Miss Fitz,' said PJ. 'What is it?'

We explained our plan to bug Putrid Pete in the hope of finding out what was going on between him and Nudgebuster & Co.

'That sounds dangerous,' said Aunt Fenula. 'Although I would like to know what's going on. They seemed very friendly earlier on, and not in a good way.'

'If it works and we're lucky, we might even find out what it is they think they're going to find at the agency,' PJ added.

There was a pause.

'Do you think the plan will work, PJ? You know all about this sort of spy stuff,' said Rory.

'Honestly? It's quite complicated, too many things can go wrong. What if Putrid Pete comes back early or Arthur loses his invisibility while he's in there? Suppose Putrid Pete doesn't meet Nudgebuster & Co. in his caravan?'

I sighed. 'We're running out of time. We need to do something, and fast.'

'Why don't you plant the transceiver on Putrid Pete?' said PJ. 'Like they do in the films?'

Aunt Fenula looked puzzled. 'So you want one of us to walk up to Putrid Pete and say, "Excuse me, Putrid, but can I plant this bug under your jacket?"'

'No!' snorted PJ. 'One of us will bump into him and plant it somewhere like under his jacket lapel or on his shirt collar.'

'He knows us too well. There's no way we can accidently bump into him,' I said.

'Not if I'm in disguise,' said PJ. She had clearly decided that she was the one for the job. To be fair, she probably was the best pick as:

1. Putrid Pete didn't know her as well as he knew the rest of us;

2. she was actually very good at this sort of thing and dangerous stuff generally;

3. if I did it I wouldn't be able to stop myself stamping on his foot or pulling his beard or something else that would give me away.

'What about PJ's disguise?' asked Aunt Fenula.

Rory grinned. 'Leave that to me!' He took out his mobile, selected a contact and moments later I heard, 'Holly? Are you free? Can you come down to the Quayside?'

I glared at Rory. 'Trust me,' he mouthed, but I glared even harder. It was bad enough I had to see Holly at school, I didn't want her anywhere near my real life. I could already hear all the stupid comments, the so called 'jokes' and 'banter' she'd direct at me. It usually ended with 'Don't take yourself so seriously, Cid – it's only a bit of fun!'

'That's great. I'll meet you at the gates in fifteen – you won't get in otherwise.'

Saturday 31 July 2:35 p.m.

By the time he ended the call I was furious. 'Why?' was all I could say.

'Don't worry, Cid. I know how you feel about her.'

'How can you have the faintest idea how I feel about her?' I snapped. 'Of all the people to involve! It's bad enough having to see her at school as it is. Her coming here is going to make it about a billion times worse.'

Okay, so with hindsight I can see I exaggerated, but at the time it felt like an understatement.

'I see how she is with you, and you're like an open book – I can almost read exactly what you're thinking.'

'How is she with me?'

'She thinks she's being funny, Cid, but I can see it hurts sometimes.'

'Don't make excuses for her! And if you can see what she's doing, why don't you ever say something?'

Rory looked very uncomfortable. He stood there, rubbing his neck and looking around Gloria's caravan. Aunt Fenula coughed and I suddenly remembered that she and PJ were still with us.

'Forget it,' I said and left the caravan, slamming the door behind me. I walked along the quayside and tried Desmond's breathing exercises. By the time I was heading back to the caravans and could see Rory and Holly in the distance I had calmed down enough to find out why Rory had decided to involve her.

'This is SO exciting,' she was saying. 'I've never been on a set before. I didn't know your family was the BUMP TV Birkwhistles. Do you know...'

And then she saw me and stopped, mid-sentence, mouth open.

'There you are, Cid,' said Rory. 'Holly's going to help us out, aren't you Holly?'

Holly's eyes became as round and wide as her mouth.

Rory put his hands on my shoulders and smiled. 'Like I said, trust me.'

Holly's expression was classic. If I'd had my phone out, I'd have taken a photo.

'How do you? ... So do you two? ... Are you? ... How come?' Eventually Holly managed to string a few words into a question. 'What's going on?'

It turned out that Holly is a very good make-up artist. Rory had got her what she needed from the make-up trailer and then been to wardrobe to get a few bits of clothing.

'I watch all those make-up and special effects videos on social media,' she explained, as she was turning PJ into an old woman before our eyes in Gloria's caravan. 'I've even made a couple myself.'

'Really?' was all I could think of saying as I reassessed what I thought about Holly. I did wince when Aunt Fenula said she's make a good addition at the agency. Holly turned around.

'Agency?'

'It's a sort of talent agency. We're the agents of the pirates who are going up against team *Screaming Skull* in the Grand Finale.'

I nodded. 'That's us.'

'I never knew!' Holly exclaimed.

'There's a reason for that,' I said.

'What do you mean?'

Rory jumped in before I could say anything. 'Only that we can't go into things for legal reasons. That's why this has to be kept secret. If you were to say anything, the whole show would have to be pulled and I'd be in huge trouble. You can't even tell Summer.'

I wanted to say 'especially NOT Summer,' but I kept quiet.

Holly nodded slowly. 'I see. Well, I won't let that happen – I love *Premiership Pirate Knockout*'.

'How long do you think she'll manage to keep all this secret?' I whispered to Rory, only not quietly enough it seems.

'I *can* keep a secret, Cid,' Holly snapped, as she helped PJ to put on the ridiculous hat that Rory had brought. It was covered in silk flowers and had a bunch of plastic grapes hanging down from it.

Rory grinned. 'That's amazing!'

I had to agree. 'I'd never recognise you, PJ. You look older than Aunt...'

'I'm only forty-seven!' Aunt Fenula snapped. 'And that is NOT old, Clematis!'

'I was going to say "than Aunt Veronica",' I lied quickly.

'PJ looks fine except for her eyes,' Holly said. 'Anyone who looks at her eyes will see they're too young for the rest of her face. The whites are especially clear and bright, but without special contact lenses there's not a lot I can do about that.' Holly paused. 'Except this,' she added.

And she adjusted the hat so that the grapes hung over the brim right in front of PJ's eyes.

'But that draws attention to her,' I said. 'Everyone will notice her.'

'Glance at her quickly, like you would in the street. What catches your attention?' Holly asked.

I laughed. 'The grapes! The grapes are so ridiculous that they're all I notice. I don't look at anything else.'

Saturday 31 July 3.26 p.m.

PJ hid behind the catering van, waiting for her signal. After a few minutes, Putrid Pete walked down his gang plank and onto the quayside. He began weaving his way through the production team's vans and stars' caravans, heading towards his own, where he rested after filming. It had a big silver star on the door. His shoulders were slumped forward, his gaze fixed on the ground eyes and his hands were in his pockets. Thankfully Fang was nowhere to be seen.

When Aunt Fenula saw Putrid Pete getting near, she gave the secret signal of a screeching seagull noise. Putrid Pete didn't look up. PJ tottered round the corner, leaning on a walking stick. As she reached him, the walking stick 'slipped' and she tumbled forwards. The plan was that as he helped her up, PJ would grasp his arm, then his jacket and while she thanked him and dusted him down, she'd stick the tiny bug under his lapel.

Looking back now, I can see the flaw in the plan: thinking that Putrid Pete of all people would help anyone, even a little old lady. Instead he shouted,

'Bosun's bones, you daft old bat! Can't you look where you're going?'

PJ grabbed onto Putrid Pete's trousers, trying to haul herself up. Instead of giving her a hand, Putrid Pete tried to shake her off. PJ was not about to let go, so he strode ahead, dragging PJ behind him. This part of the quayside was cobbled, and PJ's little old lady costume was falling away as she bumped along the ground. Finally, she let go. Thankfully, Putrid Pete didn't look back or else he'd have seen us going to the rescue.

'Well done for trying anyway, PJ,' I said.

She grinned. 'I managed to stick it to the heel of his boot, so fingers crossed, it works.'

183

All we could do now was wait. We sat in one of the outside broadcast vans nearby and tuned into the transceiver, listening to Putrid Pete's footsteps as he paced up and down his caravan.

Chapter Twenty-three

Saturday 31 July 3.45 p.m.

After about ten minutes, the silver car returned and out got Nudgebuster & Co. They burst into Putrid Pete's caravan.

'We'd have had it in our grasp if you hadn't messed up,' we heard Big Ma say. PJ, Rory, Aunt Fenula and I grinned at each other. So far, so good.

Then we heard some scuffling and a thud, followed by Mr. Nudgebuster's voice.

'Put him down, Marjorie. Dangling Pete like that is getting us nowhere.'

Then we heard another thud and a burst of coughing.

'How was I to know the little bilge rat was going to pull a stunt like that?' Putrid Pete sounded a bit hoarse.

'Don't make excuses. You're proper whingey, you are.'

'Enough!' shouted Mr. Nudgebuster. 'Calm down, Big Ma. As for you, Pete, make sure you win tomorrow. Once you've done that, the deal with Scrope will fall through, which means BUMP will go bust, which means the Miss Fitz Agency won't get paid, which means we get the property to search for as long as it takes. We're one duel away from untold wealth.'

'Think you can manage to beat Dancing Desmond?' sneered Big Ma.

'Easily!' scoffed Putrid Pete.

Then there was more scuffling and then some spluttering as Big Ma made sure Putrid Pete knew how serious she was.

'Then don't,' said Big Ma.

'Oof,' choked Putrid Pete.

'Mess,' said Big Ma.

'Ow,' coughed Putrid Pete.

'It,' said Big Ma.

'Ouch,' gasped Putrid Pete.

'Up!' shouted Big Ma.

And there was a thud.

'Do forgive Marjorie, Pete. She gets a bit carried away. It better be worth all this fuss. Which reminds me, did you find out any more about exactly what it is we' re looking for? It's all very well saying it's fabulous treasure, but what's it like? And do we know for certain it's at that agency for the Useless?'

'As it happens,' growled Putrid Pete, 'I did have some luck there. I managed to get hold of the county historian, Dr Kelvinator. She showed me some interesting records, including Jonas MacHugh's ship's log and diary. The diary mentions the Old Coaching Inn and there's a little scribble in the margins – a sketch or plan of what could be the inn back in those days.'

'Any X to mark the spot where Blind Hugh buried his treasure?' asked Big Ma.

'No,' said Putrid Pete, 'But I've been thinking. What if Blind Hugh's curse comes upon us, like those archaeologists who found Tutankhamun?'

'Nonsense, you big wuss,' scoffed Big Ma. 'Anyway, I thought you didn't believe in all that guff.'

'There's more to pirate lore than a lubber like you...'

'We've seen something like this before,' interrupted Nudgebuster. 'Do you remember, Big Ma?'

'You're right, Kenneth – I'm sure I saw handwriting like in this old ship's log – but where?'

'When we tipped that heap of bones out of his drawer – there was a pile of...'

There was a 'shush' followed by a sudden, ear splitting crunch...

Then silence.

'The bug must have fallen off,' said Rory. 'And it sounds like he's trodden on it.'

The door to Putrid Pete's caravan opened and three heads popped out, looking left, then right, then up, then down.

'I think they know they've been bugged,' I said. 'And they don't look very happy about it. I suggest we wait until Nudgebuster & Co. go and it's all died down before we leave the van.'

We didn't have to wait long before the door opened again and Mr. Nudgebuster and Big Ma left Putrid Pete's dressing room.

'I've got an idea,' said PJ. Before we could stop her she pulled the hat and wig back on and followed them. They were so deep in conversation that they didn't notice the little old lady shuffle by them and they paid no attention when she stopped by their car to adjust her sagging tights. They climbed in and drove off.

'Did you hear anything else?' I asked when PJ returned to the van.

'Not really, other than Nudgebuster & Co. don't trust Pete to share whatever it is they're hoping to find and that they don't want to share it with him anyway.'

'That's the trouble with working with crooks,' sighed Aunt Fenula. 'They can't stop thieving, even from each other.'

'At least we know why they want the agency so badly. Plus, we're one step ahead because Desmond has already made a start on the search.'

'But what if there really is a curse?' said Aunt Fenula.

'Not you too!' I said. 'We've seen how the "curse" works – skulduggery. Although a curse would explain why you made such a silly deal with Nudgebuster & Co. in the first place.'

'I didn't think there was any danger of not getting the fees for Vlad's last film. And when that didn't happen I thought the bank would help us and when they said no I thought that BUMP would pay us enough to keep Nudgebuster & Co. happy.'

Rory looked very uncomfortable.

'No one's blaming you, Rory,' I said. 'Or your dad. Come on, we've got a pirate to prepare for a duel.'

Saturday 31 July 4.50 p.m.

We all went back to the agency where the Miss Fitz cheerleaders and Team *Seahorse* were trying to help Desmond by saying things that were (a) comforting and (b) encouraging but were in fact (c) neither.

'It will be either a victory of audacious proportions or an epic demise,' said Carlos.

'It will be either an act of tremendous derring-do or a plucky last stand,' continued Barry.

'It'll either be a bloomin' miracle or curtains,' finished Clayton and drew a line across his neck with his finger.

Everyone glared at him.

'What?' he asked, eyes wide and then wandered off, muttering to himself.

Arthur offered to help, now that he had mastered invisibility. 'I'm still a bit hit and miss,' he said, 'but I'm sure I can be invisible by the time you're ready to go. I can hold Putrid Pete back or pull his hat over his eyes or trip him up.'

'But he'll smell a rat,' said Vlad. 'In fact, he'll smell much worse than a rat, Arthur. No offence, but you are truly noxious.'

Aunt Fenula gave the 'I have complete faith in you' speech and then hugged Desmond, who turned red and grinned. I gave him a recap of the 'You've beaten Putrid Pete once' talk, although I have to say I felt pretty useless. Even Prendergast sat on Desmond's shoulder and snuggled up to his cheek.

Saturday 31 July 5.05 p.m.

'Right,' said Aunt Fenula after a few moments, 'time to get down to business.'

She gathered everyone into the front office.

'We're looking either for treasure or a map that shows us where the treasure is.' She divided us up to search every centimetre of the agency buildings:

The word "treasure" got everyone excited.

'What sort of treasure?' asked Arthur.

I shrugged. 'We don't know, but it must be fabulous if Nudgebuster & Co. are willing to go to go to so much effort to get their hands on it.'

We used Desmond's plans to help us get organised. He had divided the agency buildings and courtyard into sections for search teams. We concentrated on searching the buildings, as he and PJ were practising sword fighting moves and techniques in the courtyard. I drew up a list of who was to look where.

'The chimneys need someone able to get into them. Vlad, that's you. Aunt Fenula, you can check anything that falls into the fireplace. Back office and kitchen area: Dusty and Arthur. Front office: me and Wilbur. Now for upstairs. Front store room: Carlos and Barry. Back store room: Gruff and Shuggy. Make sure you look through all the props and wardrobe too.'

'Can I swap with Gruff or Shuggy?' asked Carlos. 'I want to search the wardrobe. Clothes and costumes are my thing.'

'Exactly why you're not doing them,' I answered. 'You'll take far too long trying things on.' I hurried on before he could complain any further.

'Attic: Clayton and Spud. Finally, before you go, Desmond has made some notes about how to search, so listen up: "check on top of beams; pat wall down in case of hidden compartments and look behind any loose plaster and under any loose floorboards".'

'We'll make a dreadful mess,' said Arthur.

'If we don't find anything,' said Aunt Fenula, 'Nudgebuster & Co. can clear it up when they take the agency. If we do find the map – or better still, the treasure – any mess won't matter because we'll be able to afford cleaners and decorators.'

Vlad came into his own, searching the chimneys, even though he didn't like confined spaces. They were so dark that he was able to turn into a bat and fly up them. Unfortunately, his wings sent so much soot billowing down that Aunt Fenula, who was standing in the back office fireplace watching him, ended up looking like a chimney sweep's brush. She only did it once.

Saturday 31 July 6.20 p.m.

We had stopped for a tea break when it happened. As it looked like it was going to be our last break together, we had fresh cream cakes and toasted crumpets. I was in the FFAFA studio with Aunt Fenula, PJ and the others when, 'Where's my clever boy?'

There was a commotion as the owner of the voice flung open the FFAFA studio door and strode into the middle of the room. She was a

189

pirate captain, judging by her bellowing, no-nonsense voice, the amount of gold braid on her sleeves and her tricorn hat. Her waistcoat was a steely blue like her eyes, and she had a long plait of silver grey hair.

'There he is!' and she pounced on Desmond, who managed to look nervous and bemused all at once.

'M… Mum?' was all he managed to get out before he was swamped in an ample mother-hug. When he came up for air he was covered with purple lipstick marks.

My brain was still registering Pitiless Pearl de'Ath's grand entrance when Drastic Diego came barrelling towards Desmond (if you imagine a large barrel rolling towards you at speed you'll get the idea) shouting, 'Well done, son! I always knew Death blood coursed through your veins.'

'Death blood' would have sounded truly terrifying if we didn't already know Desmond who, moments later, had disappeared again under another enthusiastic hug. We occasionally heard phrases like,

'A proper pirate!'

'One of us!'

'Grandpa would be so proud!'

'You showed 'em, son!'

Desmond seemed to be struggling and surfaced momentarily from time to time. All we heard from him was 'But…' or 'You don't understand…'

Finally, Mr. and Mrs. Death stood back, beaming.

'Our boy defeated Putrid Pete!' Pitiless Pearl repeated this a couple of times, like she couldn't quite believe it.

'How do you know about that?' I asked.

'Your brother Marvin told us,' said Pitiless Pearl. 'I didn't believe him at first, but he said he'd got it from Typhoon Tom who'd heard it from Roger the Wrecker who knows Ruthless Ruth who's Scurvy Sam's mum and *she* said…'

'Spoilers!' squeaked Aunt Fenula. 'It's supposed to be top secret!'

Another pirate appeared. 'I've sworn them all to secrecy, madam. Pirates' Honour and all that.' He was short and round and beamed a broad smile at the rest of us before saying,

'Mungo Mump, at your service.'

190

He bowed, kissed Aunt Fenula's hand and then turned to Desmond.

'Congratulations. Defeating Putrid Pete is something worth celebrating. You have done the entire pirating community a service. Never was a pirate quite so despicable.'

Drastic Diego slapped Desmond on the back. 'Yep. Pukebreath is a nasty, sneaky, low-down son-of-a-deck-swabber, and my son is a hero!'

Suddenly Desmond shouted, 'Quiet! All of you! You don't understand. I didn't beat him in battle.'

Captain Mungo stepped forward. 'You did better than that, my lad. You outwitted him.'

'It wasn't me. You still don't understand. It was Cid's plan.' And Desmond pointed at me.

Drastic Diego looked me up and down. I think he was unimpressed.

'The best pirating is all about team work, son. Haven't I always told you that?'

'Yes, Dad, but...'

Diego wasn't having any of it. 'But nothing. You led these fine...' As he cast his eye round Desmond's crew, he faltered. 'These fine ... these ... these... er... pirates. Your crew.'.

Pitiless Pearl took her son by his shoulders and looked into his eyes.

'The fact is, Desmond, you were the only pirate captain brave enough to take on Putrid Pete. No one else dared. You laughed in the face of Blind Hugh's curse and took on the job no one else wanted. That's brave.'

'I did it to try to save the Miss Fitz Agency, not for treasure or anything.'

Mungo Mump smiled. 'So you stayed true to yourself, Desmond. That's brave too.'

Desmond opened his mouth but whatever he tried to say was swamped as introductions were made. This took a while as many needed explanations too – Wilbur's teeth, why it was not a good idea to ask Arthur to become invisible, Dusty sneezing and collapsing in a heap because he was allergic to Pitiless Pearl's perfume and so on. Finally, everyone knew who everyone was.

'So, when's the celebration?' asked Drastic Diego, looking around the room.

'Ah, Mr. de'Ath,' began Aunt Fenula.

'Death.'

'Pardon?'

'It's pronounced "Death".'

'Well you see Mr. err… Death…'

I don't know if you have ever had to call anyone Mr. or Mrs. Death, but it's not easy. Luckily Desmond cut in.

'There is no celebration. That's what I've been trying to tell you. You were all so pleased that I was one of you, a "proper pirate", that no one wanted to listen.'

'No celebration?' cried Pitiless Pearl. 'But we've brought a triple-layer-rainbow-strawberry-fudge cake. And a barrel of rum.'

Mungo Mump frowned.

'Only a small one, Mungo.'

'There's no celebration because I've not beaten Putrid Pete yet. He claimed we'd cheated, the judges couldn't agree and so there's to be a duel tomorrow to decide the winner.'

'Ah,' said Diego.

'Oh,' said Pearl.

'Yes. "Ah" and "oh",' said Desmond. 'So you've all come a long way for nothing.'

At that moment a brick came flying over the back wall of the courtyard and landed at the FFAFA studio door. There was a note tied to it.

Time's UP. We all know you're not going to win. Admit defeat.

If you're not gone by 9 p.m. then we're coming round and taking what's ours.

Kenneth & Marjorie (aka 'Big Ma')

Unsurprisingly, there were no kisses underneath.

'My guess is that Nudgebuster & Co. are trying to get their hands on whatever it is they think is hidden here before Putrid Pete gets a look in,' I said. 'Finders keepers.'

Chapter Twenty-four

Saturday 31 July 6.49 p.m.

It took a while to explain who Nudgebuster & Co. were, what they wanted and why they were communicating with us in this way.

'This isn't the first time they've threatened us,' said Aunt Fenula. 'They tried it a couple of nights ago.'

'I frightened them off with my invisibility,' said Arthur, proudly.

'Well, it was that or your stench,' chuckled PJ.

Dusty joined in. 'Don't forget the part I played. My role was vital.'

And then the chattering started. Again. I did the teacher thing and stood there, in silence, glaring, but there must be more of a knack to it than that. I expect it's one of the first things you learn during teacher training. The chatter only stopped when I gave a long, shrill whistle, which is something Miss MacLean has never done. Even Desmond looked up and he had his fingers in his ears, so I might suggest it to her, to help her with her classroom control strategy.

'Cut the chat.' I said. 'We need a plan, not a lot of hot air. So, who's got any ideas?'

'Why not call the police?' suggested Mungo Mump.

Drastic Diego stared at him. 'It's not how we pirates do things,' he said.

'In the old days, maybe, but modern pirating takes a different approach.'

'I don't hold with no modern pirating,' snarled Pitiless Pearl.

I was thinking about pointing out that she had used a double negative. After all, if she did *not* hold with *no* modern pirating, she must hold with some of it at least. I decided to keep quiet. This was neither the time nor the place.

Aunt Fenula sighed. 'I signed a contract that said if we couldn't pay back the money Nudgebuster & Co. would take the agency's property. I was desperate, but to be fair I didn't think I wouldn't be able to pay.'

'Sounds like you'll have to hand it over,' said Mungo.

'Never!' Looking at Aunt Fenula, I understood the phrase about someone's eyes being ablaze. 'I am not giving in to that ugly thug and frightful frump unless we have absolutely no choice. Even if we have no choice, when we leave we'll do it on our terms.'

'*If* we leave,' added Dusty. 'Desmond might win the duel tomorrow.'

There was an awkward silence. Desmond turned the colour of beetroot and stared at the ground. His dad put his arm round his shoulder and said, 'He might at that.'

To be honest, though, that was not what we were pinning our hopes on. I reminded everyone that we still needed a plan for 9 p.m., which gave us two hours.

'Cid's right,' said PJ. 'I say we build barricades to keep them out.'

Clayton looked up. 'They'll need to be gigantic, sturdy barricades. Madeleine pushed over the cupboard Barry and I were bundled in, remember? I'm still having nightmares about it.'

'Then there's Rocky and Herbert,' added Gruff.

Pitiless Pearl silenced Gruff with a piercing stare.

'It doesn't matter how many there are,' she said. 'We're here now. I would say that the odds are firmly against them succeeding, no matter what. Personally, I'm looking forward to meeting this Big Ma.'

The way she said the last bit, it didn't sound like it would be a polite chat over tea and scones.

'Hurrah!' cried PJ.

'Now all we need is a plan,' said Aunt Fenula. 'Cid – you're on!'

Saturday 31 July 7.02 p.m.

I sat down with PJ, Mungo Mump and Pitiless Pearl to draw up our plans. We decided a barricade across the courtyard from the Miss Fitz Agency office across to the portacabins was to be the backbone of our defence, with PJ in charge.

'We'll build it so that once they have left the office, they'll be stuck between the barricade and the gates,' said PJ. 'What are we going to use for weapons?'

194

Mungo Mump frowned. 'I'm not sure weapons are quite the thing, young lady. People could get hurt.'

'Yes, Captain Mump, us if we don't put up a bit of a fight,' I said. 'However, we don't have anything effective except PJ's sword. Desmond doesn't like his crew's swords to be too sharp.'

'Good lad,' said Mungo. 'But I take your point, Cid. We'll need something to defend the agency with.'

And so we plotted and strategized. By the time we had finalised our plans, we only just over an hour to get everyone up to speed and the defences in place.

Saturday 31 July 8.55 p.m.

Finally, we were ready. The sun was low in the sky. It was time for the last checks to make sure everyone knew what they were doing.

'Section commanders, inspect your sections and report to me,' shouted PJ, who was directing operations from on top of the barricade of armchairs, tables, an upside-down settee and all sorts of packing cases and anything else we could find.

I was in charge of the frozen food missiles to be lobbed from Aunt Fenula's flat. My team was Dusty, Barry and Aunt Fenula.

'We've over two dozen pairs of socks and tights filled with all sorts of things,' I said. 'And we've several frozen pizzas we can use like frisbees.'

'Carlos has tested the hose and turned the nozzle so it produces a powerful jet of water,' said Desmond, who was in charge of what was going on behind the barricade. 'Spud and Gruff have made a pile of rubbish bombs and the pogo stick and space hopper are ready to go. Also, the planks for rolling the bins up the barricade are in place. Oh, and Wilbur has his teeth in, although he's not wearing his glasses for health and safety reasons.'

PJ nodded. 'How about you, Captain Mump?'

Mungo was in charge of the area in front of the barricades. 'Vlad is on top of the portacabin. Shuggy and Clayton will jump out of the cupboard with those enormous water pistols. They've been messing around in the outside loo and drains. They refuse to discuss what the water pistols are filled with, but it's grey-brown and greasy looking.'

'It stinks, too,' said Pitiless Pearl. 'At least something does.'

'Oh, I forgot,' said Mungo. 'Arthur is currently invisible and says he'll try to stay that way until he's needed, just in case he can't manage to do it at the time.'

'Right,' said PJ. 'And you know what you're doing, Pitiless Pearl?'

'I wait for a signal from Miss Fitz. Then me and Mr. Death come charging into the courtyard to stop Nudgebuster & Co. turning and running. Then we'll have them surrounded, scared and beaten.'

At least that was the plan.

'Synchronise watches,' ordered PJ.

'Why?' asked Pitiless Pearl.

'I've always wanted to say it.'

Finally, we were ready to put the plan into action.

'It shows insight and guile,' said Carlos as he shook any last kinks from the hose.

'It is both shrewd and devious,' added Barry on his way up to Aunt Fenula's flat.

'It's seriously sneaky and...' but Clayton never got to finish because Shuggy shoved him in the cupboard at the front of the barricade.

'I've been wanting to do that for a while,' he said.

From my vantage point it was possible to watch everything unfold. Aunt Fenula, Barry, Dusty and I had a window each. They kept misting up (except for Dusty's) perhaps because we were hot, nervous and breathing too hard. My hands were clammy and I was worried that the large lump of frozen peas in the sock I was holding would start to melt. Before long, however, we heard Nudgebuster & Co. enter the agency office.

This was it. If we could hold out today, we still had a sliver of a chance tomorrow.

Chapter Twenty-five

Saturday 31 July 8.59 p.m.

'Cooo-eee. Anyone at home?'

Only Big Ma could make 'cooo-eee' sound menacing.

It was dusk. The warm summer air was still and carried the sounds of thudding and banging through the open windows and across the courtyard. Nudgebuster & Co. and their associates, Madeleine, Rocky and Herbert, were looking around the main agency building thoroughly.

'No one's here, Mr. Nudgebuster,' said a voice that sounded like Madeleine. 'They've wussed out.'

'Possibly, but they could be hiding. Remember what Pete said about how his crew was lured into their pathetic trap on the *Seahorse*.'

'Pathetic enough to defeat him,' hissed Barry. I shushed him. Getting angry wasn't going to help. We needed to be focused.

Suddenly the door into the courtyard was flung open.

'What have we here?'

'It's some sort of barricade, Mr. Nudgebuster,' said Herbert.

'He must be the brains of the operation,' whispered Aunt Fenula. With the enemy so close I daren't shush her, so I glared, PJ-style. It worked.

'Either that or it's a last gesture of defiance,' said Big Ma. 'It's their style – tatty and ramshackle.'

Then it all kicked off.

Saturday 31 July 9.17 p.m.

PJ jumped on top of the barricade yelling 'NOW!' and we hurled our sock missiles not only with anger but with accuracy too. The frozen chicken drumsticks and falafels were especially effective and a particularly well-aimed pizza bit Big Ma in the mouth as she tried to shout instructions to Rocky, Madeleine and Herbert.

Behind the barricade Spud was jumping on his pogo stick while Gruff bounced on the space hopper, both lobbing rubbish bombs scraped together from the bins.

'What the @*>!$?' cried Nudgebuster.

This time I really had to use those symbols. Let's just say that Nudgebuster and Co weren't happy. Unlike us. There was something satisfying watching vegetable peelings, half full take-away cartons and brown sticky ooze splatting the enemy.

Next, Carlos turned the hose on them, giving Desmond cover as he rolled the dustbins from behind the barricade up a plank to the top where he and PJ rolled them down two more planks on the other side, sending Nudgebuster & Co. flying like nine-pins in a strike.

As they got to their feet, Clayton and Shuggy burst out of the cupboard and squirted them with their water pistols.

Finally, Mr. Nudgebuster, Big Ma, Madeleine, Ricky and Herbert regained their balance, but not their dignity. It's hard to look cool, calm and collected when slops are slowly dripping down your nose and cabbage leaves are stuck to your feet.

'Where is she?' roared Nudgebuster. 'Get the addled old bat out here or I'll...'

Whatever was running down his nose dripped into his open mouth. He tried spitting it out and then made the mistake of wiping his tongue on his sleeve. Whatever it was covered in clearly tasted even more disgusting.

'I think you're the "addled old bat" he's referring to,' I said to Aunt Fenula.

I took out my phone, snapped a couple of photos and then sent a text to Pitiless Pearl.

Aunt Fenula cried, 'Coo-eee' and waved from her front door at the top of the stairs.

'Get her!' Big Ma shouted at Madeleine, Ricky and Herbert.

As they barrelled towards Aunt Fenula, Vlad whooshed down from the tree, cloak flying and fangs bared. The reflective aviator shades he was wearing as protection against any last rays of sunlight, made him look even scarier. I am not sure if Madeleine, Ricky and Herbert turned and ran or if Vlad knocked them over, but they fell into a heap at the bottom of the portacabin stairs.

'Your time is UP!' shouted Nudgebuster. He pointed at Desmond. 'That… that sorry excuse for a pirate is not up to beating Putrid Pete in a duel. I know it, he knows it, you know it. Scrope won't be buying *Premiership Pirate Knockout* so you're finished.'

Aunt Fenula smiled. 'We discovered two important things today,' she said.' One. Desmond can beat Putrid Pete as he did today, fair and square. Second, Putrid Pete is a whingey, whiny baby and a bad loser. Given those two facts, Desmond could well surprise you and beat Putrid Pete tomorrow.'

'The only surprise is that prima ballerina's a pirate at all,' snarled Mr. Nudgebuster.

Big Ma was getting agitated. 'Hand over the keys now!'

'Miss Fitz doesn't have to if she doesn't want to,' said Mungo.

'Says who?'

'Me.'

Big Ma laughed.

'And me,' said Pitiless Pearl.

Big Ma turned around. Pitiless Pearl was even taller than she was and just as powerful.

'And me,' said Drastic Diego. He was even taller than Pitiless Pearl and twice as wide.

Big Ma stopped laughing. Madeleine, Ricky and Herbert started backing away.

'I've had enough of this,' fumed Nudgebuster. 'I'm calling for reinforcements.' And he pulled an old mobile from his pocket.

Whether it was nerves or slime, he fumbled and dropped it. As he bent down to pick it up something came from nowhere and knocked him flying. He grabbed Big Ma's shoulder as he fell, pulling her on to her back. They rolled around in the mush and slops from the bins and rubbish bombs, unable to get up until Madeleine, Ricky and Herbert went to help them. Big Ma had some paper stuck to the back of her sequined, floral jacket and Mr. Nudgebuster had some chow mein noodles hanging from his shoulder, like tassels. Before they could wipe themselves down, a wolf with white, razor sharp teeth leapt from the trees at them, roaring with fury.

Unfortunately, Wilbur's landing was anything but textbook. Although he aimed in the right general direction, without his glasses he missed and overshot. He smacked into the office door and, being in mid roar, his mouth was open wide and his false teeth bit into the woodwork. Wilbur hung there for a moment before falling back onto the ground, leaving his dentures in the door. Luckily by then Nudgebuster, Big Ma, Madeleine, Ricky and Herbert were already out of the gates. In fact, it wasn't until they were half way down the alley that Mr. Nudgebuster stopped to drag the noodles from his shoulder. Then he unstuck the paper from Big Ma's back and waved it at us angrily before they both lumbered off.

Finally, Madeleine, Ricky and Herbert were bowled over by a space hopper that seemed to be flying after them. There was a cry of 'It's possessed,' and they vanished into the distance.

Saturday 31 July 9.42 p.m.

It took a long time to calm down from our victory. Even if it had only bought us another twenty-four hours before Nudgebuster & Co. took over the agency, it felt good. For once I decided Aunt Fenula's 'we'll worry about that later' philosophy was the right one. Worrying wouldn't achieve anything, especially now.

That was easy for me to say, though. Desmond sat quietly amidst all the 'did you see when I…?' and 'what about the rubbish bombs?' or 'that frozen pie hit him right on the head'.

I went over to the corner by the outside tap and slid down the wall to sit next to him on the ground.

'You OK?' I asked, immediately thinking what a stupid question it was.

Desmond gave the standard reply of, 'Yes, I'm fine. Just tired.'

'Big day tomorrow,' I said, kicking myself for saying something so lame.

Desmond nodded. We sat for a while, staring at the others celebrating yet seeing nothing.

'I can't do it, Cid.'

Desmond said it so quietly I almost missed it.

'I'm going to let everyone down. You, Miss Fitz, my crew everyone. But especially my family. They think I'm some sort of pirate hero but I'm not.'

I gulped. This isn't my kind of thing. Give me a practical problem and I'll give you a plan. Ask me to say the right thing and you're taking a big risk. Usually I go for the standard, jollying along kind of things that people say to me like:

1. 'Do your best. It's not worth worrying about.'
2. 'It's not the end of the world.'
3. 'Taking part is more important than winning.'
4. 'No one will think any the less of you.'

And most of the time these sayings are appropriate. But this wasn't most of the time.

Statements 1, 2 and 3 didn't apply. Winning was more important than anything in the world if the Miss Fitz Agency wasn't to end. And, being brutally honest, Desmond simply doing his best was not going to threaten Putrid Pete. As for statement 4, Desmond felt the exact opposite of that now that his parents had arrived and told him how proud they were that he was 'a proper pirate' at last.

'I'm not going to lie, Desmond,' I said. 'Chances are tomorrow we'll be having to pack up the agency and move on. But none of this is your fault. It's Aunt Fenula's business and she's the one who got it into this mess. It's not your job to get it out again.'

'But without Miss Fitz, where would we be? There's a reason no one else wanted to give us a chance. She got into this mess by being the only one who wanted to help us.'

I thought for a moment, then jumped to my feet.

'Right, Desmond. First things first. You've got to give it your best tomorrow so here's the plan. One, try to get a good night's sleep. Two, the duel isn't until midday, so you'll have more time to practise. I'm sure PJ and your parents will help with that. Three, if it all goes wrong, we'll go public about Putrid Pete's cheating. We'll have nothing left to lose and at least he'll get what he deserves.'

'Won't that be dangerous? I mean, imagine what some of the other pirates might do to him.'

I did imagine. And I smiled. Revenge doesn't achieve anything, but I was feeling too angry to worry about that.

'So I'd better win for Putrid Pete's sake too,' said Desmond.

That wiped the smile of my face. I had been trying to lift the pressure from Desmond's shoulders, not pile on more.

What was I saying about not worrying?

Chapter Twenty-six

Desmond, his parents and PJ were up and out early the following morning. They were down on the *Seahorse* putting Desmond through his paces before we had even eaten breakfast.

I wondered how Rory was as I sat in Aunt Fenula's kitchen, sipping my tea. I doubted his evening had been as eventful as ours. I hadn't had time to send more than a text that said, 'Catch up with you later. Here's hoping for the best.'

Aunt Fenula was even more jittery than she had been before what was being called the 'Great Agency Battle'. (Not a very catchy name.). When she made herself a quadruple layer cinnamon, sugar and banana sandwich, I knew things were bad.

It took two trips in the Miss Fitz Character Agency minibus to get everyone down to the quayside; one for the pirates, the other for everyone else. The least we could do was to cheer Desmond on.

Once we arrived I texted Rory to meet me behind the make-up caravan.

'How's it going?' I asked as soon as I saw him come round the corner.

'It's all a bit tense. Dad's so pale he's almost as see-through as Arthur. Scrope is in a very good mood, which seems to be making dad worse. Nudgebuster & Co. are acting weird, huddled together over by the catering caravan. They look like they're concentrating hard on something, which means they're bound to be plotting, and that's making me nervous, so keep your eyes peeled. Oh, and Putrid Pete is in a foul mood.'

'No change there then,' I said as I watched him go over to Mr. Nudgebuster and Big Ma. While Big Ma jumped up to meet him, Mr. Nudgebuster stuffed what looked like a large handkerchief into his pocket. I guessed that had been what they were huddled over, but the thought of what they might have been studying on it was definitely a Yuk Moment.

We were on our way over to see Desmond when a loud noise made us turn around. Putrid Pete and Big Ma were having a shoving contest and had knocked over one of the tables by the catering van, covering Mr. Nudgebuster in frothy cappuccino. Before security could arrive, the fight was over. As Nudgebuster & C. walked away Rory nudged me. 'See, I told you they were acting weird,' he said.

Meanwhile, Putrid Pete was roaring after Mr. Nudgebuster and Big Ma.

'If Blind Hugh's curse doesn't get you, I will. You'd better look out – as soon as this duel is over, I'm coming for you.'

'The odds have to be against Nudgebuster & Co if that happens,' I said. 'They might have Madeleine, Rocky and Herbert, but I've never seen such a scary looking bunch as team *Screaming Skull*.'

Sunday 1 August 9.59 a.m.

As it turned out, PJ and Desmond's parents weren't getting as far as they'd hoped with their training. When I arrived on the main deck of the *Seahorse*, Desmond was sitting on a coil of rope, his right leg jiggling up and down fast enough to wobble his hoop earring. His face looked like he'd fallen in quick-set concrete with his jaws tightly clamped.

'His "en garde" is fine,' said Drastic Diego. 'Flexible hips and strong through the thigh. He's like a rock.'

'And he can spring back from an attack with speed and grace,' continued Pitiless Pearl. 'Not that grace is important in a pirate.'

'That's the ballet-robics,' Mungo Mump explained. 'It's tough physical exercise, wonderful for strength and agility.'

There was an awkward silence.

'But?' I asked.

'But it's everything else!' Pitiless Pearl sounded exasperated. 'We can't get through to him.'

'I tried coming at him like Putrid Pete will,' said PJ. 'I think it was a bit too much. He's been sitting there like that ever since.'

I decided to let them get on with it while I went to find Aunt Fenula. She had been rehearsing the cheerleading. Hopefully their enthusiasm would see them through because their coordination and ability to follow a routine would not. And right now, Desmond needed all the support he could get.

Then I had one of those sudden thoughts that make you go frozen cold and boiling hot all at once. Putrid Pete hadn't thought it worth cheating against Desmond so far. But things were serious now. The title and prize money were up for grabs and his usual over-confidence had been his downfall in the past. I pulled Aunt Fenula to one side. I didn't want to worry anyone else.

'Suppose Putrid Pete is not as stupid as the average arch villain? Suppose he's feeling less confident now he has to fight Desmond in a duel and has decided to cheat?' I asked.

'Then we need to find out what plans he has for this duel,' said Aunt Fenula. 'Or at least make some notes on what tactics he's planning. Cid, why don't you…'

'No!' I knew what she was asking and it was too dangerous.

'But you don't know what I'm going to ask you.'

'To spy on Putrid Pete. And before you go any further, I can't think of one member of Desmond's crew who could do it. They don't do sneaky – they're all too obvious.'

Dusty had been practising his cheerleading moves away from the others with their pom-poms and had heard everything.

'I'll do it,' he said, 'to repay your kindness in rescuing me from the rubbish. I know a bit about sword fighting. I think my body used to like it. He may even have been killed in battle.'

'Are you sure, Dusty?' I asked.

He nodded. 'But I would like a lookout to keep watch for me. I feel a bit nervous since being drop kicked through the window the other day.'

Aunt Fenula has her own way of doing things, which was part of the reason we were in this mess. She looks at the world in her own way. If she were rich, people would say her ideas were eccentric. But she's not, so people say they're daft instead. Her plan of using Prendergast to help Dusty find out if Putrid Pete was deciding to cheat probably falls into this category. He's not the most obliging bird at the best of times. He's also vain and crochety. 'Crochety' is a sharp, snappy, angry kind of a word and Prendergast was a sharp, snappy, angry kind of a parrot.

On the other hand, we didn't have much time and I didn't have any better ideas.

We had to approach Prendergast in the right way, though. I bigged up the role – the hero who saves the day, that sort of thing. I had all but run out of things to say when Aunt Fenula tickled him under the chin and told him he was a 'big, strong, handsome bird.' And that was it. He agreed. Aunt Fenula clearly had some mysterious power over parrots.

Prendergast, of course, wanted make-up and a costume so we did him up as a seagull with a false beak. I made Team *Seahorse* swear not to laugh on pain of swabbing the decks with a toothbrush. They managed it, although Clayton had to suck in his cheeks.

Sunday 1 August 11.25 a.m.

We used one of those coin operated telescopes to watch as Dusty and Prendergast made their way to the enemy ship so we looked like tourists rather than spies. Dusty managed to clamber up the side of the *Screaming Skull* while its crew was busy cheering on Putrid Pete as he practised his sword skills. Prendergast perched on the crow's nest, then he flew down to the rails along the quarter deck.

'Let me look,' said Aunt Fenula, grabbing the telescope from me.

'What's happening?' I asked.

'Prendergast is circling over the ship. Dusty is crawling behind some barrels, trying to get nearer without being spotted. He's got his note book and pencil between his teeth.'

'I hope he doesn't fall apart under the stress of it all,' I said. 'That'd give the game away.'

Aunt Fenula described Dusty's progress along the deck of the *Screaming Skull* until he was crouched next to a large barrel behind the pirates, who were sitting on old sacks. He had a good view of Putrid Pete from there.

Suddenly, Prendergast squawked.

'What's happening?' I grabbed the telescope back from Aunt Fenula. Vicious Vince was walking towards where Dusty was hiding.

The squawk had made Dusty jump and I guess his rattling alerted the pirates. Vince grabbed Dusty's skull, putting his hook through the eye socket, which made me wince. I don't know if Dusty could feel physical pain or if it were the shock, but he collapsed in a heap. Prendergast flew off.

Sunday 1 August 11.50 a.m.

With ten minutes to go until the duel, I ran back to the *Seahorse*, where Desmond was practising with his father's sword.

'I thought he'd be happier with one that was sharp,' said Pitiless Pearl. 'But he's even more scared. He's landed one or two blows, but more by luck than judgement.'

I watched Diego give Desmond a few last pointers. Desmond stood, rigid, nodding and biting his lip. Finally, he said, 'Come on, son. You're a Death. You can do it. It's in your blood.'

Mungo's advice was a little different. 'Be true to yourself, Desmond. Do your best. Be your best.'

Pitiless Pearl sighed and whispered to me (not very quietly).

'He's not going to win. It's time to face facts.'

Indeed, it was. I stopped him before he headed down the gangplank.

'Look, Desmond. You have to do this. Dusty's in trouble. He was doing a reccy on Screaming Skull to make notes on Putrid Pete's tactics, but he got caught. Prendergast escaped.'

My phone buzzed. It was a text from Aunt Fenula. I read it out.

'Putrid Pete is threatening unspeakable things to Dusty unless Desmond gives in now and says PP's won.'

Desmond stopped and looked at the ground.

'Putrid Pete said that did he?'

I nodded. 'I guess that means he thinks you're in with a chance.'

Desmond's face did that funny thing when you're scared and holding back tears but trying to be brave.

'But Cid, I'm not good with a sword. I'm not cut out for this sort of thing. This is not who I am. I'm a dancer, an entertainer.'

'Can't you pretend you're starring in a show? A musical or ballet perhaps. Imagine the deck is a stage. The spotlight is on and Dancing

207

Desmond de'Ath is top of the bill.'

Desmond seemed to slip into a trance. He began mumbling.

'The theatre. A show. Music and dancing. Be true to myself. Be my best.'

Then suddenly he turned to me and said, 'I'm not a pirate, Cid. I'm not going to pretend.'

And with that, he marched down to the main deck. There was nothing I could do. It was too late.

Sunday 1 August Midday

Moments later, Putrid Pete was glowering down at Desmond, who was strangely calm.

'Is he... smiling?' asked Drastic Diego.

'Err... yes,' replied Pitiless Pearl, before shouting 'Let 'im 'ave it, Son!'

We were all gathered on the *Seahorse* because, in Putrid Pete's words, it would give 'Dezzy the home advantage as he needs all the help he can get.' The Miss Fitz Agency cheerleaders had been asked to stick to cheering rather than doing anything more adventurous.

Rory shouted, 'Action!' to Delia, who started filming. He blew a whistle and the duel began.

Putrid Pete snarled, showing what was left of his yellow teeth.

'So you're not going to help Dusty, your skinny friend? So be it. I'll keep him. The ship ought to have a real screaming skull on board, after all.'

I didn't like to think about how Putrid Pete would get Dusty to scream. Desmond, however, remained calm. He smiled and didn't say a thing and that *really* annoyed Putrid Pete.

'Come on then,' he said, swiping in Desmond's direction with his sword.

Desmond didn't seem in the least concerned. Instead, he did a couple of warm-up stretches. Putrid Pete laughed.

'That won't help you now,' he said.

Desmond smiled and paced a little. He didn't seem to be in any hurry, whereas Putrid Pete was getting angrier by the second. With a growl Putrid Pete leapt forward and – swoosh – lunged at Desmond. Desmond leapt backwards and he missed.

Swish! Putrid Pete slashed at him. Desmond twirled several times, quickly, on the spot and Putrid Pete missed again.

Putrid Pete was getting more and more worked up, but Desmond was relaxed. It was all very odd. Then whoosh – Putrid sliced at him but Desmond pirouetted to the side, so he missed him again.

Aunt Fenula was smiling. The Deaths were dumbfounded. Team *Seahorse* were looking at each other, open mouthed. The Miss Fitz cheerleaders were cheering loudly enough for all of us. Rory looked at me, and mouthed, 'What on Earth…' I shrugged and then started to enjoy the show.

Desmond was tying Putrid Pete up in knots. One moment he had jumped up on the capstan, the next he had leapt over the open hatch, leaving Putrid Pete teetering on its edge as he tried to hit Desmond with his sword.

Team *Screaming Skull* fell silent as they watched their captain slash this way and that, hitting nothing but the rigging or the deck.

By now, Putrid Pete was huffing and puffing. 'Will you stop prancing around? Stand still and fight like a pirate!'

'What's the matter?' laughed Desmond. 'Can't you keep up with me?'

When Putrid Pete swiped high, Desmond ducked. When he swiped low, Desmond jumped over his sword. It was utterly amazing. Even Desmond's parents started laughing and shouting 'You show him, son!' and 'Go Desmond!' At one point, Pitiless Pearl nudged Mr. Scrope and said, 'That's my boy, you know.'

Desmond literally ran circles around Putrid Pete, darting this way and that until he had him so confused that he was facing in the wrong direction. Desmond tapped him on the shoulder. Putrid Pete turned around, panting and drooping. His sword was dangling from his hand and Desmond made a final twirl, kicking it to the deck as he went.

Now I got it: 'I'm not a pirate, Cid. I'm not going to pretend.'

Desmond picked up Putrid Pete's sword and gave it back to him. Team *Seahorse* and the Miss Fitz Agency and everyone at BUMP went wild.

'Now,' Desmond said. 'I'd be obliged if you would return Dusty to us.'

Normally Putrid Pete would mock Desmond for saying something like 'obliged'. Instead he went mad and started shouting over and over,

'You CHEATED! You're a CHEAT! I demand a rematch. I won!'

Desmond was not only calm now; he was very confident.

'I think you'll find that parrying and avoiding your opponent's blows are key to sword fighting. I did nothing against the Pirate Code, old or new.'

Putrid Pete looked over to Nifty Nikolai, who shrugged and shook his head.

Putrid Pete glared at Desmond.

'If you want to see that manky pile of old bones again,' snarled Putrid Pete, 'then you'll give me the prize money, the title of *Pirate Champion* and say you cheated.'

'But I didn't cheat.'

'It's up to you. If you don't do as I say, I'll keep him. Like I said, I could do with an actual screaming skull. And I'll make sure he screams all right.'

Desmond paled and his expression drooped. He dropped his sword and sat down on the ground, arms on his knees and his face buried in his arms.

I signalled to Delia to cut the filming.

Chapter Twenty-seven

I wasn't sure what to do next, so I went to find Rory. He was with his father, who was being threatened by Nudgebuster & Co. Desmond winning was NOT what they wanted at all. Mr. Birkwhistle was fitting in as many words as possible before the threats began.

'I'm as surprised as you are,' he was saying. 'I thought you'd be happy. Desmond's won. Mr. Scrope will sign the television deal for the States. You'll get your money back.'

My mouth interrupted before my brain had caught up with it.

'I can tell you why they're unhappy. If Desmond had lost, they'd have not only got your business. The Miss Fitz Agency would have gone bankrupt too and they would have ransacked it looking for something valuable they want.'

Big Ma wasn't very convincing when she said, 'Something valuable? At the Miss Fitz Agency? All you have is a lot of tatty, broken relics. And that applies to your belongings as well as your clients.'

She started laughing at her own joke but, yet again, my mouth took charge.

'We know we have something of great value. Something that you want is hidden on our premises. Something that you were looking for when you turned our place upside down.'

'Is that so?' asked Big Ma.

'Yes.'

'I don't believe you.'

'It's true.'

'Where is it then?'

Big Ma must have thought I was stupid.

'Wouldn't you like to know?' (Translation: 'I have no idea, but you have just told me I was right. There is something worth a lot more than

£20,000 at the Miss Fitz Agency.')

Suddenly Mr. Birkwhistle started blurting out all sorts of things I didn't want to hear.

'Now I think of it, perhaps Captain de'Ath has broken a rule. Or we could have a re-match? There must be something we could do.'

I didn't understand why Mr. Birkwhistle was so upset until I noticed Rory, with Big Ma looming behind him, her hands clamped on his shoulders like one of those amusement arcade claw cranes gripping the big prize.

'You're in quite a state, Mr. Birkwhistle. I think we'd better look after Rory while you sort this mess out.'

Rory was struggling, so Big Ma grabbed his arm and held it behind his back. He winced. Mr. Birkwhistle was frantic.

'I can fix it, I swear, but please, give him back.'

'I'm sure you can,' sneered Nudgebuster. 'But Rory will be an incentive for you.'

By this time, Aunt Fenula, PJ, Team *Seahorse* and the Deaths had joined us. Fang and Prendergast flew overhead, circling each other.

I saw Pitiless Pearl nod at Drastic Diego and make a letter 'C' with her fingers. Apparently it meant 'Plan C' but I only found that out later. What happened next was so fast I can only remember snapshots:

- Pearl rushing Big Ma and sending her flying.
- Drastic Diego grabbing Rory and flinging him at Mr. Birkwhistle.
- Team *Seahorse* surrounding Rory and his dad and Desmond actually slapping Scurvy Sam's wrist when she tried to grab Rory again.
- Fang swooping at Desmond but being chased away by Prendergast!
- Aunt Fenula hand-bagging Nudgebuster again – she can move fast when she wants to.
- A fight breaking out. I'm not sure who won but Pitiless Pearl and PJ were bonding over scaring Putrid Pete's crew stupid – not that they had far to go.

The next thing I remember clearly was an ear achingly high-pitched screech coming from the *Screaming Skull*.

'Aieeeeeee!'

It was loud enough to be heard even above Clayton yelling 'Bundle!' as he piled on top of a heap of assorted pirates. We looked up to the *Seahorse* to see Putrid Pete holding up Dusty's skull in one hand and his thigh bones in the other.

'Give in now or I'll smash these bones into pieces so small it'll take you months to glue him back together again.' Then he laughed. 'Well, crew, what do you think? We'll be the only pirates to have a real skull and cross bones.'

'Unhand him, you scoundrel!' declared Desmond, clearly feeling much more like himself again. I can come up with about a hundred words to describe Putrid Pete and all of them are much ruder than 'scoundrel.'

'You tell 'im son!' shouted Pearl, shaking her fist at Putrid Pete, who was now dangling Dusty's skull over the side of his ship.

'Help!' squeaked Dusty.

'Say I won! I don't care what you do with Nudgebuster & Co.,' Putrid Pete yelled. 'I had nothing to do with any of their scheming.'

'Liar!' shouted Aunt Fenula.

'Prove it!'

'Help!' squeaked Dusty.

'Let's ask Mr. Nudgebuster and Big Ma,' said Rory. 'They weren't looking too friendly with you by the catering caravan.'

'Yes,' I agreed. 'Now Desmond has won, they'll admit you cheated. That way Mr. Scrope won't buy *Premiership Pirate Knockout*. And that means BUMP won't get paid, so we won't get paid and Nudgebuster & Co. get what they've been after all along – the Miss Fitz Agency and the treasure that's hidden there.'

'Ha!' laughed Putrid Pete from the bow of his ship. 'You won't dare ask them!'

'Oh yes we will,' shouted Aunt Fenula, giving Putrid Pete a thin-lipped, toothy, smug smile as her eyes narrowed into a glare that would stop a bullet. 'If you don't agree that Desmond won and hand back Dusty, that's exactly what we'll do. We'll have nothing to lose.'

But when we looked round, Mr. Nudgebuster and Big Ma had disappeared. We were just in time to see their limo screeching out of the dockyard gates. Putrid Pete smirked.

'Now what?' he asked, still smirking. Now I know why teachers tell you to 'wipe that smirk / silly grin off your face.' That was what I wanted to do to Putrid Pete, with an iron wool scrubbing pad.

'Help!' squeaked Dusty, no longer dangling over the side of Putrid Pete's ship, but tucked under his arm, which couldn't have been pleasant as Putrid Pete got that name for a reason – 'Putrid' means so much more than 'smelly.

'It'll be interesting to see what some of the other pirate crews you went up against do when they find out you cheated them,' I said. I know I'd sworn not to tell, but Dusty was in danger and if we were going to lose everything, then we were going down fighting.

'And we do have proof to show them,' Rory added.

That did the trick. The smirk vanished as Putrid Pete came over very twitchy. Then he snapped, waving Dusty's skull around as he shouted a new threat.

'I don't know what you think you're doing, but if you want to see your friend returned to you with all his pieces intact, it'll cost you the prize money.'

Sunday 1 August 1.21 p.m.

What a time for Graffham H Scrope IV to turn up!

'I heard a commotion. What on Earth is happening, Birkwhistle?' But Mr. Birkwhistle was too exhausted to answer Mr. Scrope. And anyway, he had no idea. He'd been standing behind Aunt Fenula all this time, gently swaying and staring into space.

'It's all part of the final episode, Mr. Scrope,' said Aunt Fenula. 'A bit more drama.'

'But I can't take any more drama,' murmured Mr. Birkwhistle, and he slumped against an embarrassed Pitiless Pearl.

Mr. Scrope ignored him. 'So Putrid's about to get his comeuppance, eh?'

Aunt Fenula nodded. 'He's kidnapped one of Desmond's crew in a last ditch attempt to make him give in.'

'Why? Desmond's already won?'

Aunt Fenula opened her mouth, then shut it again.

'Well?'

Aunt Fenula opened her mouth, then shut it again. Before anyone could say or do anything else Shuggy shouted, 'Look! Desmond's standing on the *Seahorse* and he's got the plank out.'

Aunt Fenula looked at me. I shrugged. I had no idea what was in Desmond's mind.

'I think our Desmond is putting Plan B into action,' said Drastic Diego.

'Captain Death is using Plan B, Mr. Scrope,' said Aunt Fenula, as if she had an idea of what it was about. Still, it seemed to satisfy Mr. Scrope.

'Make sure you get all this Plan B stuff on camera,' Mr. Scope said to Delia. 'We could have the makings of an even greater grand finale that we thought.'

I hoped so.

We all watched as Desmond turned and walked away from the plank. A long way away. The *Screaming Skull*'s crew started jeering, but then Desmond turned round. He loosened his shoulders, took some deep breaths and focused, ignoring the jeers. I suppose he was used to them. Everyone fell silent. I grabbed Rory's hand, or maybe he gripped mine. But we held on tight as Desmond started to run towards the plank.

Then the remaining Miss Fitz cheerleaders began chanting.

'Des-mond! Des-mond! Des-mond!'

Team *Seahorse* joined in.

'Des-mond! Des-mond! Des-mond!'

'What does he think he's up to?' said Vicious Vince.

'P'raps he's going to do some synchronised swimming,' Scurvy Sam chuckled. 'With the sharks.'

Desmond ran faster and faster, leaping onto the plank but not slowing down. By now everyone was staring, open mouthed.

'Look out, Cap'n,' shouted Scurvy Sam.

Putrid Peter laughed. 'I'm not afraid of that dancing donkey!' he shouted back.

As Desmond reached the end, he jumped as high as he possibly could, like he was on a diving board, and pirouetted through the sky in a majestic arc over to the poop deck of the *Screaming Skull*.

What happened next took only a few seconds. Putrid Pete opened his arms wide and beckoned Desmond with a shout of, 'Come on, if you think you're hard enough,' while Scurvy Sam and Vicious Vince shouted 'Move, Cap'n, you're standing right where he's going to…'

Whump! Desmond smacked into Putrid Pete, grabbing his jacket to try to stop himself, but it was too late. Desmond's landing slammed them both into the side of the ship with such force that he catapulted into the sea taking Putrid Pete with him. Luckily, Dusty's skull fell to the deck spinning on its crown, his thigh bones nearby.

'Men overboard,' cried Spud, as Desmond and Putrid Pete hit the water with an almighty slap and splash.

Putrid Pete was clawing at Desmond in the water, pushing him under. Team *Seahorse* was furious.

'He's trying to drown our captain!'

'It's not that,' yelled Scurvy Sam. 'Captain Pukebreath can't swim!'

We could hear Desmond shouting at Putrid to 'calm down' and 'stop splashing'. It didn't do much good. Putrid Pete was putting everything he had into panicking. Every time Desmond fought his way back to the surface, Putrid Pete's thrashing arms knocked him back below the waves. Then they both disappeared and the water stilled, except for a few bubbles popping to the surface. It only lasted a minute or so, but it seemed much longer. Suddenly they bobbed up again, gasping and coughing. Putrid Pete's panicking had worn him out so that Desmond at last managed to swim to the dock side, pulling Putrid Pete with him.

A moment or two later Desmond stood on the quayside barely visible in the middle of a group hug surrounded by cheering pirates and Miss Fitz cheerleaders. Putrid Pete stood shaking and shivering, probably from both cold and fright. Water trickled off him to form a little puddle and, as it dripped down his face, he gurgled, coughed and sniffed. It wasn't possible to tell if his sniffing was down to crying or not. His eyes certainly looked red.

Sunday 1 August 1.40 p.m.

Desmond fought free from the crowd and walked over to Putrid Pete. He held out his hand. For a moment Pete looked like he was going to sneer, but then I realised he was actually attempting a real smile. No wonder he didn't do it that often. He took Desmond's hand and shook it. Desmond winced at the tight grip. Then Putrid Pete spoke through chattering teeth, 'You s-s-saved my life, Captain de'Ath. And acc-according to my code I'm f-f-forever in your debt.'

'Think nothing of it, my dear chap.' Despite everything, and even though he was soggy with sea water, Desmond was still in full 'Desmond mode'.

'As for the other b-b-business,' Putrid Pete continued as Vicious Vince wrapped a blanket around his shoulders, 'I w-w-want nothing more to do with it, or them. You have my w-w-word as a senior member of the Professional Pirates' and Swashbucklers' Association.'

'Them?' asked Desmond. 'You mean Nudgebuster & Co.?'

Putrid Pete nodded.

'What about "it"?' I asked. 'You said you didn't want anything more to do with "them, or it".'

Putrid Pete looked over each shoulder before fixing a glassy-eyed stare on Desmond – and yet not on Desmond. It was like he was seeing something standing right behind Desmond's shoulder.

'B-blind Hugh brought me to this end, no doubt about it. Without Desmond here, I'd have drowned.' Putrid spluttered and coughed up more sea water. 'Well, I don't need warning twice. Blind Hugh's curse is real and if you pay any heed to me you'll all stay well clear. Now, let that be an end to it. I've nothing more to say on the matter.'

Then Putrid Pete turned to his crew, his voice finally recovered from the shock and sea water. 'As for you lot, you're all going to have some ballet lessons. And there'll be...' he turned to Desmond '... ballet-robics is it?'

Desmond nodded.

'Ballet-robics every morning before breakfast.'

There was muttering from Team *Screaming Skull*.

'But...' began Scurvy Sam.

'Silence in the ranks,' snarled Putrid Pete. 'Or you'll be swabbing the decks with cotton buds.'

In some ways it was comforting to know that Putrid Pete hadn't had a complete personality change after his experience. I don't think I could have coped with that on top of everything else.

Mr. Scrope watched all this open mouthed, which was deeply unpleasant as he kept chewing his bubble gum all the while. He turned to Delia, the sun glinting off his mirrored sunglasses, and said, 'Did you get all that about Blind Hugh and spirits and curses and all?'

Delia nodded.

'What's Blind Hugh and the curse all about? It could make a great TV series. Or even a motion picture!'

Aunt Fenula patted Mr. Scrope's arm before Delia could answer, 'You heard what Putrid Pete said. Best steer well clear of curses and the like in my experience. Too much of a business risk for a start.'

Mr. Scope nodded, then shook Aunt Fenula's hand hard enough to make her bingo wings wobble. It's not that Aunt Fenula is especially flabby, but she's not very muscly.

'I gotta hand it to you, lady, you guys know how to put on a good show over here,' he said. 'I'm glad I stayed around to see what was in store. The audience at home will go wild for *Premiership Pirate Knockout.*'

Aunt Fenula smiled.

Then Graffham H. Scrope IV beckoned his lawyers, who had folders of thick documents under their arms.

'Get over here, Birkwhistle!' Mr. Scrope said. 'We've got a deal to shake on and contracts to sign.'

Sunday 1 August 12.15 p.m.
Trouble Scale 0

Mr. Birkwhistle was so dazed that Rory had to lead him over step by step.

Graffham H. Scrope IV slapped Mr. Birkwhistle on the back. Hard.

'You took it right to the wire,' he said. 'I have to say, I doubted you once or twice there – but it's sensational! It's gonna be a big hit in the US. In fact, I reckon it'll go global.'

'We told you we'd deliver, Mr. Scrope,' said Rory on behalf of his dad who was still trying to recover his breath after all the pats on his back. 'And Miss Fitz,' Rory called out as he headed over to Mr. Scrope's limo, 'the money will be transferred into your bank account by the end of the day.'

'Thank-you Rory, and thank your father, too,' Aunt Fenula called back – and then she smiled and winked at Mr. Birkwhistle. Aunts!

Meanwhile, Team *Seahorse* was still celebrating its captain.

'Desmond the Vanquisher!' said Carlos. 'My faith in him trouncing his nemesis never so much as wavered.'

'Desmond the Conqueror! continued Barry. 'My trust in him overwhelming his archenemy never so much as wobbled.'

'You fibbers!' finished Clayton. 'We all doubted him. And we shouldn't.' And with that, he wiped away a little tear.

I suddenly felt very tired and in need of banana split with all the trimmings. And I could think of a lot of trimmings – fudge pieces, chocolate sauce, whipped cream, fresh strawberries, cookie dough, mango slices…

'Come on,' said Aunt Fenula, as if she could read my mind. 'Let's celebrate. It's on me.'

There was an enormous cheer. 'To the ice cream parlour!' shouted Aunt Fenula. There was another cheer as we all headed to the dockyard gates. Suddenly, we heard a shout.

'Oi! What about me.'

We looked around.

'Hey! Over here, on the deck with my thigh bones.'

Dusty!

'And don't forget the rest of me, either.'

Sunday 1 August 2.52 p.m.

It took three goes for Dusty to finally pull himself together with all the bones in the right place and the right way round. He had been through quite an ordeal and we all wanted to know what it was like on the *Screaming Skull*.

'Everything is the newest, the best, the most expensive there is. But it feels… wrong. It's all cold, sharp, soulless.'

'Were you frightened?' asked Gruff?

'I'd be lying if I said I wasn't. Especially when Putrid Pete had my head in his hands. And he kept on asking me "where is it?" And when I said "what?" he threatened to drop kick me over the side. So I told him if he did that, he'd never find out because I was the only one who knew where it is. Then he said "what is it?" And I told him if he didn't know, I wasn't about to tell him.'

'So where is it, Dusty?' asked Shuggy. 'You can tell us.'

'And what is it?' asked Spud.

Dusty sighed. 'Don't you two start. I'll say it one more time, so listen carefully: I... DON'T... KNOW.'

'Then why tell Putrid Pete you knew where...' PJ began.

'Because I didn't want him to drop kick my skull! There's only so much a skeleton can take. It's bad enough that I had to get rid of the lovely thick, goatskin parchment I'd been lining my drawer with. It was so comforting – smooth and warm, great for keeping out drafts. They really get into your bones, you know. But after Nudgebuster and Big Ma had ransacked...'

At that moment I had a heavy, ice-cold shock pulse through me like a snowball dropping from my head into my stomach and then sliding down my legs into my feet. I interrupted Dusty in mid-flow.

'Parchment? Are you sure?'

'Of course. I remember parchment from when my body was alive. Mind you, that was at least a couple of hundred years ago.'

'Was there anything on it?'

'Not much. Some tiny handwriting and what looked like a plan or map. Most of it looked like scribble.'

'Think carefully, Dusty,' I said. 'What did it say?'

'I don't know.'

'Dusty!'

'Do you read your bedding, Cid?'

'Fair point.'

'What did you do with it?'

'I put it in the dustbin.'

I stopped suddenly, causing a pile up of pirates behind me.

'Then it must be...'

Aunt Fenula, the Deaths and Captain Mump took a few seconds to realise that no one was following them. They stopped and turned round. I hurried up to them, the others right behind and bundling into me again.

'That's what Nudgebuster and Big Ma were huddled over,' I said to

Aunt Fenula. 'It's what they didn't want Putrid Pete to see. They've worked it out.'

'Slow down, Cid. You're not making much sense.'

I tried to slow down but all the words rushed out at once, scrambling and shoving each other until they spewed out in a big heap. My brain couldn't keep up, so my mouth didn't stand a chance. 'It's why Nudgebuster & Co. left so quickly – Dusty's drawer, the parchment, the rubbish, Big Ma's jacket. They've worked it out, the writing on the document. They know exactly where the treasure is buried. We've got to get to the agency ASAP.'

'Nope,' said Aunt Fenula, 'I didn't follow any of that.'

'Except,' said Pitiless Pearl, 'that we need to get to the agency double quick.'

Chapter Twenty-eight

Sunday 1 August 3.22 p.m.
Trouble Scale At least 8! Heading for 9?

We made quite a sight running down the main street – PJ led the charge, with Aunt Fenula and me puffing behind her. Following us were pirates in various shapes and sizes, a flying hat (complete with veil), a wolf wearing glasses, a skeleton whose skull couldn't quite keep up with the rest of it and, bringing up the rear, a cloud of noxious haze.

We rushed back to the agency but we were too late.

As we walked through the main office, we could hear muttering and scraping. There, in the courtyard, were Mr. Nudgebuster and Big Ma. He had a spade, she had a pickaxe. Madeleine, Rocky and Herbert were nowhere to be seen. Big Ma was next to a large hole that had been dug against the outside loo wall. Mr. Nudgebuster was standing in the loo's doorway. Judging by the smell, he had been digging a hole on the other side of the wall in the loo itself. At least I hoped that was what it was.

They were too focused on their work to hear us walk into the courtyard.

'You don't give up, do you?' I said.

They jumped and dropped a thick, yellowing piece of paper. Big Ma went to stamp on it but her back was too stiff and I was too quick. I grabbed it before her flowery Dr Martens hit the cobbles.

Although Nudgebuster and Big Ma were too large to cower, they somehow looked smaller. They said nothing and stuck together, warily eying the Deaths – even Desmond.

'This is what I was on about,' I said to Aunt Fenula. 'It's Dusty's old drawer lining. It was tipped out along with him when Nudgebuster & Co. "visited" on Wednesday. Later, when Putrid Pete showed them the documents he'd found in the records office, they realised they'd seen what they were looking for here. But Dusty had thrown it in the bin.

During the Agency Battle, we used rubbish bombs and Desmond rolled the bins at dear Kenneth and Marjorie over there. Remember when Wilbur sent them flying? When Big Ma got up she had paper sticking to her back? That was the parchment!'

Aunt Fenula nodded. 'Yes, Nudgebuster peeled it off her jacket when they ran down the alleyway. He waved it at us.'

'Yes. I thought he was angry. In fact, he was waving it in a "nyah, nyah, we've got it" sort of a way.'

'So why did they fight with Putrid Pete?' asked Desmond.

'Stop talking like we're not here,' snapped Big Ma. I ignored her.

'Putrid Pete got enough of a glimpse of the parchment today to know what it was. That's why they fought earlier. He also knew that if Desmond beat him in the duel, and Team *Seahorse* won, Nudgebuster & Co. would sneak off to the agency straight away to get the treasure for themselves before anyone missed them.' I looked at Desmond. 'The fact that Putrid Pete was so worried about Nudgebuster & Co. doing that means he must have known you were in with a good chance of beating him.'

Desmond grinned. 'He must have done.' Then he peered over my shoulder. 'That's definitely a treasure map. And thanks to Mr. Nudgebuster and Marjorie, we know exactly where to look.'

Mr. Nudgebuster and Big Ma snarled threats at Desmond, but he stood his ground.

'What's that written on the back?' asked Vlad, fluttering around under the map.

'Jonas Hugh MacHugh. Captain, the *Keel Hauler*,' Dusty said.

Drastic Diego and Pitiless Pearl gasped. 'Blind Hugh!'

Pitiless Pearl smiled. 'Do you remember I used to tell the kids stories about him, Diego? The same ones told to us when we were kids, they were, passed down through pirate families for generations.'

'Those tales gave our kiddies nightmares more than once, I can tell you,' said Drastic Diego.

'Mind you, Desmond wasn't scared by them, was he?' Pitiless Pearl ruffled Desmond's hair. 'He thought Blind Hugh needed some lessons in manners and etik... ettyketty...equitek...'

'Etiquette,' said Desmond. 'You told us those stories to scare us into practising our pirate cursing and helping out around the ship.'

'You always refused to curse,' said Diego.

'But I always helped out around the ship.'

'You were a good boy,' said Pitiless Pearl. For a moment I thought I saw a tear in her eye, but it was probably the twilight catching her glitter mascara.

All this while Nudgebuster & Co. had stood by quietly, glancing at each other from time to time, sometimes raising an eyebrow. I think they were trying to signal each other.

Drastic Diego looked at them.

'I'm a fair sort of pirate, so I'm going to give you a choice. You can either carry on digging while we watch and hand over anything you find. Or you can run away now and never darken the Miss Fitz Agency again.'

'You can't...' shouted Mr. Nudgebuster. Then he stopped. He had finally realised he was out of options.

'No,' I said. '*You* can't. Whatever it is you hoped to find here, there's nothing more you can do about it. So you might as well do as Mr. Death says.'

'What about what we're owed?' snarled Big Ma.

'It'll be in your account by tomorrow morning.

Nudgebuster & Co. hesitated.

'Would you like to be thrown over the wall or will you walk out?' asked Pitiless Pearl.

It didn't take much consultation for Nudgebuster & Co. to decide they'd take the second option. They tried to make the first few steps dignified, which wasn't easy because they smelled disgusting and looked worse. Then they ran, turning only for Mr. Nudgebuster to shout, 'You haven't heard the last of us.'

Big Ma did the fist-waving as she was far scarier.

'Gertcha!' At least I think that was what Pitiless Pearl shouted as she, Diego and Desmond took a couple of paces towards them. Nudgebuster & Co. finally fled.

Sunday 1 August 4.36 p.m.

Aunt Fenula looked at the mess in the courtyard and said, through a pinched nose, 'I think we ought to clear this up, fill in the holes.'

'I think we ought to make the most of the work they've done,' said Drastic Diego. 'Looking at the map, I think they were pretty close to finding whatever they were looking for. It's got to be in one of these holes either side of the loo wall. It must have been buried before the loo was put in.'

It wasn't going to be pleasant, but we knew Diego was talking sense. We decided to draw straws to see who would carry on digging inside the loo, but Desmond said he'd never ask anyone to do anything he wasn't willing to do himself, so he pulled his neckerchief *and* his ruffles up over his nose and started shovelling sloppy sludge from the hole. Drastic Diego helped, for which we were all grateful. The stench was enough to make me retch. It was even worse than Arthur, the Invisible Man.

I don't know if you've ever used an outside loo, especially an old one, but you'd have to have been completely desperate to use ours. It was almost a historic artefact and hadn't been used for years. It was in a small, damp, stone building with unpleasant looking brown crusts on the iron pipework and cistern. It had a long chain with a wooden handle and when Aunt Fenula lifted the wooden toilet seat she let it drop again immediately. Gruff wouldn't go anywhere near it because of the spiders' webs. I can't say I blamed him. There were a lot of the thick grey kind that look like candy floss and stick to your clothes.

Outside Pitiless Pearl organised Team *Seahorse*. Aunt Fenula and I watched, stunned, as they did what they were told without any complaining, stalling or skiving. Aunt Fenula, PJ, Vlad, Dusty, Wilbur, Arthur and I watched from a distance and fetched anything that was needed – mainly tea.

It was only an hour before Desmond called out, 'I think I've found something.'

It would have to come from the hole inside the loo! With Drastic Diego to help, he managed to loosen the packed down soil around a small, wooden chest. It looked and smelled more than a bit suspect, so we took it into the courtyard and hosed it down before we opened it. Inside was an even smaller casket and a parchment scroll on which was a rhyme. Aunt Fenula read it out loud.

'*Cursed am I who found this, for it's brought me misery.*

Its hypnotic power is far too great, to return it to the sea.
It drove me mad until I lost whatever I held dear.
It ruled me like a tyrant, controlling me by fear.
This casket holds a secret like a coffin in a grave,
And it will only open for a pirate strong and brave.
And if you are, dear reader, this pirate bold and true,
You'll see this thing for what it is and know what you must do.'

'It's Blind Hugh's curse,' said Pitiless Pearl. 'No doubt about it.' Then Pitiless Pearl shuddered, which scared me. If she was afraid, it must be something terrifying.

'What can you tell us about it?' I asked.

Drastic Diego sat down on an upturned bucket and we all gathered round. The stench didn't matter anymore. It was as if something had smothered it, or turned off our sense of smell.

Chapter Twenty-nine

Sunday 1 August 5.45 p.m.
Trouble Scale rising?

'Blind Hugh was first mate on Captain Tarquin Terror's ship. It was the richest pirate ship of its time, which was over 300 years ago. The ship sank – some say it was overloaded with treasure – and Blind Hugh was the only survivor. Of course, he wasn't blind then. He was obsessed with the treasure that went down with the ship. Years later he managed to swim down to the wreck. There was no diving equipment in those days and he refused any help. He had to hold his breath, so it took dozens of dives for him to get much. Anyway, one day he found something he'd been looking for especially. It was said to be worth more than the rest of the treasure put together. That was the last dive he made.'

'So where does the curse come in?' I asked.

'Hugh became so attached to this valuable thing that It took over his life. He wouldn't tell anyone what It was, or let them see It. He trusted no one and drove away his family and friends. It is said that Hugh would sit staring at this treasure for hour after hour and It gradually robbed him of his sight. They say he went blind first, then mad. Finally, he put It in a silver casket inside another box, because Its hold over him was so strong.

'Well, on his death bed he made his last remaining relative, his great nephew, promise to It throw back into the sea. Blind Hugh told his great nephew that if he didn't, he'd be sorry because the thing cursed whoever had It.'

'Let me guess,' I said. 'It was never thrown back into the sea.'

'So the legend goes. His great nephew tried and tried to open the casket, but couldn't. He became so obsessed with opening it that he lost his job, his house – everything. He too died friendless and penniless. So did his great-nephew's son and granddaughter. All they knew was that there was something of tremendous power and incalculable value in the casket. It seemed to cast a spell over whoever owned It, even from inside the casket. I guess you could say it sort of hypnotised them.

Anyway, eventually the granddaughter ended up the same, without a friend or penny to her name until she and her little boy were sent to the debtors' prison. Before they were taken she buried the casket and left a coded message in a secret panel in her house that gave directions to where It was buried. The message was found a hundred years later. Since then It has "disappeared" and reappeared many times. Often fakes and forgeries, of course. Some claimed to have decoded it, but nothing ever came of their claims.'

Pitiless Pearl took over. 'One of the rumours was that the chest with the casket in it had been buried in this town. Other rumours said London, Glasgow, the Caribbean, Marseille, Cyprus, Cape Verde – almost anywhere you care to mention.'

Aunt Fenula looked around at us.

'It sounds like scary stuff,' she said. 'What should we do?'

Sunday 1 August 6.12 p.m.

Everyone stared at each other. There was silence. I shrugged. 'It must be valuable if Nudgebuster & Co. and Putrid Pete wanted to get their hands on It.'

'Do we open the casket?'

'It depends on whether you believe in curses I suppose, Miss Fitz' PJ said.

Aunt Fenula bit her lower lip. 'I really don't know what to believe. If the curse is true whoever manages to open the casket could be in great danger. If it isn't then that person will be fabulously rich.'

'What about if we all open the casket together?' I said. 'If the contents are that valuable I think it's called treasure trove and I don't know if we'd be allowed to keep it. We'd have to hand it over to the government. That's the law.'

Drastic Diego was not impressed. 'That doesn't sound very fair. And people wonder why pirates keep their treasure a secret.'

I got out my phone to double check.

'It says on this website that the finder gets half the value of the treasure trove when they hand it over. The landowner gets the other half.'

'In that case,' said Aunt Fenula, 'let's agree to open it, tell the authorities and get the cash reward. We found it on our property.'

We took a vote. The only person against was Desmond, which didn't really surprise anyone. We huddled around Aunt Fenula as she tried to slip the catch on the casket.

'It must be stiff, Cid. You have a go.'

I couldn't either. Nor could PJ.

'It says in the poem that the casket has to be opened by a strong and brave pirate,' said Shuggy. 'In which case, I should be able to do it. You're not pirates.'

But Shuggy couldn't either.

'Ha! If it said the most boastful pirate, you'd have stood a chance,' said Spud. 'Give it here.'

The casket wouldn't open for Spud. Or Gruff. By the time Clayton wanted a turn, Drastic Diego took it off him.

'No offence,' said Drastic Diego, 'but I wouldn't say you and your crew mates are the strongest or bravest pirates here.'

So then Diego tried. The catch on the casket did move a little, but not enough. He tried a second and third time, but it wouldn't budge any further.

'Give it to Desmond,' said Pitiless Pearl.

Everyone stared at her for a moment as if they had misheard her.

'Desmond?' said PJ.

But Desmond didn't want to do it.

Aunt Fenula smiled her best smile at him. 'Please, Desmond,' she said. 'Think what the agency could do if it had more funds.'

'I don't agree with any of this,' said Desmond, taking the casket.

'Even if you find the most precious treasure you have ever seen?' asked Shuggy. 'What will you say then?'

'I'll say that it should be thrown into the sea, like Blind Hugh wanted all those years ago. It seems whatever It is has brought misery to everyone who ever had it. Nothing is worth what happened to Blind Hugh and his family.'

'I can't see Desmond succeeding where you've all failed,' said PJ.

'No offence, but the pirate must be strong.'

'It depends what "strong" means,' said Clayton.

Wise words from Clayton? There was certainly something strange going on.

I looked at the scroll. 'It'll open for you, Desmond. I'm sure of it.' And I read the last four lines out again.

'This casket holds a secret like a coffin in a grave,

And it will only open for a pirate strong and brave.

And if you are, dear reader, that pirate bold and true,

You'll see this thing for what it is and know what you must do.'

'Go on,' said Pitiless Pearl. 'You've proved you're strong and brave in your own way. Where other pirates see treasure, you see something more important. Otherwise you wouldn't have offered to give Miss Fitz whatever you dug up in the treasure hunt. She told me what you said and it made me so proud.'

She looked at Mungo Mump, who had been standing back, watching what was going on but saying nothing.

'You taught him well, Mungo.'

Desmond took the casket and the catch slipped open with ease.

Sunday 1 August 7.00 p.m.

Inside, nestling in red velvet, was the largest jewel I had ever seen. It would have filled the palm of my hand, but when I tried to lift It out, it wouldn't budge.

Pitiless Pearl gasped. 'It's a blue diamond. It's priceless.'

It's... mesmerising,' declared Carlos.

It's'... alluring,' added Barry.

'It's not,' finished Desmond. 'It's Blind Hugh's curse.'

'Oi,' said Clayton. 'It was my turn. I always go next.'

But no one was listening to him. Carlos and Barry were right, It was mesmerising and alluring. In fact, we were all spellbound by the blue diamond. It was cut so that it sparkled like the sun on the summer sea. The evening was still bright but we had turned on all the courtyard lights to help us see where we were digging, yet the diamond glowed more brilliantly than any of them. We were bathed in blue light. This is all very poetic, which is not usually my style, but the blue diamond has that effect. Nothing else seemed to matter at that moment. When Aunt Fenula spoke she sounded as if she were in a dream.

'How can anything that beautiful be a curse?'

'And so valuable,' whispered Pitiless Pearl.

Carlos reached out to touch it but pulled his hand back quickly, as if he had been scalded.

'Think what you could do with the money, Captain,' he said. 'Surely It's worth...'

Desmond was the only one not spellbound by the blue diamond he held. He cast a slow look around at us.

'Can't you see what It's doing?' he said. But all we could see was the jewel he held.

Desmond snapped the casket shut, snapping us back into the real world at the same time. I shook my head to clear it from that fuzzy feeling you get when woken from a deep sleep.

'Wow,' said PJ. 'That jewel is quite something. I could sit and stare at It all day.'

Dusty nodded. 'Imagine owning It. You'd be the envy of everyone.'

'Everyone would want to be your friend,' said Arthur. 'No matter how badly you smelled,' he added.

Desmond shook his head. 'I can't believe what I'm hearing. Why would you want the kind of friend who only likes you because you're rich?'

Fair point. I prefer the kind of person who will stick with you when everything goes wrong. Someone like Rory had turned out to be.

'But if It's treasure trove,' said Shuggy, 'we won't keep the jewel but we will get a ship-load of money. Think about what we could do with it!'

Desmond opened the casket again and once more we fell under the jewel's trance. He took It out and held It up, lighting the courtyard in a bright blue glow. First Spud and then Gruff tried to take It from him, despite their fingers being burned, but the jewel wouldn't budge.

Desmond put the jewel back onto Its red velvet cushion and shut the casket again.

'It is beautiful,' he said, 'but that doesn't hide the fact that It's Blind

Hugh's curse. If you can't see the effect It has on you, I can. No matter where It's kept, the temptation to take It will be too great and whoever does, well there's no telling what would happen to them or what It might make them do. Those stories about Blind Hugh's family aren't fairy tales to frighten children with, they're true.'

'But...' Carlos got no further.

'Hush, me hearty,' said Drastic Diego, patting him on the shoulder. 'It's Desmond's decision. Even the jewel knows that.'

Desmond looked at Aunt Fenula. 'What do you think, Miss Fitz? It was found on your property. That must make It yours.'

'I think that Desmond knows what to do. That's why the jewel chose him.'

'In which case,' said Desmond, 'I think it's time to walk back to the quayside. I'll take a speedboat and return the jewel back where It belongs. I'd like you all to promise to go down on to the gun deck of the *Seahorse* and stay there for ten minutes, so you don't see where I'm going.'

'Don't worry, Desmond. Anyone who doesn't will have me to answer to.'

'Thanks, Mum. They wouldn't dare.'

Chapter Thirty

Sunday 1 August 9.03 p.m.

The sun was setting as Desmond finally started up a speedboat he had borrowed from Mr. Scrope, who kept one with his yacht. We were all sitting on the gun deck of the *Seahorse* in a circle, facing inwards, and listening to the sound of the speedboat engine fade as Desmond took Blind Hugh's curse out beyond the bay and into the open sea. We kept our word and none of us looked to see the direction in which he had gone.

'It has been a night of stirring passions and gallant exploits,' sighed Carlos.

'It has been a night of high romance and noble deeds,' added Barry.

'I've come over all gooey,' finished Clayton. 'I love you guys.'

And he pulled a protesting Carlos and Barry into his arms and squeezed them so tightly that they couldn't speak, although their faces were saying 'Help me!' We didn't.

Monday 2 August 1.28 a.m.

It was the early hours of Monday morning when we arrived back at the Miss Fitz Agency. Drastic Diego put his arm around Desmond's shoulder.

'So, son, what's it to be?'

'What's what to be?'

'Your future. Swashbuckling or entertaining? Pirate or dancer?'

'You wouldn't mind?'

Pitiless Pearl smiled. 'It's taken us a while to realise it's not up to us, but we've got there.'

'But, you can't leave us,' Gruff gasped. Shuggy clasped his hands like he was praying. Spud crossed his fingers on each hand, closed his eyes and mouthed 'No, no, no.' Carlos covered his face with his hands. Barry bit his lip. Clayton jiggled his legs.

'I've always wanted to be a dancer. Entertaining people makes me happy, it makes them happy – and that's very important.'

Team *Seahorse* groaned.

'But other things, other people are important too and I love pirating with my crew.'

Team *Seahorse* cheered.

'And dancing pirates are going to be the Next Big Thing, aren't they Miss Fitz?'

Aunt Fenula nodded. 'Apparently even Team *Screaming Skull* have been convinced of that. And, Desmond, when *Premiership Pirate Knockout* goes out, you and Team *Seahorse* are going to be huge!'

'Clayton's already there,' sniggered Barry, but everyone ignored him.

As everyone went inside for cocoa (Desmond had banned rum, and it was his celebration) Aunt Fenula gave me a hug.

'You're quite something, Cid.'

'So are you.'

'I guess we're finally at zero on your patented trouble scale?'

'I'd say we're at about 2.'

'Two? Why not zero?'

'I've looked at the agency's accounts,' I said. 'And I know who you've got on your books. But I reckon we might be able to make it work.'

THE END

Printed in Great Britain
by Amazon